CHILDREN

of LIGHT

CHILDREN

of LIGHT

ROBERT STONE

ALFRED A. KNOPF New York 1986

THIS IS A BORZOI BOOK
PUBLISHED BY ALFRED A. KNOPF, INC.

Portions of this work were originally published
in *Esquire*, *The Paris Review*, *Playboy*, and *Tri Quarterly*.

Library of Congress Cataloging-in-Publication Data
Stone, Robert.
Children of light.
I. Title.
PS3569.T6418C5   1986   813'.54   85-45602
ISBN 0-394-52573-6

Manufactured in the United States of America
FIRST EDITION

The author gratefully acknowledges a grant from the National Endowment for the Arts and a residency at the Villa Serbelloni through the generosity of the Rockefeller Foundation.

CHILDREN

of LIGHT

Waking, he saw aqueous light on the blue-white ceiling—the morning sun reflected from the swimming pool just outside the window. The moment he raised his head the poison struck; thirst, nausea, a barbed pain behind the eyes. When he turned he felt the warm girl beside him, naked, belly down. He reached out, and with the lightest touch his sodden state could bring to bear, ran his fingers along the small of her back, over her buttocks and firm thigh. In his first moments of consciousness, he had not been able to remember who it was there. The touch of her cool young skin brought recollection quickly enough.

As gently and silently as he could, he climbed out of bed and padded across the tiles to the chair on which he had piled his clothes the night before. He did not want to wake her, wanted to be alone in spite of his loneliness.

Dressed, he went out through the bedroom door and found himself in her enormous kitchen. It was stark white, gleaming with steel and glass, resplendent with morning. At the tap, he drank long and breathlessly, resting his elbows on the cold edge of the sink. He wet his hand and rubbed his face. When he looked up he saw brown mountains through the kitchen window, a steep ridge crowned with mist commanding a neat green valley. It was a shimmering day, dappled with promise.

"Fucking California," he said aloud. He was still half drunk.

Even after twenty years he was not immune to California mornings. He supposed they must represent the pursuit of happiness to him.

He closed his eyes and gripped the sink. His eyes were swollen. They want pennies, he thought. Pennies over them. He took a deep breath, swallowed and drew himself erect.

Now go, he told himself.

3

Adjoining the white kitchen was a small dining area. A little spiral sculpture of a stairway led down to the living room, where he had left his bags. He opened his suitcase across the sofa and rummaged through it for clean socks, underwear, a fresh shirt. Gathering up the clothes, he went to the spare bathroom and locked himself in against the fulsomeness of the morning. He turned on the shower, trying to calm himself with the familiar sound of the spray. His hands trembled. He was about to be afraid.

Instantly he was sick, vomiting into the fixture, sweating, dysenteric. Purged for the moment, he sat down on the covered toilet seat, holding his head in his hands. Desolation.

Of course he was poisoned. He had been poisoning himself for weeks.

As he stepped into the shower, he caught sight of himself in a mirror on the door of the medicine cabinet. The thing itself. Unaccommodated man. He did not let his gaze linger.

Standing under the veil of warm water, he began to recite. He made his voice large, comically orotund:

"Thou art the thing itself," he declared to the tiny white room. "Unaccommodated man is no more than such a poor bare forked animal as thou art."

He felt better then, but only for a while. A wave of regret had massed and was advancing on him; he had hardly time for breath before it ran him down. Bitterness—stifling, sour, the color of jaundice, gagging him.

"Pour on," he declaimed, "I will endure. On such a night . . ." He stopped and fell silent.

At times like the one he was presently enduring, Walker, who was a screenwriter, would think of the days behind him as a litter of pictures. Light on the water, his wife at twenty, a sky, a city, his children at tender ages. One remembered image or another might move him almost to tears, then presently the emotion stirred would seem trivial and false, like some of the scenes he had written. His phantoms of conscience, his deepest regrets would appear petty, vulgar and ridiculous. These moods afforded Walker a vision of his life as trash—a soiled article, past repair. Observing things compose themselves into this bleak spectacle, Walker would wonder if he had ever had the slightest acquaintance with any kind of truth.

He held fast to the safety bar in the shower stall. What we need here is a dream, he told himself, a little something to get by on. For the past few weeks, he had been getting by on alcohol and a ten-gram stash of cocaine and he had begun to feel as though he might die quite soon.

Showered, he stepped out of the stall, dried himself on the guest towel and, avoiding the mirror, checked out the medicine cabinet. To his sharp delight, he found a little tube of Valium beside a bottle of vitamin B complex. The perfect hostess, he thought. A marvelous girl.

When he had helped himself to a five-milligram tablet of Valium and some B complex, he stepped on the bathroom scale, closed the cabinet and was confronted once more with his own image. Men Walker's age were held to be responsible for their faces, a disquieting notion. But his was hardly a mask of depravity. He drew himself erect and stared it down. Just a face, quite an ordinary one. Caught, he squinted to examine the creature in the glass. It was his business to know how he looked; he worked as an actor from time to time. He looked, he decided, like a man in his forties who drank. For most of his life he had appeared younger than his age. Perhaps it was just the light, he thought. He looked away and stepped on the bathroom scale.

Walker found that he weighed just over one hundred and seventy pounds, which he thought not bad for one his height and build. He poked two fingers under his rib cage on the right side, checking for evidence of liver enlargement. Everything seemed as usual there.

Stepping off the scale, he blundered into his reflection yet again. This time he was paralyzed with the fear of death. He turned away and leaned against the wall, closing his eyes, taking deep deliberate breaths. It took him some moments to calm himself. His inner resources were in some disarray, he thought. Valium would have to serve in the present emergency. Another line from *Lear* came into his mind: "he hath ever but slenderly known himself."

For the first time in his articulate, thoroughly examined life, Walker wondered if that might not be true of him. Not possible, he decided. He knew himself well enough. It was the rest of things that gave him trouble.

He dressed. Returning to the kitchen, he half filled a water glass with vodka, then poured clam and tomato juice mixture over it. Walking carefully down the stairway, he sprawled beside his suitcase on the light gray sofa and savored the cozy impeccability of Bronwen's living room. When he had taken a few sips of his drink, he reached into the lining of the case and drew out the fold of pink notepaper that contained his ready-to-hand cocaine. He set the envelope on the coffee table in front of him but left it unopened.

How well she lives, he thought, for one so young. He himself was homeless and had been so for more than a month.

Walker worked in the film industry, having come into it seventeen years before as an actor. He had gone through the Hagen-Berghof studios with the thought of learning the theater and becoming a playwright. A few years later he had written the book and lyrics for a very serious and ambitious musical version of *Jurgen* and been astonished to see it fail utterly within a week. There had never been a play and he had come to realize that there would never be. Walker made his living—quite a good one—chiefly as author, adjuster or collaborator on film scripts. During the past summer, he had been acting again, on stage for the first time in years as Lear. Over the years he had advanced in station within the old black fairy tale. At different phases of his life he had played Cornwall's servant, then Cornwall, then Kent, finally the King. He was still up on Lear-ness, chockablock with cheerless dark and deadly mutters, little incantations from the text. They were not inappropriate to his condition; during the run of the show his wife had left him.

Drink in hand, he went up the stairway again and stood just inside the bedroom door, looking in at the young woman. Such a nice house, he thought. His jaw was tight with anger. Such a pretty girl.

He leaned in the doorway and watched her. She lay facing him, her red-blond hair partly covering her eyes, her lips parted over long cowgirl's teeth. She slept on, or pretended to. A deep blue silk sheet was gathered about her naked body; she was sheathed in it.

Bronwen was a writer, a midwestern girl honed smooth by early success and the best of California. Observing, or rather ogling, her at rest, Walker was stirred in equal measure by lust and resentment.

Basically, they disliked each other. They were both, in their diverse ways, performers, comics; much of their companionable humor turned on mutual scorn.

She had written three short novels, witty, original and immensely pleasurable to read. Bronwen was nothing if not funny. Each of her novels had been received with great enthusiam by reviewers and by the public; she had become famous enough for Walker, to his deep inward shame, to take a vulgar satisfaction in his liaison with her. She was intelligent and coldhearted, a spiky complex of defenses mined with vaults of childish venom and hastily buried fears. Kicked when she was a pup, Walker would say behind her back. The game they played, one of the games, was that she knew his number. That his stratagems to please, his manner of being amusing, the political sincerities that remained to him were petty complaints to which she was immune. Others might take him seriously—not she, the hard case, worldly-wise.

He ran his eyes over her long frame and wondered if she knew he knew about the pistol she kept in the wicker chest beneath her bed, wrapped in a scarf with her Ritalin tablets. Or whether she knew his number well enough to imagine the measure of his rage, or the murderous fantasies that assailed him—of destroying her, transforming her supple youth to offal, trashing it.

He was immediately stricken with remorse and horror. Because he liked her, really, after all. He must, he thought; there had to be more than perversity. She was funny; he enjoyed her wit and her high spirits. And she liked him—he was sure. She could speak with him as with no other friend; she respected his work, she had said so. It occurred to him suddenly how little any of this had to do with the terms of the heart as he had once understood them; love, caring, loyalty. It was just a random coupling, a highbrow jelly roll. Might

she imagine that violent fantasies beset him with herself as their object? She might well. She was very experienced and knowing; she had
his number. And the Lord knew what fantasies she spun round him.

Back in the living room, he found his wallet on the sofa where he
had been sitting. It was thick with bills, jammed in haphazard. He
remembered then, having almost forgotten it in his malaise, that he
had won a great deal of money at Santa Anita the day before. He had
gone with Bronwen; it was a glorious day and they had lunched at
the clubhouse. Walker had scored on the double, a perfecta and an
eight-to-one winner. His take was over a thousand dollars, the largest
amount of money he had ever won at the track. It had paid for dinner
at the San Gabriel Ranch and it would pay a week's rent at the Chateau. He had been living at the Chateau Marmont since the closing of
Lear, having rented his house in Santa Monica. He did not care to be
alone there.

Walker caressed the disorderly wad between thumb and forefinger.
The touch of the wrinkled bright new bills gave him a faint feeling
of disgust. He took out a hundred, examining the lacy engraved illu-
mination at its border. Then, on an impulse, he rolled the bill into a
cylinder, laid out a line of his coke and blew it. Nice. He sniffed and
rubbed his eyes. Confidence. A little surge for the road. Immediately
it occurred to him that in the brief course of his waking day he had
consumed Valium, alcohol and cocaine.

We need a plan, he thought. A plan and a dream, somewhere to
go. Dreams were business to Walker, they were life. Like salt, like
water. Lifeblood.

He touched the tip of his index finger to the surface of the coffee
table, capturing the residue of cocaine that remained there, and rubbed
it on his gum.

Go, he thought. It seemed to him that if he did not go at once death
would find him there. He stood up and packed his suitcase, leaving
the small fold of cocaine on the table as a house present. He had plenty
more in the case.

Stacked on the mantel above the fireplace were Bronwen's three
novels; Walker found that each was engagingly inscribed to him. The

drill was for him to take them and leave a note. He turned the topmost book to the back jacket and looked at Bronwen's picture. Her eyes were fixed on the middle distance, her lips were slightly parted, her cheekbones high and handsome, her chin dimpled. She looked hip and sympathetic and fingerlickin' good. He placed the book back on the mantelpiece and left it there. Then he put on his sunglasses, picked up his bags and went forth into the morning.

As he drove the freeway, KFAC played Couperin, the *Leçons de Ténèbres*.

Walker thought of himself as a survivor. He knew how to endure, and what it was that got you through. There was work. There were the people you loved and the people who loved you. There were, he had always believed, a variety of inner resources that the veteran survivor might fall back on; about these he was no longer so sure. The idea of inner resources seemed fatuous mysticism that morning. He had drugged and drunk too much, watched too many smoky reels of interior montage to command any inner resources. It was difficult enough to think straight.

As for work—after weeks of living on his nerves it would take nearly as much time of disciplined drying out before he could begin to face a job. And love—love was fled. Gone to London. The thought of her there and himself abandoned made his blood run cold. He put it out of his mind, as he had trained himself to do since Seattle. He would deal with it later, he would do something about it. When he was straightened out. A dream, he thought. That's what we need.

He left the freeway at Sunset and parked in Marmont Lane behind the hotel. At the desk he bought the morning's L.A. *Times* and *Variety*. He rode up to the sixth floor in the company of a famous German actor and two stoned young women.

The air in his apartment held a faint scent of stale alcohol and undone laundry. He opened the leaded bedroom windows to a tepid oily breeze. Below him were the swimming pool and the row of bungalows that flanked it. Dead leaves floated on the surface of the dark green water. The pool gardens smelled of car exhaust and eucalyptus.

This time it was not going to be easy to get straight. He would have to go about it very skillfully. Above all he would have to want to. There would have to be a reason, and Walker knew that inquiry into his reasons for surviving would bring him into dangerous territory. The world in general, he had conceded at last, required neither him nor his works. His wife was gone—for good as far as he knew; his children were grown. He was going to have to pull out for his own reasons, alone and unrequired, in a hotel in West Hollywood. The taste of death and ruin rose in his throat again.

He decided not to think about it. In order to postpone thinking about it he opened his suitcase, took out the tubular talcum container that held his cocaine and tapped out a small mound of the stuff onto the smooth dark marble of his bedside lamp table. He did it up with the hundred-dollar bill. Fine, he thought. For the moment he had obviated motivation; he was the thing itself again. The thing itself shortly came to self-awareness in the kitchen pouring out a shot of vodka. Perplexed, Walker looked at the drink he had prepared. He sniffed, drew himself erect and emptied the glass into the sink drain. He had made a luncheon engagement with his agent and keeping the appointment was all he owned of purpose. He must at least postpone the next drink until lunch. A small gesture toward renewal, nothing ambitious.

Drinkless, he went into his living room, turned the television set on, turned it off again and began to pace the length of the room.

This is where we begin, he told himself. We reinvent ourself. We put one foot in front of the other and we go on.

In a moment he went back to the bedroom and did another line. Then he leaned back on the bed and stared through the balcony windows at the still surface of the pool five stories below.

From somewhere amid the damp greenery of the garden, a mockingbird was trilling away, sounding a little fife march. For a fraction of a second Walker was beguiled by a shard of memory, the tiniest part of an old dream. It was gone too quickly to be pinned down.

He got to his feet and went to stand at the window. The bird song came again, under the rush of traffic, stirring recall.

He had gone away from the balcony and was sitting on the bed with the telephone in his hand when the memory surfaced. He put the receiver down and turned to the window. The bird trilled again.

He was remembering Lu Anne Bourgeois, whom the greater world called Lee Verger. She had been half on his mind all the previous spring, but Seattle, the show and the dreadful events of the summer had swept everything away.

Years before, when he and Lu Anne were young and fearless, in the days of mind drugs and transfiguration, they had invented a game together for bad nights. In fact, it was not so much a game as a state of mind to be indulged and they had called it Bats or Birdies.

Bats or Birdies was played in the worst hours before dawn. Winning entailed holding your own until morning, making it through the night with your head intact to the moment when bird song announced the imminence of first light and day. That was Birdies. Losing was not making it through, losing your shit. Bats. Mockingbirds, with their untimely warbles at ungodly hours, upset the game, making you think that it was morning and you had won through when in fact you were still fast in the heart of night.

He thought of Lu Anne and his heart rose. She was pale. She had dark blue saintly eyes and a smile that quivered between high drollery and madness. Nine years before, she had been nominated for an Academy Award in a supporting role; her subsequent career, like Walker's, had been disappointing.

Long ago, during their time together, Lu Anne had given him Kate Chopin's novel *The Awakening*. Its setting was Louisiana in the late nineteenth century; Lu Anne was a Louisianan, Chopin's book had been a favorite of hers. He had written a script, and every day of its writing she had been with him or in his expectation, so that when the principal character of Edna Pontellier was defined in scene and dialogue, Lu Anne inhabited it utterly. In those days they had dreamed of doing it together but it had not turned out that way.

Time passed. The book was discovered by academics and declared a feminist document. Lu Anne had acquired a new agent, who was vigorous, female and literate. About a year and a half before Walker committed for the Seattle *Lear*, ten years after his last revision of the script and six since his last conversation with Lu Anne, a package had been put together.

A young director named Walter Drogue had been engaged. *The Awakening* would be Drogue's fourth picture; he was generally accounted intelligent, original and aggressive. His father, also named Walter Drogue, was one of the industry's living Buddhas. A director himself for almost fifty years, Drogue senior had been publicly caned, fired upon by sexual rivals, blacklisted, subpoenaed and biographied in French. The father's name, it was felt, added luster to his son's project, and the son's price, like Walker's and Lu Anne's, was not immoderate.

A producer of some probity took the picture over. One of the majors was induced to finance and distribute. It was all perceived as prestigious, timely and cheap. There was a real possibility that the interests involved might find themselves in control of a well-made picture that would generate good reviews, awards and, with the right handling, a favorable profit line. A vestigial social impulse was being discharged. Somewhere, deep within the Funhouse, they had opted for a calculated risk.

After shooting most of the summer in New Orleans, the production had moved, for convenience and economy, to the Drogues' favorite Baja location at Bahía Honda. The elder Drogue had been filming there for many years and had bought hotel property through a nominal Mexican owner. Thus he was able to serve as factor to his own productions.

As far as Walker was concerned, it was a little late. He had been asked down and declined. Probably, he thought, to their relief. There was also the matter of Lu Anne, his dark angel. They had survived their last outing but it had been close. They had survived because they were both young then and married and motivated and skilled survivors. It would not be the same now.

But stoned, abandoned, desolate—Walker found himself listening to birdcalls and thinking of her. His heart beat faster. It had not been quite six years, he thought. She had kissed him casually. He imagined that he could recall her touch and when he did it was the woman he had known a decade before who presented herself to his recollection.

She was married again, to a doctor; she had children. His business now was to save himself and his own marriage, restore his equilibrium. What we need here is less craziness, he told himself, not more.

Then he thought: A dream is what I need. Fire, motion, risk. It was a delusion of the drug. The production's location office number was in his black book. He found himself with his hand on the phone.

Yours in the ranks of death.

Trapped within some vertiginous silence, he dialed the far-off number. At the first ring he hung up in terror.

A few minutes later, it seemed to him that he was perfectly well again. When he picked up the telephone it was to confirm luncheon with his agent's office.

At the agency, he got Shelley Pearce on the line. She was Al's assistant, a Smithie who had gone through the Yale Rep some years after Lu Anne. She had been a student of Walker's at an acting workshop; he had gotten her her first job, as a gofer on a production at U.A. He had introduced her to Al.

"Hello, Gordon," Shelley said. She sounded glad to hear from him and he felt grateful.

"Where were you?" he said. "Every night I searched that sea of pale immobile faces. No Shelley."

"You kidding, Gordon? *King Lear?* You think I got time for that shit?"

He laughed.

"Yes, Gordon," Shelley said, "yes, I was there. I saw you. You were wonderful."

"How's that?"

"Wonderful, Gordon. Wonderful, O.K.?"

"I thought so too," Walker said. "I felt underappreciated."

"Didn't you see the L.A. *Times?*"

"Acceptable," Walker said. "But faint."

"Don't be greedy," Shelley said. "Al will bring you some clippings to slaver over at lunch."

"Why don't you and I have dinner tonight?" he asked her suddenly. "Why don't we go to the San Epo Hotel?"

She was silent for a moment.

"How are you, Gordon? I mean, how are you doing?"

"Not so good," he said.

"Sure," she said. "The San Epo, sure. Sunset. Know when sunset is? It's in the paper."

"I'll call the Coast Guard."

"You drinking?" she asked. "You better not stand me up."

"I'll be there," he said.

A rriving at Musso and Frank's, Walker settled in at a banquette table and ordered a martini. Keochakian came in fifteen minutes late to find him ordering a second.

"Bring me one too," Al told the waiter.

Keochakian studied his client. He had hard, unconfiding eyes behind thick tinted glasses, the face and manner of a Marseilles *numéro*.

"How are you, Gordon?" He shook Walker's hand and gripped his shoulder. "How are Connie and the kids?"

"They're dead, Al."

The agent looked at him without expression.

"Hey, that's funny, Gordon."

"You always ask. I wondered if you were listening."

Keochakian bared his teeth.

"I always listen. I want to know. I'm a family man. I'm not like you, you fuck. They're wasted on you."

"Connie left me," Walker said.

"I don't believe that," Al said. "It's impossible and I reject it."

"She left me a most eloquent letter. A bill of particulars. She seemed very determined. She's in London."

"Know what I think? I think she'll come back. I'm sure of it. If you want her to." Keochakian sipped his drink and grimaced. "I presume you want her to."

Walker looked down at his folded hands and nodded slowly.

"Face it, man. Without her you're fucked. You'll go down the tubes. You have to get her back."

"She has her pride."

"Now you know," Keochakian said.

"I can't talk about it today," Walker said. "I'm too scrambled."

"That's fine. But when you do want to talk about it let me know, because I have a few things to say on the subject and I have the right to an opinion."

Walker chewed his lip and looked away.

"So what do you want to eat?" Al asked.

"Since we're having martinis," Walker said, "I'm thinking liver."

"The liver is good," Al said. He signaled for a waiter and was attended at once. They ordered. Under his agent's disapproving eye, Walker called for a half bottle of cabernet.

"Tell me about Seattle."

"I could spend the rest of my life doing *Lear*," Walker said. "I'd like to do it all. The Fool. Gloucester, Cordelia. The fucking thing is bottomless."

"Shelley saw you."

Walker smiled. "She said. She's my turtledove."

"Would you like to work?" Al asked. "I have something good."

"When?"

"They'd want to test this week. But they asked for you specifically, so I think that's just a formality." He was frowning. "Are you tied up or something? Why is it important when?"

Walker made no answer.

"You into something? Will you have a script for me?"

"No," Walker said. He cleared his throat. "I thought I'd go down to Bahía Honda and look in on *The Awakening*."

Al squinted through his green-shaded glasses and shook his head. "Why?"

Walker shrugged. "Because it's my baby. I want to see how they're treating it."

"I thought we went through this," Al said. The waiter brought the wine for Walker to taste. When it was poured out, Keochakian covered his own glass with his hand to decline it. "I thought a decision had been made and I thought it was the right one."

"I've decided I want a look-in."

"A look-in," the agent said, a toneless echo.

"Make my presence felt."

"They don't want you down there," Al said.

The main course arrived. Walker poured himself a second glass of wine.

"They asked for me once," Walker said.

Keochakian took his glasses off and shrugged. "They didn't care, Gordon. Walter thought he might pick your brain a little but he certainly doesn't need you now. He'll think you're crowding his act."

Walker picked up a fork and looked at his plate.

"I'd like to, you know."

"They won't pay. They don't require you."

"I'll pay. I'll go as a civilian. For the beach."

Al addressed his liver and onions.

"I think this is unprofessional."

"I don't see why," Walker said. When he began to eat he found that he was very hungry. "It's not unheard-of."

"You're going to see Lee Verger," Keochakian said. He was avoiding Walker's eyes.

"It would be nice to see Lu Anne. Look, I've got some stake in the picture. Why shouldn't I go down?"

"Because you work for a living," Al said. He spoke very slowly and softly. "And I have work for you."

"I'm not ready," Walker said vaguely.

"It's a fun part. It's big. A faggoty intellectual villain. You'd have a blast."

"I feel the need to go down to Mexico for a while. When I get back—I'll be refreshed. I'll be able to work."

Keochakian leaned his knife and fork on his plate.

"Let me tell you something, Gordon. If you show up on that set you'll be digging your own grave."

Walker laughed bitterly.

"You think it's funny, fucker?" Keochakian asked. "You know how you look? You're sweating fucking alcohol. You think I can't see your eyes? You think people in this business don't know what drunks look like?"

"I'm quitting tomorrow, for Christ's sake."

"Oh," Al said with a humorless smile, "quitting tomorrow. That's nice. That's good, Gordon. Well, I suggest you do that, pal. And I suggest you leave Lee the fuck alone." He put his fork to the meat, then set it down again. "I mean, go retrieve Connie. Lee doesn't need you. You're the last thing she needs. Whereas Connie for her own sick reasons does."

"I need a trip. Travel is therapy for me."

Al looked at him and leaned forward across the table.

"If you're ever unable to work, put yourself in a hospital."

"Please, Al."

"Gordon," Keochakian said, "ten years ago this might have been a joke but it's not a joke now. Take the cure, man. People do it all the time."

Walker put a hand to his forehead.

"You have the money. Do yourself a favor. Get out of circulation and dry out. Go East. New England. It's autumn, they have some good places there, you won't see anyone you know."

"I'd go bananas," Walker said. "A place like that."

"Maybe it has to be done, Gordon."

"Well," Walker said in a placatory manner, "we'll see how it goes."

A busboy came and removed their plates. Walker poured wine.

"Too bad you won't do this thing I have for you. It might get you television."

"Is that what I want?"

Keochakian's eyes seemed to glaze. He stared into space and scratched his chin.

"I think I'll grow a beard, Gordon. A goatee, what do you think?"

"Good, Al. That'd be good."

"Don't you dare go down there," Al said. He shook his finger before Walker's face. "Don't you dare undo all the work I've done."

"Sure, Al," Walker said. "Hey, what work, man?"

"Fuck you, Gordon."

Walker waited, half expecting him to stand up and leave. They both sat tight, facing one another.

"We made a very favorable deal, financially," Al said calmly.

"My best fee," Walker said. "A record."

"Exactly. We also dealt with some typical Walter Drogue–like ploys."

"Did we?"

"Yes, we did, Gordon. You may remember his concern over the feminist perspective."

"I wasn't aware of it."

"Walter was worried about the absence of a feminist perspective. He gave us a lot of shit about this. Know what was on his mind?"

"I can guess."

Keochakian smiled thinly.

"He wanted a writing credit. Not for some broad—for him. He saw the script was good. He thinks the thing might go. He wanted a writing credit for his vanity and to jack more points out of them."

"Well," Walker said. "Walter's a great feminist."

"Definitely," Al said. "I hear his father was an even greater feminist. Anyway, that fucking ball would have rolled seven ways from sundown but it would have stopped on a writing credit for Walter Drogue. We were able to checkmate these numbers. We saved your points and credit."

"He never heard of the novel before I did the script."

"He thinks he did."

"This time last year," Walker said, "he thought *The Awakening* was a mummy movie. Now he thinks he wrote the book."

"That's how he is, Gordo. And if you go down there and act like a rummy and mess with his actress you'll play right into his hands. He thinks he can swallow you with a glass of water."

"Did he say that?" Walker asked, smiling.

"Words to that effect. And they're all running scared because Dongan Lowndes is down there doing a big magazine piece on the filming. They're afraid he'll make assholes out of them and screw the project."

"Well," Walker said, "how about that?"

Dongan Lowndes was a novelist whose single book, published eight years before, Walker much admired. In the intervening years, Lowndes had turned to nonfiction writing for quality magazines. Most recently he had been writing on such subjects as Las Vegas crooners, self-publicizing tycoons, fatuous politicians and the film industry. He wrote well and bitterly and they feared him.

"Does he think he can swallow Lowndes too?"

"They're hoping to charm him."

"Maybe with Lee, huh?"

"This is a Charlie Freitag production, Gordon. You know Charlie. He figures . . ." Keochakian raised his eyes heavenward. "Christ, who knows what he figures? He's a culture vulture. He thinks it's a class picture and he thinks Lowndes is a classy guy. He thinks he'll get a friendly piece and it'll be good for the picture."

"Whereas in fact Lowndes can't get it on to write and he hates to see people work. He'll nail them to a tree."

"Tell Charlie," Al said. He watched Walker sip his wine. "Hey, you're a little bitter too, huh?"

"Lowndes is a fine writer," Walker said. "I hope he never writes another novel in his fucking life."

"Terrific, Gordo. You're just what they need down there. You can hassle Lee and piss on the press. Get drunk, start fights. Just like old times, right?" He leaned across the table and fixed his Vieux Port stare on Walker. "You'll hurt people. You'll hurt yourself. I'm telling you to stay away."

"I'll think about it," Walker said.

"Please," Al said. "Please think."

He took a file folder full of press clippings from his attaché case and handed them to Walker.

"Enjoy yourself. Sober up. Call me in a couple of days and we'll talk about what you should do." He called for the check and signed it as the waiter stood by. "I mean, what if Connie comes back or calls and you're off fucking up somewhere? Don't do anything. Don't go anywhere until you're sober."

They went out. It had turned into a Santa Ana day with a dry comfortless breeze, a hot hazy sky. At the corner of Bronson, Keochakian took hold of Walker's lapel.

"People are watching you," he said. "Always. Evil people who wish you bad things are watching. You're not among friends." He turned away, walked a few steps and spun round. "Trust no one. Except me. I'm different. You can trust me. You believe that?"

"More or less," Walker said.

On the way back to West Hollywood, he stopped at his health club, had a swim and read his reviews in the sauna. The reviews were, in the main, good. One of them was good enough to drive him out of the heat with angina pains. It called his performance a revelation. "Walker's anguished king, descending from impotent frenzy to an almost fey, childlike madness, comes as a revelation to those familiar only with his street-smart movie turns."

He thought it cheering, although the pains rather worried him.

Back at the Chateau, he packed up, left a wake-up call and took a short nap. His dreams were stormy. An hour later he was south of Long Beach in rush-hour traffic.

Deep into Orange County, he pulled off the San Diego Freeway and cut over toward the coast road. On his left, the future of southern California was unfolding; he passed mile upon mile of development divided into units by redwood fencing and bougainvillea, mock vil-

lages centered on a supermarket and a Bob's Big Boy. Every half mile
or so a patch of stripped, empty acreage awaited the builders and
better times.

On his right, through some realtor's stratagem, the land was un-
improved. Herefords grazed in fields of yellow grass; wildflowers and
manzanita flourished. From somewhere came the smell of orange
trees, as though it were spring and twenty years before. The nearest
groves were miles away now.

He drove into fog among the dry hills, the warm wind died away
and on the coast it was gray and cool. He felt better suited.

On the coast road, he turned south. For a few miles it was all
suburban maritime; there were condominiums with marinas, dive
shops, seafood restaurants. Further down the Herefords wandered
among undulating oil-well pumps, a landscape of tax deductions.

At seven-fifteen, half an hour before sunset, he was pulling into
San Epifanio Beach, the last repair of untranslated seediness in the
county. The beach had oil rigs offshore and an enormous German
Expressionist power plant on the city line. There was a fishing pier
borne seaward on spindly pilings in defiance of the Pacific rollers, the
far end of which vanished into enshrouding fog. At right angles to
the coast road, garnished with a rank of rat-infested royal palms, ran
the lineup of tackle stores, taco stands and murky cocktail lounges
that was the beach's principal thoroughfare.

Walker braked at the intersection to let a party of surf punks cross.
The slashes of green or orange in their close-cropped hair reminded
him suddenly of the patch of white that had appeared in his brother's
hair following rheumatic fever. The four youths glared at him with
impersonal menace as they went by.

Three blocks beyond the main drag rose the San Epifanio Beach
Hotel, a nine-story riot of exoticism that dominated the downtown
area. It was a shameless building from another age, silent-movie Spanish. With its peeling stucco walls, its rows of slimy windows and soiled
shades, it was a structure so outsized and crummy that the sight of it
could taint the nicest day. Walker was fond of it because he had been
happy there. He had lived in the hotel years before in a room beside

an atelier where a blind masseur cohabited with Ramon Novarro's putative cousin. He had been married there, in the dingy ballroom, amid cannabis fumes.

Walker pulled over into the guest parking lot. A tough-looking little Chicana with a ponytail, a baseball cap and bib overalls handed him a claim ticket.

He went past the theater-style marquee over the main entrance and walked round to the beach side of the building. Several empty tables were arranged on a veranda overlooking a nearly deserted park. At the far end of the park four black teenagers, stripped to the waist, were playing basketball. Nearer the hotel, some Hare Krishnas from Laguna were chanting for the entertainment of two elderly couples in pastel clothes.

Walker ambled across the park to the beach. The wind was sharp, it had grown chilly with the approach of sunset. The declining sun itself was obscured in dark banks of cloud. Walker watched the waves break against the dark purple sand. Once he had seen porpoises there, seven together, playing just outside the break line of the surf. He had been standing in the same place, on the edge of the park around sunset. His wife had been beside him. His children were digging in the sand and she had called to them, pointing out to sea, to the porpoises. It had been a good omen in a good year.

He walked along the sand until he felt cold, then climbed back to the park up a dozen cement steps that were littered with plastic carriers and beer cans and smelled of urine.

The wall of the corridor between the main entrance and the inner lobby of the San Epifanio was covered in worn striped wallpaper against which were hung ghastly seascapes at close intervals. Once past them, he strolled into the candlelit gemütlichkeit of the Miramar Lounge, all nets and floats and steering wheels. There was not much sunset to be seen through the picture windows but the lights were low and the bar and adjoining tables fairly crowded. The customers were middle-aged, noisy and dressed for golf—a hard-liquor crowd. Walker took the only vacant stool at the bar and ordered a Bloody Mary. The drink when it came was bitter, hefty with cheap vodka. Strong drinks were a selling point of the place.

On the stool next to Walker sat a blond woman who was drinking rather hungrily of her gin-and-tonic and toying with a pack of Virginia Slims. She appeared to be in her early thirties and attractive, but Walker was not certain of either impression. He was not altogether sober and it was difficult to see people clearly in the lighting of the Miramar Lounge. That was the way they liked it there.

At the entrance to the bar, adjoining the corridor through which he had passed, was a phone booth, one from the old days decorated with sea horses and dolphins in blue and white tile. After a moment, Walker picked up his drink and went to the phone booth. He took out his black book with its listing of the Baja location numbers and his telephone credit card.

He took a long sip, held his breath and dialed. The resonance of submarine depths hummed in the wires as he waited for the ring. When it came, he closed his eyes.

When the telephone rang she was outside, in a lounge chair on the sand, looking into the afterglow of sunset. Her children were playing with their father at the water's edge; she had watched the three forms darken to silhouettes in the dying light. The soft honey glow of the children's bodies had faded in the quick dusk; now their scamperings and her husband's thin-limbed gestures against the radiant foam and magenta sky suggested puppetry to her. It was an ugly thought and she forced it aside. She let the phone ring until she saw that her husband had heard it; knee deep in light surf, he had turned at the sound. She stood up and took her sunglasses off.

"I'll get it," she called to him.

She jogged up to the open door of their bungalow, wiped her sandy feet on the straw mat and rushed to the phone.

"Lu Anne," said the voice on the far end when she answered. "Lu Anne, it's Gordon. Gordon Walker."

She had known, she thought, who it would be. Watching the sun go down she had been thinking of him and thinking that he would call that night.

"Hello? Lu Anne? Can you hear me?"

His voice sounded from the receiver in her hand as clearly as though he were there in Mexico, somewhere in the same hotel.

"Lu Anne?"

Slowly, guiltily, she replaced the receiver.

It had grown dark in the stone bungalow. The only light came from fading pastel sky framed in the doorway. She sat on a high-backed wicker chair looking out. In the darkness behind her she could feel a presence gathering. A confusion of sounds rang in her ears and among them she heard Walker's voice saying her name. Watchful, perfectly still, she stayed where she was until she saw a figure in the doorway. At first she thought it had to do with the things that were manifesting themselves behind her back; she watched fascinated, virtually unafraid.

"Señora?"

She knew who it was then.

"*Sí, sí*," she said, and she reached out for the light that was right over the phone. "Hello, Helga. Good evening."

Helga Machado was the children's nanny, supplied by the production unit through the hotel. A stout, pale, heavy-browed young woman, she watched Lee Verger with caution and a formal smile.

"Now," Helga said, "I may take the children for their dinner. Or else I can come back a little later."

Lu Anne was blinking in the sudden light. The wariness in Helga's expression did not escape her.

"Well," she said cheerfully, "let's see. Why don't we call them and they can go to dinner and I'll say good night to them when we get back."

"Very good, señora."

Lu Anne went past Helga and through the doorway. At the water's edge, Lionel and the children were still playing in the darkness. The shallows flashed phosphorescence where they ran.

"David and Laura," Lu Anne called to her children. "Dinner time, you-all."

She saw the dim figures fall still, listened to her little son's protesting moan. They would be early to sleep. If she missed them that evening there would be only the shortest amount of time available for goodbyes in the morning. She and Lionel were to dine that evening at Walter Drogue's casita. It was a courtesy—a farewell meal for Lionel—and there had been no chance of declining.

When the children came up from the beach, Lu Anne led them into the bungalow and bent to them, holding each by the hand. They were only a year and a half apart; David was five and Laura seven. They had their father's red-blond hair a shade darker, and their mother's blue eyes.

"You guys go with Helga and wash off all the sand and salt. Then you eat your dinners like good children and you can go see *The Wizard of Oz* in the suite."

Thus bought off, the children murmured assent.

"Laura," Lu Anne called after her daughter, "don't forget your glasses, honey. Or you won't be able to see the movie."

"If I had contacts," the little girl said, "then I'd never forget them."

Going out, Helga and the children stopped to talk with Lionel, who had come up from the beach. She listened as he joked with them.

"Who was it?" Lionel asked her when he came inside. He was over six feet in height and dramatically thin, with a long face and a prominent nose. His hair was thinning, the sun-bleached strands pasted across his tanned scalp. Lee was facing the dressing-table mirror; Lionel watched her in the glass.

"Oh," she said, "it just rang and stopped. It must have been the switchboard or something."

Her husband took off his bathing suit and stood beside her at the mirror rubbing Noxzema on his face and chest. Their eyes met.

"Take your medicine, love?" he asked.

There was a look he had when he asked about the medicine. A stare. It made him seem cruel and unfeeling although she knew perfectly well that he was neither.

"Can't you tell?"

"I'm sorry," he said. "I'm like an old woman about it. I'll stop."

She had stopped taking the pills ten days before. Held her breath and stopped. Sometimes her old pal Billy Bly gave her something to get her through the night. She felt quite guilty about it but she was convinced it had to be done. They were ruining her concentration. They were ruining everything.

"You've seemed very well," Lionel said. "I mean," he hastened to add, "you've seemed happy. That's what it comes to, I suppose."

"I've been working," she said. "Nothing like it."

"It's good, isn't it? This." He meant the film.

"Yes. I mean I think so. Edna—I love her."

"Do you think she's you?"

"Are you asking me that as a doctor?"

He had a way of seeming especially serious when he was joking. Sometimes it was hard to tell.

"As a fan."

"Well, of course she isn't me. I mean," she said with a laugh, "things are tough enough as they are."

She looked up at him in the mirror and saw him smile. He reached out and touched her shoulder and she put her hand over his. After a moment, he went into the bathroom and she heard the shower go on.

If he wanted to, she thought, he could count the pills. Then he would know. She looked at herself in the highlighted mirror, bent toward her own image.

A month before, she had done a face-cream ad that was running in the women's magazines. They had asked her because she was visible again, working. It was an over-thirty-five-type ad and doing it had proved to be a good idea because in it she looked smooth and sleek and sexy. She had given the photographer a face she associated with

Rosalind in *As You Like It*, whom she had played at twenty-three in New Haven.

Lu Anne looked into the mirror at her Rosalind face, stared into her own eyes. There were people, she thought, who must be studying the magazine ad, looking into the eyes.

There would be nothing compromising there. Rosalind was nothing if not sane. Lee Verger loved her above all women.

Rosalind in the looking glass smiled, a tiny curve of the lip on one side. I am Rosalind who can strike you lame with reasons and be mad without any.

Lee Verger smiled back into her mirror. A circus taste bubbled up in her mouth. She thought of a voice but never heard it, only imagined what the voice might say. She closed her eyes and made a fist and rested her forehead on it.

When Lionel came out of the bathroom she straightened up. He had dressed after his shower in white duck trousers and a Filipino wedding shirt; he glowed. He stood beside her again, just where he had stood before, combing his sparse red-blond hair, humming "Don't Cry for Me, Argentina."

"How are you?" he asked after a minute.

"I'm all right," she said, smiling for him. "Mostly tired, I guess. Those period clothes, poof . . ." She shook her head. "It makes you feel for those women back then. The stays. The pins."

"Have you stopped taking your medication?"

"Oh, honey," she said, "please don't."

"I'm very sorry," Lionel said. "Truly I'm sorry to press you. But I must know."

"Did you count them?"

He hesitated. "I had a quick look."

Aware of his displeasure and his eyes on her, she bent her head in shame. Presently, he reached out a hand and began to massage the back of her neck. She could not relax. His touch, the strong fingers kneading the base of her skull, seemed perfunctory and unloving, a fidget.

"You don't know what it's like," she said.

"No. Look," he said softly, "you were acting guilty." He pursed his lips, embarrassed. "If you feel guilty it can mean something's wrong."

"You don't know what it's like to try and work behind the fucking things. Your eyes hurt, you can't use them. Your head weighs a ton."

Lionel took his hand away. "Really, I wish we'd had this out earlier."

"Lionel," Lu Anne said, "I want to try something. I'm finding the drug very hard to work behind and I want to try cutting it for a while."

She looked up at him but his gaze was fixed on some place behind her. He was avoiding her pleas, her sickness. He wanted it simple, done with pills. She supposed she could hardly blame him.

"When did you stop?"

"A week ago," she said. "More than a week."

"And you feel all right?"

"Yes."

"You haven't been hallucinating?"

"Oh, Lionel," she said. She affected a dismissive shudder and a condescending smile.

"Don't bullshit me," he said fiercely.

"I'm not. I've been fine."

"Are you sure?"

"Yes," she said.

"If you stop taking your medication," Lionel told her, "I can't go."

Lu Anne took a deep breath, looked in the mirror and covered her eyes.

"Are you hallucinating now?"

"No," she said.

"Look at me!"

She was staring at the tiled floor. Suddenly she raised her head and looked him in the eye.

"What do you expect to see?" she asked him coldly. "Do you expect to see it?"

Lionel removed his glasses and wiped them on a Sightsaver. He rubbed his eyes.

"As though," she said, "it soiled my eyes. And I should avert them from the doctor's godlike gaze."

"I'm very sorry," Lionel said. "Sometimes I get so frightened I can't function."

She watched him turn away confounded and her heart filled with pity for him and with love.

"It's my enemy," he said, and she thought she heard a throttled sob in his voice. He was looking at her. He was dry-eyed. "It frightens me. I hate it."

She walked up to him and took his right hand and kissed the knuckle of his forefinger, which was callused where he chewed it in his terrors and rages. They were endured, she thought, for her.

"You are my hero beyond fear," she told him. "My knight."

"I've finally come to think of it as evil," Lionel said. "That's a term I've always resisted."

"As unscientific," Lu Anne suggested with faint malice.

"As meaningless. As a word belonging to false consciousness."

"It doesn't have a moral. This . . . condition. Not of the kind you're comfortable with."

"Evil," Lionel agreed, "is not the sort of term I'm comfortable with." He raised his spectacles toward the overhead light and inspected their surfaces. "How extraordinary that the thing should be metabolic. Like gout."

"An undigested bit of beef," Lu Anne said, "like Jacob Marley's ghost. An underdone potato."

Lionel slapped the back of his neck so savagely that Lu Anne started.

"Here I am, see, a specialist in medical practice. In my specialty there are two, maybe three basic pathological conditions. For Christ's sake," he cried, "maybe just one. I can't heal it. I can barely treat it. I don't even have a fucking insight into it." He released his neck and stared wildly into the mirror. "I should go about with a bowl of leeches. I should have become a bloody palmist."

She went to him and touched his cheek. "To each his doctor," she declared. "This is mine." She felt him fighting off tears; somehow he always succeeded. She herself had begun to cry.

Wise as he was, he could not cure her. A part of her rejoiced in that as freedom; the part, she had no doubt, that was mad, bad and dangerous to know. It rejoiced in refuge from his mastery, his shrewdness and compassion. There was a wood through which he could not pursue her with healing arrows and a dark tower of retreat.

"So," he said after a moment, "I'm supposed to leave in the middle of a picture while you go off your medication. What happens then?"

"I'll hassle it."

"Will you indeed?"

"Lionel," she told him, "it's like trying to work behind any drug—grass, Valium, cocaine. You don't know what you're doing. You don't know what you're like." His heavy-browed stare did not seem unsympathetic. "I mean," she went on, "I can't use my eyes. I feel like a droid. It might be neat for having tea with Alan Cranston, but as for work—well, why hire me? They could have anyone. Plenty of people can give a lousy performance without the use of drugs."

"I see your point," he said impatiently.

"What about tardive dyskinesia? Have we talked about that?"

"Lu," Lionel said, "don't worry about tardive fucking dyskinesia. Worry about flipping out. Worry about a second Vancouver." He stood up and paced the bungalow. "I mean, actual straitjackets, right? Actual padded cells. Want to try it Mexican style?"

"I want to stop," she said wearily. "I want to go to work like a normal human actress. I would like to try a little cautious experiment along the lines of . . . trying to do without it . . . for a little while."

"I can't let you do it while I'm away," Lionel said. "The risks are too high. We're away from home. You could have a very bad experience."

He sat down on the bed beside her. She took his hand and looked into his eyes.

"We always agreed that a time would come when I would have to try it alone," she told him. She swallowed and licked her lips, mannerisms she had drilled away, never to be used except intentionally, in character. Well, she thought, I am acting for him now. Perhaps she always was, day in, day out. Perhaps away from the shadows and the Long Friends it was all acting. There was no Lee Verger after all.

So dreadful and frightening was the thought that she doubled her grip on his strong lean hand.

"This is the time," she said. "While the kids are with you. While I'm doing something that I feel so strong about. Man, I want to put my pills aside and be that woman and be me."

Lionel said nothing. She gripped his hand but did not look at him.

"Trust me, love. Trust me and I'll make you proud. It'll be me and it'll be beautiful."

Something in his continuing silence troubled her.

"I mean," she said, "if anything goes wrong because I'm off the pills, won't there be warning signs?"

She heard his dry, bitter laughter. Gently he disengaged his hand from hers, stood up and went to sit in one of the wicker rocking chairs the kids had dragged in from the porch. The chairs were props, strictly speaking, but so comfortable that everyone who could misappropriated them.

"I've been seeing the warning signs all week," Lionel said.

"You never told me."

"I hoped . . ." he began. "I knew you'd stopped. I hoped."

"And were you wrong?" she demanded of him. "Were you wrong to hope?"

He shrugged. "What do I know?" He leaned back in the rocker, his sandaled feet on the bed, his eyes closed. "I hoped."

She went and knelt beside his outstretched knees. He had fallen silent again; it seemed the silence held a message for her but she could not make it out.

"It was a miracle we didn't blow it all in Vancouver," he said at last. "A miracle we kept it under control. They could have been reading about it in every supermarket line in America."

"I was mostly drunk," Lu Anne said contritely.

"I was there," her husband told her. "You were drunk and off your medication." He kept his eyes closed and wiped his brow. "That goes together with you."

"You have to trust me," she said. "This is the time."

More silence. Then he took his legs down and stood, raising her gently beside him.

"Do you think that your performance has improved since you stopped taking those pills?"

She smiled. "I think that's one of the signs you've seen. You've been going to dailies, Lionel. You know it has."

"Christ," he said.

"I don't want to give it up," she cried at him. "I'm on top of the world. I don't want to take them anymore." She turned away weeping. "And be a slave and lose my work and our sex life, a zombie. I don't want to, Lionel."

"It's true," he said. "Your performance has changed." His voice was soft and remote as though he were speaking to an observer or to himself. "You look different in the rushes."

She laughed and turned on her heel.

"I photograph alive now! I have feelings and I can get them out there. I mean, it's so hard with just a camera, Lionel. But I'm doing it now. Acting, it's called. Acting and sort of acting." She exchanged another secret smile with Rosalind in the lighted mirror. "Sometime," she said, "you should get Blakely to show you his collection of old-time rushes. He's got a trunk full of tests and dailies from the old times—the golden age stuff, the old-time stars. Man, if you want to see people working ripped, tranqued and wasted, get him to show you them. Like Monty Clift. The junkies and alcoholics and the controlled crazies." She touched her breast like a penitent. "It's fascinating, Lionel, but it's not pretty." She had been speaking with her back to him; when she turned around he was gone. But he had only stepped out on the veranda. The dusk had given way to starry night. They had lighted the tiki torches along the perimeter of the beach.

Clenched-fisted, his jaw set, he stood with his back against the adobe wall.

"I have an odd superstition," he told his wife. "I keep thinking that one day I'll look over my shoulder—or turn a corner—and one of those things will be there, waiting for me. One of the things you see."

"They have a name," she said. "To neutralize them."

"Don't say it." He cut her off quickly. "Never utter it."

"All right," she said. She looked at him and suddenly understood what the silences had meant, the quick slides from anger into resignation, from obsessive possessiveness to indifference. "Dr. Kurlander told me the same thing. To not say it out loud."

He was going to walk. The surgical touch that passed for tenderness, the shifting moods—that was what they meant. He was tired and he was through with her. Eight years of patient martyrdom and at last he was saving himself, looking after number one. And why not? she thought. It was failure all around, his and hers.

A small electric lamp, styled like a gaslight, gave off a soft light beside their veranda door. The night sky was ablaze with stars. He never turned toward her as she watched him across the shadows.

"I want you to stay in close touch with Kurlander," Lionel told his wife. "I'm going to telephone him and he'll be checking in with you every day. If you're in trouble call him. You can't afford to stop the medication altogether, you'll crack up. But if you take one fifty every morning and one fifty at night you might keep things the way you are at the moment. Remember, you may experience a bad attack as elation."

"So," she said, "if I start feeling too good I'm in trouble."

"You won't feel good long. But don't panic and go back to your regular dose." He turned to the cream-colored wall and struck it. "No booze, no grass, no dope—sorry. When shooting ends, go straight back to your regular dose. In the future," he said, reaching toward her, "who knows? They may come up with something that works as well with fewer side effects. You may stop being crazy. One of us may die."

"There would still be the other," she said. "There would still be the kids."

"The bomb might fall."

"Oh, trust me, love," she said. "Trust me and I'll give you some-thing beautiful."

Lionel smiled. "A movie."

"Don't you like movies, Li?" she asked him wryly. "I tell you, babe—even if they have to take me off this set in a blanket I'm going to work."

He stayed braced against the wall, immobile. She stared at him, knowing he would not turn, that he was afraid of her madness. Sweet Lionel, she told him silently, I'm gonna kiss the ground behind your fading shadow. Only let me keep my children.

"You mustn't cry," he said when he faced her at last.

She wiped her face with the back of her hand.

"Why do you stay with me?" she asked him after a while.

"Because," he said, "to me you are life. And I will not give up on life. It's as simple as that."

For a moment she thought she must be wrong, that he would not go. Then he kissed her, lightly once and then hard on the lips, and then released her. After that she knew he was lost to her.

That's the way you give up on life, she thought. But you go right on living.

"And you," she asked him. "You'll be all right?"

"Oh yes," he said.

She nodded, knowing it was no less than the truth. He would suffer and then he would be all right. And I'll sing your song alone, *mon cher*, she told him. If I can keep my children. One of the things gathered itself up in the dimness at the unlighted end of the veranda.

There were four children, counting the dead, and she did. The little golden ones, Lionel's perfections. Charles, the dead one, in cus-tody of the Long Friends. A girl who looked like her and whom she hardly knew, who lived in Baton Rouge with her ex-husband, Robi-taille, because Momma was crazy in California. She slid her hand down the inside of Lionel's arm, tracing the warm silk, and held his hand, the hand of the man who was getting his courage up to leave her. They stood together for a while and Lionel said with a theatrical flourish: "Well! We may live in hope of our fashionably late dinner, eh? If we don't starve to death first."

She was able to summon a polite smile.

Lionel sniffed the perfumed air. "Think I'll have a walk," he said. "Conceal myself and spy out the preparations for the feast. I can't even remember the way, it's so long since we were asked together."

"It isn't hard to find," she told him. "It's at the end of the left-hand path. At the top."

"Where else?" Lionel said, and went out into the darkness. "I mean dinner with Walter Drogue—we've really arrived, wouldn't you say?"

"Absolutely," Lu Anne said. "Landmarks crumble, baby, but when you say dinner with Walter you're saying all you can say. It should be on the Universal Tour."

She watched him set out for the path; the taste of his betraying kiss was still warm on her lips. She was getting the universal tour. As he strode out of sight she considered herself as life, its deserving stooge and representative.

The Long Friends were gathering in the dark; she felt beyond fear or anger.

She had done her best—she felt sure she had. Lionel had done his, a tough, resolute, truly loving man. She thought she heard little Charles crying; she raised a hand to her mouth. Everyone had done their best.

She must not hate him; it was wrong and no good would come of it.

Then it occurred to her that Gordon Walker must be coming down.

Walker did not try to place the call again. He picked up his drink from beside the telephone and went back to his barstool.

She might have been on the line, he thought. Perhaps it was only a thrill of fear she felt at the sound of his voice. Perhaps calm resolution and refusal. Perhaps someone else had picked up the phone.

But it was Mexico, Mexican phones. As likely as not he had spoken into a dead line, into an unheeding, untroubled past. There was so much to be said, he thought, for leaving things alone.

Beside him, the blond woman on the neighboring stool had put a cigarette to her lips, supporting it with a bridge of fore and middle finger. It seemed somehow a quaint gesture, suggestive of *film noir* intrigue. Walker's hand was on the lighter in his jacket pocket, but he checked the impulse. He did not want to pick her up. And although he was curious about her, he did not feel like forcing conversation.

He studied her in the candlelight. Not bad for the San Epo, he thought. She seemed free of the principal undesirable qualities common to pickups at the lounge, in that she was neither a prostitute nor a man in drag. She seemed, in fact, a fresh-faced, confused and vaguely unhappy young woman who had no business on a San Epifanio Beach barstool. He was about to give her a light out of common politeness when, from somewhere behind him, a flame was thrust forth and she inclined her cigarette to receive it. She smiled uncertainly over Walker's shoulder and murmured her gratitude. Walker, who had not turned around, found himself listening to merry masculine laughter of an odd register. A voice boomed forth, subduing all other sounds in the place.

"I've recently had the opportunity to visit Mount Palomar," the voice declared with a dreadful earnestness, "and was devastated by the sheer beauty I encountered there."

Such a sound, Walker considered, could only be made by forcing the breath down against the diaphragm, swallowing one's voice and then forcing the breath upward, as in song. He listened in wonder as the voice blared on.

"Everywhere I travel in California," it intoned, "I'm—utterly dazzled—by the vistas."

He's raving mad, thought Walker.

"Don't you find your own experiences to be similar?" the voice demanded of the young woman at the bar. It was a truly unsettling sound, its tone so false as to seem scarcely human.

To Walker's astonishment, the woman smiled wider and began to stammer. "I certainly . . . yes . . . why, I do. The vistas are ravishing."

"How pleasant an experience," brayed the voice, "to encounter a fellow admirer of natural wonders."

With as much discretion as possible, Walker turned toward the speaker. He saw a man of about fifty whose nose and cheekbone had been broken, wearing a hairpiece, a little theatrical base and light eyeliner. Returning to his drink, Walker cringed; he had feared to see a face to match the voice and that was what he had seen. It was a smiling face, its smile was a rictus of clenched teeth like a ventriloquist's. The thought crossed his mind that he was hallucinating. He dismissed it.

"So few," the man enunciated, "truly see the wonders nature arrays before them."

How true, thought Walker.

The man eased himself between Walker's stool and the lady's, taking possession of her company and presenting a massive shoulder to Walker, his defeated rival. Walker moved his stool slightly so that he would still be able to see her.

"I know," the woman said, with an uneasy laugh. "The average person can be blind to beauty. Even when it's right in front of them."

Walker sipped his drink. The neighboring dialogue was beginning to make him unhappy. Abandoning his observation of the two newly friends, he turned to see that Shelley had come in. She was standing in a doorway that opened to the windswept terrace; she was smiling, she had seen him. A tan polo coat was thrown over her shoulders, she was wearing pants to match it and tall boots. Under the coat she wore a navy work shirt and a white turtleneck jersey. Her dark hair was close-cropped.

She waved to him and he watched her make her way through the bar crowd. When she was by his side he stood up and kissed her.

"You look pretty tonight, Shell," he said into her ear.

"You look pretty too, Gordo." She cupped her hands around her mouth and croaked at him. "Why are we whispering?"

Walker put a finger across his lips and moved his eyes toward the couple on his right. Shelley peered at them, then looked at Walker with an expression of anticipatory glee. Her black eyes were so bright he wondered if she had been doing drugs.

"Do I discern a visitor to our shores?" the big man inquired in his awful voice. "Great Britain, perhaps?"

The young woman, who spoke with the accent of southern Indiana or Illinois, hesitantly explained that she was not a visitor from abroad.

"What a surprise," the man had his voice declare, while his heavy face did surprise. "Your impeccable pronunciation convinced me you must be from across the water."

Walker looked away. Shelley was hiding behind him on the stool, resting her chin on her hands, grinning madly at the bottles behind the bar.

"Let me see," sounded the man through his morbid grin. "The eastern states, perhaps. I have it. I suspect Boston is the key to your refinement."

"No," said the woman. "Illinois is my native state." She giggled. "I hail from the central region."

Walker glanced at Shelley. She was batting her eyes, doing an impression of goofy cordiality.

"Ah," honked the big man. "How charming. The land of Lincoln."

They listened as he introduced himself as Ulrich or Dulwich or something close. "May I offer you a cocktail?" Ulrich or Dulwich asked gaily. "The night is young and we seem kindred spirits."

Shelley put a hand on Walker's arm. She had seen a free table. They got up and went over to it.

"How come you never say anything like that to me, Gordon? How about offering me a cocktail?"

He called a waitress and ordered Shelley a White Russian, which was what she claimed she wanted. Before the waitress could leave with the drink order Shelley called her back.

"Do you see that man at the bar," she asked the girl, "the big one with the blond lady?" The waitress followed Shelley's nod. "We'd like to buy him a drink."

"Cut it out, Shelley," Walker said.

"When you give him the drink," Shelley said, "tell him we're putting assholes to sleep tonight. And we got his number."

"Shut up," Walker said. "Forget it," he told the waitress. The waitress was tall and dark, with a long melancholy face. One side of her mouth twitched in a weird affectless smile.

"You," she said to Shelley, "you used to work here, right?"

Shelley wiggled her eyebrows, Groucho Marx–like.

"That's right," Walker said.

"So," the girl asked, "you don't want me to . . . ?"

"Of course not," Walker said.

"I myself hail from Tougaloo," Shelley said to Walker. "May one inquire where you yourself hail from?"

"It's so gruesome," Walker said. "It's like a wildlife short."

"What animal is he, hey, Gord?"

"I don't know why we come here anymore," Walker said.

"I bring you here to listen to dialogue," Shelley said. " 'Cause I'm your agent's gal Friday. It's my job."

"It's so fucking depressing."

"Slices of life, Gordo. That's what we want from you. *Verismo*."

"Do you see that guy? Does he really look like that? Is it something wrong with me?"

"No," she said. She spoke slowly, judiciously. "It's a wildlife short."

"She doesn't see him."

"She doesn't seem to, no."

"It's loneliness," Walker said. He shook his head. "That's how bad it gets."

"Oh, yeah, Gordon? Tell me about it."

"I hope," he said, "you didn't get me down here to pick on."

"No, baby, no." She patted his hand and smiled sadly. She shook her head vigorously and tossed her hair, and made mouths at him.

He watched her, wondering if she were not on speed. Of course, he thought, it was difficult to tell with Shelley. She was a clamorous presence, never at rest. Even quiet, her reverie cast a shadow and her silences had three kinds of irony. She was a workout.

"What are you doing with yourself, Shelley?"

"Well," she said, "sometimes I have assignations in crummy ocean-front hotels. Sometimes I get high and go through the car wash."

"Going to open your own shop soon?"

She was watching the man with the voice and his companion. She shrugged.

"I'm not sure I want to be an agent, Gordon."

"Sure you do," he said.

"Look," Shelley said, raising her chin toward the man, "he's gonna light a Virginia Slim. His balls will fall off."

A squat man of sixty-odd passed by their table, carrying an acoustic guitar.

"Hiya, Tex," he called to Shelley. "How you doin', kid?"

"Hi," Shelley replied brightly, parodying her own Texas accent. "Real good, hey."

The older man had stopped to talk. Shelley turned her back on him and he walked away, climbed the Miramar's tiny stage and began to set up his instrument.

"That fuck," she told Walker. "He thinks he's my buddy. When I worked here he practically called me a hooker to my face."

"I can't remember how long ago it was you worked here," Walker said.

"Can't you, Gordo? Bet that's because you don't wanna. Eight years ago. When I left Paramount." She sipped from her drink and turned toward the picture window. The last light of the day had drained from the sky but no lights were lighted in the Miramar Lounge. "Yes, sir, boy. Eight years ago this very night, as they say."

"Funny period that was."

"Oh, golly," Shelley said. "Did we have good times? We sure did. And was I fucked up? I sure was."

"Remember gently."

"Clear is how I remember. I had little cutie-pie tights. Remember my cutie-pie tights?"

"Do I ever," Walker said.

"Yep," she said. "Little cutie-pie tights and I wanted to be an actress and I wanted to be your girl. High old times, all right."

The elderly man with the guitar began dancing about the little stage. He struck up his guitar and went into a vigorous rendering of "Mack the Knife" in the style of Frank Sinatra.

"That rat-hearted old fucker," Shelley said. "I don't know if I can take it."

"How come he called you a hooker?"

"Well shit, I guess he thought I was one." Her eyes were fixed on the singer. "So I called him on it. So he cussed me out and fired me. Now I'm his old friend."

"And you a rabbi's daughter."

"Yeah, that's right, Gordon. You remember, huh? It amuses you."

"The rabbi's raven-haired daughter. Makes a picture."

She blew smoke at him. "My father was a social worker in a hospital. He was a clinical psychologist but he had been ordained. Or whatever it's called."

Walker nodded. "You told me that too, I guess."

"I told you it all, Gordo. The story of my life. You're forgetting me, see?"

He shook his head slowly. "No." He was aware of her eyes on him.

"Hey, you don't look too good, old buddy. You looked O.K. in Seattle."

"I been on a drunk. This is what I look like now."

"You're nuts, Gordon. You live like you were twenty-five. I'm supposed to be a hard-drivin' player and I'm not in it with you."

"It's a failure of inner resources. On my part, I mean."

"You better be taking your vitamins."

"Connie left me," Walker said.

He watched her pall-black eyes fix on his. She was always looking for the inside story, Shelley. Maybe there was more to it, he thought. Maybe she cares.

She drew herself up and studied the smoke from her cigarette. Her mouth had a bitter curl to it; for a moment she was aged and somber.

"Well," she said, "wouldn't I have liked to hear that eight years ago."

"I'm sorry you didn't get to hear it eight years ago," Walker said. "You get to hear it now."

She smiled, a thin sad smile.

"Actually," she said, "Al told me."

"Ah. So you knew."

"Yes," she said. "I knew."

"Hard-ass, aren't you?"

"Come off it, Gordon. You can't cry on my shoulder. It's a fucking ritual. She'll be back."

He turned away from her. The candlelight and the red and green lanterns were reflected in the seaward picture window, together with the faces of the customers. In the glass, everything looked warm and glad, a snug harbor.

"I hope you're right."

She only nodded, holding her faint smile.

"Maybe I shouldn't take it seriously," Walker said. "But I think I do."

A ripple of anger passed across Shelley's face, shattering her comedy smile. Her brow furrowed.

"Do you, Gordon? Then why the hell are you . . ." Her voice was trembling. She stopped in the middle of a word.

"What, Shell?"

"Nothing. I'm not getting into it." She was facing the bar and her gaze had fastened once more on the crooning seducer and his fair intended. Her eyes were troubled. "Look at him, Gordon. He eats shit, that guy. He's a hyena. Let's take him out." She turned to Walker and seized his sleeve. "Come on, man. You can do it. You would have once. Punch the son of a bitch."

"I'm on his side," Walker said. "He's a *bon viveur*. He's a sport like me." He picked up the drink beside his hand and finished it.

Shelley Pearce shook her head sadly and leaned her head against her palm.

"Oh wow," she said.

"I suppose we could effect a rescue," Walker said. "We could hide her out in our room."

"Our room?" She might have been surprised. He thought her double take somewhat stylized. "We have a room?"

"Yes, we have a room. Should we require one."

"How many beds it got?"

"How many beds? I don't know. Two, I guess. What difference does it make?"

Shelley was on her feet.

"Let's go look at it. I think I want to swim in the pool."

"The pool," Walker said, and laughed.

She laughed with him.

"That's right. Remember the pool? Where employees weren't allowed to swim eight years ago tonight? Got your bathing suit?" She worried him to his feet, clutching at his elbow. "Come on, come on. Last one in's a chickenshit."

He got up and followed her out, past the bar. As they went by, the crooning man gave them a languid eyes-right.

"Do you enjoy great music?" he was asking the blond woman. "Symphonies? Concertos? Divertimenti?"

They rode the automatic elevator to the top floor and followed the soiled carpet to their door. The room behind it was large and high-ceilinged with yellow flaking walls. The furniture was old and faintly Chinese in ambiance. The air conditioner was running at full power and it was very cold inside. Walker went to the window and turned it off. Two full-length glass doors led to a narrow terrace that overlooked the beach. He unlocked the bolt that held them in place and forced them open. A voluptuous ocean breeze dispelled the stale chill inside.

"This is neat," Shelley said. She examined the beds, measuring her length on each. Walker went out to the hall to fetch ice. When he returned, she was on the terrace leaning over the balustrade.

"People used to throw ice," she told Walker. "When I worked the front tables people would throw ice cubes at us from the rooms. It would make you crazy."

She came inside, took the ice from Walker and drew a bottle of warm California champagne from her carry bag. As she unwired the wine, she looked about the room with brittle enthusiasm.

"Well," she said, "they sell you the whole trip here, don't they? Everything goes with everything." Her eyes were bright.

"You on speed, Shell?"

She coaxed the cork out with a bathroom towel and poured the wine into two water glasses.

"I don't use speed anymore, Gordon. I have very little to do with drugs. I brought a joint for us, though, and I smoked a little before I went out."

"I wasn't trying to catch you out," Walker said. "I just asked out of . . . curiosity or something."

"Sure," she said, smiling sweetly. "You wondered if I was still pathological. But I'm not. I'm just fine."

"Do you have to get stoned to see me?"

She inclined her head and looked at him nymph-wise from under gathered brows. She was lighting a joint. "It definitely helps, Gordo."

Walker took the joint and smoked of it. He could watch himself exhale in a vanity-table mirror across the room. The light was soft, the face in the glass distant and indistinct.

Shelley's cassette recorder was playing Miles Davis' "In a Silent Way." She took the joint back from Walker; they sat in silence, breathing in the sad stately music. The dope was rich and syrupy. After a while, Shelley undressed and struggled into a sleek one-piece bathing suit. He went to hold her but she put the flat of her hand against his chest, gently turning him away.

"I want to swim," she said. "I want to while I still know about it."

Walker changed into his own suit. They gathered up towels and their ice-filled champagne glasses and rode the elevator down to the pool.

The light around the San Epifanio Beach pool was everywhere

besieged by darkness; black wells and shadows hid the rust, the mildew and the foraging resident rats. There were tables under the royal palms, pastel cabanas, an artificial waterfall.

Walker eased himself into a reclining chair; he was very high. He could feel his own limp smile in place as he watched Shelley walk to the board, spring and descend in a pleasing arc to the glowing motionless water. Across the pool from where he sat, the candles of the lounge flickered, the goose clamor of the patrons was remote, under glass. In a nearby chair, a red-faced man in a sky-blue windbreaker and lemon-colored slacks lay snoring, mouth agape.

Shelley surfaced and turned seal-like on her shoulder, giving Walker her best Esther Williams smile. He finished his champagne and closed his eyes. It seemed to him then that there was something mellow to contemplate, a happy anticipation to savor—if he could but remember what it was. Easeful, smiley, he let his besotted fancy roam a varicolored landscape. A California that had been, the pursuit of happiness past.

What came to him was fear. Like a blow, it snapped him upright. He sat rigid, clutching the armrest, fighting off tremors, the shakes. In the pool a few feet away, Shelley Pearce was swimming lengths in an easy backstroke.

Walker got to his feet, went to the edge of the pool and sat down on the tiles with his legs dangling to the water. Shelley had left her champagne glass there. He drank it down and shivered.

In a moment, Shelley swam over to him.

"Don't you want to swim?"

He looked into the illuminated water. It seemed foul, slimy over his ankles. He thought it smelled of cat piss and ammonia. Shelley reached up and touched his knee. He shook his head.

"You O.K.?"

He tried to smile. "Sure."

In the lounge, the musical proprietor was singing "Bad Bad Leroy Brown." Light-headed and short of breath, Walker stood up.

"I think I'm feeling cold," he called to Shelley.

She paddled to a ladder and climbed out of the pool.

"You don't look good, Gordon. You're not sick, are you?"

"No," he said. "It's just the grass. It's all in my head."

They went upstairs holding hands. Walker took another shower, wrapped a bathrobe around himself and lay down on the bed. Shelley Pearce stood naked before the terrace doors, facing the black mist-enshrouded plane of sky and ocean, smoking. A J. J. Johnson tape was running—"No Moon at All."

When the piece ended she started the tape over again, scatting along with it under her breath. She went back and stood at the window like a dancer at rest. The back of one hand was cocked against her flexed hip, the other at a right angle from the wrist, holding her cigarette. Her head was thrown back slightly, her face, which Walker could not see, upturned toward the darkness outside.

He got off the bed and walked across the room and kissed her thighs, kneeling, fondling her, performing. His desire made him feel safe and whole. After a few minutes she touched his hair, then languidly, sadly, she went to the bed, put her cigarette out and lay down on her side facing him. He thought she wept as they made love. When she came she gave a soft mournful cry. Spent, he was jolly, he laughed, his fear was salved. But the look in her eyes troubled him; they were bright, fixed, expressionless.

"Hello," he said.

"Hello, Gordon."

"Some fun, eh, kid?"

"Just like old times," Shelley said.

"Why did you ask me about the beds?"

" 'Cause I work for a living," she told him. "I need a good night's sleep. If there was only one bed I'd have to drive home."

"You treat yourself better than you used to."

"Yeah," she said. "Everybody treats themselves better now. You're supposed to." After a moment she said, "Hey, Gordon, how come you're sniffing after Lee Verger?"

"Come on," Walker said. "Don't."

"I'd like to hear you tell me how that's a good idea."

"It's my script," Walker said. "I gave it my best. I want to see her do it. In fact, I want you and Al to set it up for me."

"Al doesn't want to do it, bubba."

"Do it on your own. Play dumb. Tell him you thought it was O.K."

"Why don't you take a rest?"

"I don't rest," Walker said.

"I knew you'd pull this," she said. "Al told me about your lunch. I wasn't surprised."

"Did you call them?"

"I called Charlie Freitag's office and I spoke with Madge Clark," Shelley said in a lifeless voice. "I guess they'll put you up for a day or two. Charlie likes you. Charlie likes everybody. They have to work it out with the location people, so it'll take a little time to fix." She stared at him with a vexed child's stare. He avoided her eyes.

"How about giving other people a rest? Like Connie, huh? Or Lee. Why don't you give her a rest?"

He only shook his head.

"She's a fucking psycho."

"That's your story, Shelley."

"Oh yes she is, Gordon. She's just as crazy as catshit and you better leave her alone."

"I want to see her," Walker said.

"You belong in a hospital," Shelley Pearce told him.

He smiled. "Your boss told me the same thing."

"Sure," Shelley said. "We're in league against you." She got up and walked to the foot of the bed and leaned against the bedboard. "You know what crazy people like most, Gordon? They like to make other people crazy."

"You have it wrong," Walker said, "you and Al."

"Her husband is with her. Her kids too. You want to walk into that?"

"I want to work," Walker said slowly. "I want to get back into it. I need a project I care about. I need to work with people I care about."

"You're so full of shit, Gordon."

"Don't be vulgar," Walker said.

"You're an assassin, man. You don't even care if you don't get laid if you can make some woman unhappy."

She stood beside the bed shielding her eyes from the harsh lamplight, then turned her back on him, folded her arms and walked toward the balcony with her head down.

"Every time I see you, we talk about your love life, don't we? We never talk about mine."

"How's your love life, Shell?"

"Thanks for asking," she said.

"Seriously."

"Seriously?" she asked, rounding on him. "Well, it does just fine without you in it. I get along without you . . ."

"Very well."

"Yeah," she said. "That's the line. I get along without you very well." She turned toward him and on her face there was a pained half smile. "It's absolutely true. No question about it."

"Good," Walker said.

She had turned away again, toward the blackness beyond the window; she was singing:

"I get along without you very well,
  Of course I do."

She sang it twice over, snapping her fingers, straining for the key. He watched her come over to the bed.

"Wanna sing along with me, Gord?" She raised his chin with her palm. "Except when autumn rain . . ." she sang. "Da dum de da da dum. Remember, Gord?"

"No."

"No," Shelley said. "Naw. Well, that's good, Gordon. 'Cause then I don't have to worry about you. Or you about me."

"Oh, I don't know," Walker said with a shrug. "People should care."

"Is that what you think, Gordon?" she asked. "You think people should care?"

"Perhaps," Walker suggested, "you find the sentiment banal?"

"No, no," Shelley said. "No, baby, I find it moving. I find all your sentiments moving." She lay down beside him. "You want to fuck some more? Or you too drunk? Tell momma."

Slowly Walker leaned forward, took the champagne bottle from beside the bed and drank. "Stop it," he said quietly.

"Yes," she said. "Yes, all right." She took the bottle from his hand. "Why her? Why Lee?"

Walker shook his head. "I don't know."

"You think you invented her," Shelley said. "You're going to be sorry."

"No doubt," Walker said, and shortly went to sleep.

A sweet expensive tropic darkness had enveloped the Villa Liberia; it was included in the budget and thought to enhance production values. Beyond the tiki torches stood illuminated fences and armed men. These, together with the jacaranda, reminded Lionel of South Africa, of Houghton and home.

To the sound of a gentle surf, Lionel climbed the hotel's elegantly turned stone pathway until he stood upon a broad parapet that commanded the rows of bungalows and the main buildings with their interior gardens and swimming pools. In the lagoon, below and to his left, a few dories swung at anchor, lighted for night fishing. Southward along the coast, beyond the wire, were the lights of the village.

At the parapet, the path divided. A shallow ramp descended to the shadowy beach; a flight of coral-colored steps climbed toward the casitas on the higher slope. Lionel leaned against the stones of the rail and took out a cigarette.

In the morning he would be flying home—Los Angeles, then Rio, then Johannesburg. He had been eight years away. Neither of his children had seen their grandparents. Nor had they seen the beautiful scourged land, the winter roses, apartheid. Thinking about the trip, he was charged with excitement over the children's impending discovery and his own return. They would lose their innocence there, pick up a small portion of the real world's burden, learn fear. It was not all so sanitized there as at Bahía Honda.

He smoked and considered his fear and the fear his children would inherit. He and Lu Anne had talked about the danger. They had agreed it was remote, that the Night of the Long Knives was unlikely to come in that very month of that very season as if only to engulf their children. Luck rarely ran that hard. Yet, he thought, someone's luck would run out there. Sometime, sooner or later, someone and their children, traveling in that country, would awaken in the night out of luck.

For the moment, it was a phantom terror. He was not afraid for himself or for the kids, not really. His long-term apprehensions were serious ones; for his parents too old to run away again, his married sister and her boys, old friends of all colors with complacent styles or dangerous politics. So many of the people who had shared his youth —in Houghton, Durban, the Cape—had become politically involved and he could only imagine the lives engagement imposed on them.

He was a rich doctor in Los Angeles, a world away; a Hollywood shrink, a cliché. Married to an actress whose name would be vaguely familiar in Pietermaritzburg or Maclear or Aliwal North.

Then it struck him how happy, how joyful he was to be going away. He lit another cigarette and watched the twinkling dory lights.

He stood and smoked and considered the petty emotional squalor which was his present stock-in-trade. So aroused was he that it took him some little time to understand that the true source of his excitement—his happiness, in fact—was that he would be getting away from her. From her closely reasoned madness, her nightmare undersea beauty and deluded eyes.

He was startled from this insight by the sound of a woman's laugh-

ter. The laughter was so loud and confident and heedless, so alien to
his lonely despair that it surprised him to anger. Looking up the slope,
he saw in the fairy glow of the patios a blond woman with her back
toward him. She was seated on one of the low, tiled walls that sur-
rounded the whirlpool baths and she appeared to be naked. So far as
he could make out, she was wide-shouldered and slim-waisted, attractive in the latest of California styles, the style which was orthodoxy
on that production. The girls all looked a bit alike to Lionel. Drawing
nearer, he saw that there were two men sitting chest deep in the
whirlpool on which the woman rested.

Inadvertently, Lionel had blundered into the director's compound.
He began to back away along the path he had followed but, uncannily,
one of the men spotted him in the darkness. He heard his name called.
He recognized the man as Walter Drogue. The woman was Drogue's
wife, Patty.

"Lionel," Drogue called to him. "*Bienvenidos!* Come over and have
a drink."

Lionel trudged self-consciously toward the patio. At his approach,
Patty rose from the edge of the Jacuzzi and hastily draped herself in
a burgundy-colored beach robe. The second man in the tub got to his
feet and climbed for dry land, making no attempt to cover his nakedness. He was an elderly man, grizzly of chest and scrotum, his frame
slack and emaciated. He took a chair and observed Lionel's approach
with black gypsy eyes, watchful and expressionless.

The director stayed where he was in the tub, smiling contentedly.
He was deeply tanned. His dark hair, moistly pasted to his forehead
like Napoleon's in a cognac ad, was worn short, shaven about his neck
and ears in an almost military fashion.

"Lionel," Drogue declared, "you and Patty know each other."

"Of course," Lionel said. "Good evening."

"Hi," Patty said, raising her amber eyes to him.

"This is my father, Walter senior," Drogue told his guest, indicat-
ing the naked old man, who had taken a chair beside Patty Drogue.
"He'll be with us for the next ten days. Dad, this is Lionel Morgen,
Lee Verger's husband."

Walter Drogue senior was a man from the mists of legend, a contemporary of Walsh and Sturges and Hawkes. The introduction of this celebrated figure did not put Lionel any more at ease. He felt offended by old Drogue's nakedness. Drogue senior did not offer his hand but instead placed it, all venous and liver-spotted, on his daughter-in-law's caramel shoulder.

"Well," Lionel declared, with a fatuous enthusiasm that chafed in his own hearing. "I'm certainly privileged to meet you, Mr. Drogue."

"Yeah?" old Drogue asked.

"I was just spying out the way, you see. We haven't been up here in the dark."

"I'm glad you came," Walter Drogue the younger said. He had descended to chin level in the whirling green water. "Give us a chance to rap informally. Just ourselves. What would you like to drink?"

Desperate as he was for escape, Lionel decided a drink might be welcome. And indeed there were things for him and Drogue to talk about apart from the general company. The presence of Patty and the old man would have to be endured.

"Well, I won't say no," declared Lionel affably. "If I could have a whiskey? A scotch?"

He had hardly spoken when Patty Drogue disengaged herself from the old man's pawings and hurried into the bungalow.

"So," Drogue junior said from the depths of his whirlpool, "couldn't take it, huh?"

Lionel looked down at the immersed director and chose to conclude that he was being good-naturedly teased, as an outsider.

"Actually," he said, "I've been enjoying myself enormously."

When Patty Drogue came out again, she was carrying a tray heaped with bottles and glasses and shakers filled with ice. Lionel, to demonstrate an easy manner, took up a bottle of unblended scotch and poured himself an undiluted measure.

"That's good," the younger Drogue said. "It's a pretty crazy way to pass whole weeks. Especially if you're not really playing. As a rule, locations and spouses don't mix."

"We've been all right," Lionel said. "I don't think we've been in each other's way, Lu and I." He glanced across the pool and saw that both Patty and old Drogue had settled into pool chairs. Apparently no conversations went unwitnessed in this family circle. "And I see you bring Mrs. Drogue." The whiskey was as smooth as good brandy. Lionel drank rarely but this glass warmed his blood.

Patty Drogue laughed. Her laughter had an unsettling edge, as though he had said something ridiculous.

"That's true," Walter said. He too seemed to be suppressing a secret hilarity. "I always bring Mrs. Drogue."

Lionel assumed an expression of self-assured amusement to show that he could join in the fun.

"South Africa," young Walter Drogue said, "South Africa's easier to handle?"

Lionel held his smile.

"You have to understand that my parents live there. My mother got there from Europe in the very nick of time." He was silent for a moment. "And of course they're quite anxious to see their grandchildren. At their age they can't count on too many visits."

"I didn't mean to put South Africa down, Lionel," Walter said. "I mean—why should you carry the weight? You left, didn't you? To practice here."

Lionel was growing tense. He finished his drink, and before he had a thing to say about it, Patty Drogue brought him another.

"I left," he said. "I suppose I could have stayed and joined the Resistance. I mean . . . friends of mine did. But my parents wanted us all to go. Myself and my sisters."

"Your parents loom large in the picture, huh?"

"You should talk," Patty Drogue said casually to her husband.

Walter junior shrugged good-naturedly. The older Drogue watched her with his blank cautious eyes.

"Silence, exile, cunning," old man Drogue said from the shadows. "And you get to hear the bellyaches of rich Americans. Your parents should be proud of you."

"Wherefore do we lecture Lionel?" Walter Drogue asked charitably. "We've been showing our films to segregated houses out there. We used to do it in our own South. We have plenty to answer for."

"I realize that Mr. Drogue spent time in prison," Lionel said, belching on his drink. He was afraid he might appear obsequious. "Perhaps I'm not made of the same stuff."

"Perhaps," old Drogue said. "I was indicted. I never did time. Life is made of perhaps. Perhapses."

"Lay off him," the younger Drogue said. "He's not getting paid to take this shit from you. Go pick on a qualified professional." He turned sympathetically toward Lionel. It seemed to Morgen that a pattern was emerging in which each of the Drogues would seize an opportunity to protect him from the others. Perhaps even the old man would rally to his defense at the next attack. He glanced into the dark corner where old Drogue was lurking; it seemed, after all, unlikely.

"Don't let him demean you, Lionel. He thinks he invented political commitment. He thinks he invented facing the slammer."

"Well," Lionel said, "it's true enough about me. I've had friends go to the slammer for fighting apartheid but I'm quite untouched."

"You know what the cons say?" old Drogue demanded of them. "They say never trust a man who hasn't done time."

"You don't have to place your trust in me, Mr. Drogue," Lionel said. "I'll be on my way in the morning."

"There were bets down on whether you'd finally leave or stay," young Drogue told him. "Weren't there, Pat?"

"Do I have to say how I was betting?" Patty Drogue asked plaintively.

"Bets?" Lionel asked. "I don't see why anyone was betting. We knew from the start how long I'd be here. I mean, your girls bought my tickets."

"Yeah, sure," Drogue said. "But we thought under the gun you'd be more flexible about it."

"My schedule is not flexible in the least, Walter. I've taken all the hospital leave I can manage. I was back and forth to New Orleans a dozen times. It's taken me a year to organize my appointments in time for this trip."

Young Drogue gave him a long cool look and shrugged amiably. Patty stared into the surgical green light of the whirlpool bath. The old man was invisible within the patio's toy jungle.

"We haven't changed our plans," Lionel said. "I don't see why that should surprise anyone."

Walter emerged naked from the lighted pool and slipped into a boxer's silk robe that had YOUNG DROGUE embroidered across the back. The Drogues' collective nakedness had begun to repel and embarrass Lionel. In his experience, the clothed party held the advantage in mixed encounters. Within the Drogue compound, this principle seemed to have been reversed.

"O.K.," Walter Drogue the younger said.

"So," Lionel said, "as I am on my way out, I thought we might speak privately for a bit."

Young Drogue sat down on a plastic chair and stretched, yawning luxuriantly. "What a good idea," he told the psychiatrist. "Patty," he told his wife, "bring me a drink, please. And bring the good doctor one. And the aged P." Walter Drogue the elder swore audibly from his corner of darkness.

"We exploit Patty a little," Walter explained to Lionel. "She wouldn't have it any other way."

"I'd like to speak privately," Lionel said.

"This is privately, Lionel," Walter Drogue said. "This is as private as we let it get."

"It's about Lu Anne," Lionel said.

"No shit?"

"I think I just wanted to know . . . from a second source, as it were, how things were going."

Walter gave him a soft smile. "Fine, Lionel. Things are going fine."

"She's quite good, isn't she?"

"Oh, I think that would be an understatement, Doctor. She's always good, your Lu Anne. But this is something else."

"And the picture? Your feeling about the picture is good as well?"

"Lu Anne and I are the picture," Walter Drogue said. "We two together. And we're good enough to eat."

"I've been seeing dailies as soon as they come in," Lionel told Walter Drogue, "and I'm terribly impressed."

"We're sitting on a treasure, my friend. We're going to astonish the world."

Patty returned with another tray of drinks.

Lionel wiped his glasses. His head ached with the whiskey.

"I thought . . ." Lionel began. "I wanted to be sure everything was all right with her."

The director was silent. Lionel drained his glass.

"Would you like another?" Patty Drogue asked.

"Oh no," Lionel said. "Not now."

"She likes bringing drinks," Walter Drogue explained.

"It's my way of atoning," Patty said.

"Tell me what you think," Walter Drogue said soberly. "You're her husband, you've been living with her. You're a . . . specialist in human behavior. How do you think she's doing?"

"I don't think that since she left the stage she's been so involved in a show," Lionel said.

"Surely," Drogue said, looking about with his bright-eyed smile, "this is good news?"

"Well," Lionel said, "yes."

"But . . . ?"

"Her eyes," old man Drogue said from the shadows. "I remember her eyes from when she first came out here." They all turned toward him. "It didn't show up in her glossies," old Drogue went on. "You could turn the page right past her. Up on the screen, her eyes, they'd fucking lay you out. I remember," he said. "From when she first came out here."

Lionel stared at his huddled figure in the darkness, trying to think of something to say.

"Before sound," old Drogue said, "they would have loved her eyes."

"Even you don't go back that far," Patty Drogue told the old man

playfully. "Can you really say 'before sound'?" She did a bass imitation of his rasp.

"He was here before sound," her husband told her. "He worked
on *House of Sand*."

"You look at their eyes from those days, you'll see eyes." He grunted,
a laugh or the clearing of his throat. "They came from tough lives."

"*House of Sand*!" Patty Drogue declared. "I love it! I love it," she
told Lionel, "when they say 'before sound.' "

"That was the last one Everett French did. He was a lush then. I
cut it for title inserts."

"That's romantic," Patty Drogue said. "Everett French losing his
shit to gin. Fitzgerald-like."

"So *you* tell *me*," young Drogue said, addressing himself to Lionel.
"How's my actress and your lady wife?"

"Listen," Lionel said. He was holding on to Walter Drogue's silken
sleeve, the sleeve of his boxer's robe. When he saw the Drogues staring
at his hand he took it away. "There is a certain kind of artist, don't
you think," he asked them, "who might be described as a *halluciné*?"

"Dickens," Patty Drogue said with enthusiasm. "Joan Miró. What
do you think, Walter?"

Young Drogue's *faux naïf* smile tightened.

"Sure," he said, turning the very word to bitter mimicry. "Dickens
and Joan Miró."

"Wagner," old man Drogue said from his unseen perch. "Mahler.
Max Reinhardt."

Lionel was impressed at their erudition. "Those are all," he said,
"wonderful examples."

"How about another drink?" Patty asked.

"No, no," Lionel said. "Your guests will be here. I've got to get
back shortly to pick up Lu Anne."

"Bela Lugosi played Hamlet for Reinhardt," the elder Drogue in-
formed them. "They called him the greatest Hamlet of the German-
speaking theater."

"But over here," Patty Drogue pointed out, "Abbott and Costello
were waiting for him."

"Because he was a junkie," Walter said, still smiling. "Because it was Hollywood."

"Well," Lionel said, "that's how I see Lu Anne."

"As a *hallucinée*, right, Lionel?" Patty asked. "Not as a junkie."

"No, no," Lionel reassured Mrs. Drogue. "As a *hallucinée*."

"Like Dickens," young Drogue suggested.

Lionel paused a moment, then laughed politely. "Well, I don't have to tell you this, Walter, I'm sure. But some performers put a tremendous emotional investment into their roles. They can't hold back. They pay a very high price for their work."

"And that's Lu Anne, isn't it, Lionel?" young Drogue asked.

"Well," Lionel said, "yes. I mean, I don't know that much about acting—how it works from inside. It's a mystery to me. Like all mysteries, I find it a bit frightening."

"You're a philosopher, Lionel. A student of the mind. And you think the price of this performance might be a mite high for your wife in her sensitive condition. The scenes we're shooting from now on are some of the most intense in the script. It's a shame you can't stay for them."

"I'm sorry," Lionel said. "I thought I was performing yeoman's service putting in so much time down here. I was led to understand location shooting would be over by now."

"That was last year."

"Yes. Well, last year is when I arranged for the journey. Originally we thought we'd go together. My parents have planned around it. The kids' schoolwork has been arranged for. Why are you treating me like a deserter?"

"Come on, Lionel," young Drogue said. "I'm not doing that. Do you know who Gordon Walker is?"

"He's the scriptwriter."

"Did you know he was coming down?"

"I heard something about it," Lionel said. No one had breathed a word to him.

"Old pal of Lu Anne's, right? Sort of a second Dickens?"

"I know who he is," Lionel said. "I know he went out with Lu Anne. What are you suggesting?"

Young Drogue displayed opened palms. "Hey, Lionel, I never suggest. If I want to say something I just up and say it."

"It sounded to me," Lionel said, "as though you were implying something that's none of your business."

"Not at all, Lionel. Nothing of the kind. You have to leave, so you'll leave." He sighed. "I just thought everybody should understand everybody else's feelings. See, we're Californians. Compulsive communicators. We're overconfiding and we're nosy. Don't mind us."

"I wouldn't worry about Gordon Walker, Lionel," Patty Drogue said soothingly. "I mean, there's much less sex on movie locations than a lot of people think."

Lionel turned to her blankly. "I beg your pardon?"

"Ah, let him come," young Drogue said. "Maybe tension will enrich her performance? Think so, Lionel? I think it's possible. Anyway," he told Lionel good-humoredly, "I can swallow that asshole with a glass of water."

"She'll be all right," Lionel said. "We've agreed it's time for her to handle it alone."

"No second Vancouver?" Drogue asked delicately.

"She'll be all right," Lionel said.

"And you've got Kurlander covering in case of emergency, right? He's agreed to come down if necessary?"

"That was privately arranged."

"Should we put him on the payroll?" Drogue asked. "We might do that."

"I've taken care of it. I don't think you'll need him."

"I'm really glad we had this talk," Drogue said. "So we could find out where we stood. By the way, have you read the script?"

"Of course," Lionel Morgen said. But he had not. He had glanced at the Chopin book and leafed through a few of the scenes his wife was to appear in. That was all. He was instantly appalled at his own defensive lie.

"We thought you'd stay," Patty Drogue intoned sweetly. "We thought you'd decide Lee needed you and stay."

"I offered to stay," Lionel said stolidly. "In spite of the difficulties. She agreed that I should go."

"Well," young Drogue said cheerfully, "you're the doctor."

There came the clatter and rustle of arriving guests ascending from the terraces below.

"Great eyes," old Drogue said. Lionel's own eyes had grown accustomed to the shadows and he saw that in the alcove where old Drogue was, a hammock had been strung between two date palms and the old man sat astride it. He looked, Lionel thought, like an old parrot on a stick swing. "But her pictures don't make money."

Lionel thought of his wife's eyes and of his own image in them. "She said," Lionel told them, "that if she couldn't finish this one without me she was through."

"That settles it, then," young Walter Drogue said. He advanced and put his arm around Lionel's shoulder. "You want to get our leading lady and bring her on up, right, Doc? Can't have a party without her."

Patty Drogue was wheeling an entire dollyful of canapés over the cobblestones of the patio.

"Make way," she called. Her voice echoed over the hillside as she greeted the arriving guests across darkness. "Hello, you guys. Help yourselves to drinks while we get changed."

Walter Drogue was walking Lionel to the path, holding him in an embrace. At the top of the pink steps, Lionel swept Drogue's arm from his shoulder and started down, slowly and silently, ignoring the people going by. He came to the parapet at which he had stopped on the way up to watch the lights.

Drogue's expensive liquor churned in his guts. For one self-loathing moment, he imagined he could smell his own cologne but it was only some overripe sweet odor of the place.

She had called him her knight and he was leaving her to them. He was numbed with his own betrayal. In their way, although they had it wrong, they were right to despise him. He loved her. But her madness was too much for him. It was stronger than he was, and evil.

Evil, a word attaching to false consciousness.

Now he would go, with his children, and in his faraway country he would think about it and he would see.

In the meantime, he recalled with a shudder, there was dinner to be endured. Dinner with the Drogues.

Dinner with the Drogues took place under the stars. Lionel was silent and vague. People who did not know him did not realize that he was drunk and thought he might be deaf or even a little slow, like someone recovering from a cerebral injury.

Lu Anne for her part had never seen her husband so utterly besotted. More like a drunken cricketer than a medical Svengali with his schizoid Trilby in tow. Those among the guests who had come to see him spoon-feed her got to watch her half carry him down the path to their casita.

In the bedroom, she had to undress him, practically put him in bed. He was not there at all, no more for her than for anyone else. She worked hard not to think about his leaving and she was tired and a little drunk and that helped.

Once, as they lay together, the full moon visible through the casita's window, he reached out and took her hand. If she saw or heard anything, he told her—anything that might not really be there—she was to press his hand and wake him. Slim chance of that, she thought. They were already gathering. But that night at least she would sleep.

Well after she was certain he had passed into oblivion, he startled her by taking her hand again.

"I have discovered," he announced, "the exact way in which America made sex obscene."

"What?"

Intrigued, she struggled toward waking. But he had gone to sleep again, his hand still pressed to hers. So she was alone in the darkness.

In solitude. What a beautiful word, she thought. And beautiful in Spanish, *soledad*. It was the name of a prison.

Still holding her husband's hand, she began to pray.

In the dingy coffee shop, Walker took a breakfast of rye toast and tea. A hard steady rain drilled against the panes of the seaward windows. The ocean-borne wind rattled the ornate rusted fastenings that secured them and rainwater seeped through the rotten moldings to form small puddles on the checkerboard floor.

He smoked and watched the rain, ignoring the morning paper spread out on the unsteady table before him.

Shelley had gone while he was still asleep. She had left a note commanding him to stay in town until he heard from the agency and to call her that afternoon.

After a few minutes, he took his newspaper upstairs to pack and outwait the rain. As soon as he had closed the door behind him, he set about running more cocaine. He had no sure purpose for the day, only the dream of going south. The dream provided him a happiness against all reason, it was succor and escape. Coke turned it adamantine, to mythic longing. As he stood at the window over the rain-soiled sea, his blood quickened at the prospect. He felt then that it was all he had.

The rain increased. Walker paced the length of his room. He had begun to think about his script for *The Awakening*, sustaining a glow of proprietary satisfaction. He had not looked at it for many months. Suddenly now, a prisoner of the morning rain, he lusted after the thing and it occurred to him that in the addled state to which he had reduced himself he might have forgotten to bring it along. He brought his suitcase out of the closet and quickly found his two copies in their blue bindings. He picked one out and seated himself in one of the room's musty elephant-colored armchairs to read it over. As soon as he turned the cardboard cover an airmail envelope slid from between the pages and landed in his lap.

The envelope contained a month-old letter from his younger son at prep school. He had received it just after the closing of *Lear* in Seattle, tucked it away with the scripts in token of a determination to respond, then forgotten it.

Walker sat looking at his son's unanswered letter, smarting with guilt and shame. So stricken was he that he nearly put it aside. Ever since his sons had left home he had written them regularly, demanding replies. Even when his older boy, Tom Moore who was called Deak, had stopped writing or phoning back—had, in effect, stopped speaking—Walker had gone on writing, composing what he himself called sermonettes. That he had forgotten Stuart's letter was a measure of the low place in which he found himself.

"Dear Parents," Stuart Walker had written. "When I woke up this morning I asked myself where's my change of season? Here it's mid-September and the sugar maples are turning awesome colors. Everything's the way it's supposed to be except me because I'm just not *feeling* it . . ."

Walker folded the letter, put it aside and went to the suitcase for his book of telephone numbers. He looked at his watch: it was nearly twelve in Maine and he might catch his son in the dorm between his last morning class and lunch. When he had found the number he dialed it and asked the boy who answered for Stuart Walker. His son came on the line.

"Christ, kid," Walker said, "I'm sorry I didn't answer your letter. Things have been confused. I've been busy."

"I guess that's good, huh?"

"Yeah," Walker said, trying to sound as though it was good. "Better busy than not."

"Hey, Dad," the boy said. "You know Mom was here. She was on her way to London."

"That's right. How was she?"

"She was really funny about it."

"Was she indeed?"

"Really," Stuart told his father. "She was a riot. Good old Mom."

"Good," Walker said cautiously. His son was opaque, a politician. "So it was all pleasant?"

"She was fine," Stuart said. "You don't have to worry about her."

Walker felt a wave of simmering anger rise in his breast. He mastered it quite easily.

"When you wrote you said . . . you said . . . you weren't feeling the change of seasons. I wondered . . . whether, you know . . . everything was all right with you. And if you were down . . . whether you still were. And if . . . I was hoping," he stammered on, "that it was better."

"Right," the boy said. "Well, that was a couple of weeks ago."

Yes indeed, Walker thought. How tidily this kid kept score. Deak never did, never in the same relentless fashion. Nor did Walker himself. His wife did but her way was gentler. She was forgiving. Her younger son was not.

"Sure," Walker senior said. "Of course."

"I think I was down because I'd just been hanging out with Deak. You know how he's been."

Walker knew something about the way his son Deak had been for the past year and his heart went cold with fear.

"He doesn't write or call us," Walker said to his younger son. The taste of a whine hung on his lips, a savor of special pleading. "We don't know how it is with him."

"Sometimes I get mad at him," Stuart said. "Then I get brought down, you know, and I wish there was something I could, like, tell him. But what can I tell him? It was always Deak who told me what was what."

"What I worry about," Gordon Walker said, "is drugs." It was painful for him to say it; his sons knew his ways well enough. Yet it was what he worried about.

"Yeah," Stuart said, and no more.

Walker hesitated.

"Well," he finally asked, "should I worry?"

"No," the boy said without conviction. "I don't think so."

"Is he dealing?"

"You have to ask *him*, Dad."

"I thought," Walker said, "because we both loved him . . . we might . . . as it were . . . take counsel together."

"Oh," Stuart said. "Oh, for sure."

Walker bit his lip.

"Did your mother see him?"

"Yeah. We went to dinner in Portland."

"Good," Walker said. "How was it?"

"He was a little wasted," Stuart said. There was a suggestion of good-natured laughter in his voice.

"Oh God," Walker said aloud.

"I think we ought to get together all of us. We might all go over to London. Deak would go for that."

"I don't know about that," Walker said.

"I guess," Stuart Walker said, "I'm being naive."

Walker sighed. "I'm glad you enjoyed your summer of stock."

"Oh yeah," the boy said, "it was excellent. They asked me back, O.K.?" For the first time in their conversation Stuart seemed to speak without calculation. "Next year, wow, am I looking forward to that."

"And you'll be in the school play this year?"

"Hey, Dad," Stuart said, "are you kidding? You know I'll be in it. They don't call it the school play," he added. "They don't like that. They call it Masquers. Because we're all so preppie pre-professional here."

"I suppose," Gordon Walker said, "that's what I'm paying for." He heard his son laugh politely.

"Listen, kid," he said. "Take care of yourself. I'll see you at Christmastime."

"How will we do that this year, Dad?"

"I don't know. I'll call you. And Stu—" he called before the boy could hang up. "If you hear from Deak—if you see him—tell him for Christ's sake to call me."

After a few minutes he took up Stuart's letter and read it through again. Reading it oppressed him; when he had finished it he was left with a mixture of depression and anxiety that felt for all the world like grief.

The letter was a good one, observant, witty, boyishly rueful. There was a little about the opening of term and a few cautious lines about Deak that were at once concerned and humorous. Most of it recounted Stuart's adventures with a summer theater company in Rhode Island. He wrote tellingly about the two plays that had been done—a ten-year-old Broadway comedy and *Ah, Wilderness!* He described his humiliation at being scorned for his youth by girls his own age who competed for the older actors. He described, without names, the artful, courteous and good-natured manner in which he had turned aside the advances of a homosexual actor who was an old friend of his father's. He wrote about the audiences, the town, the adolescent social scene, about a drama student whose name was Blanche and who had called him an odious buffoon. It was a delightful letter. Any reader would conclude that its author was openhearted, generous and affectionate—all of which Walker knew well his younger son was not. Tom—Deak—the older boy, was all those things, or had been once.

Stuart Walker had talent and his parents' good looks. He was unusually literate for a seventeen-year-old and successful at school. But it was as an actor that he truly dazzled. At fifteen he had performed on the Off-Broadway stage in the limited run of a surreal English drama. Since that debut he had been offered parts on the average of two a month. His summer theater experience had been intended by his parents as an exercise in humility and he had not objected. He was preternaturally wise, would wait, study longer, listen and learn. At times Walker and his wife would look on their younger son with superstitious dread, so bright did his possibilities appear.

In his oceanside hotel room, Gordon Walker examined the letter once more. He realized now one of the reasons that he had not answered it on receipt, unconfronted at the time but plain enough now. The letter had provided Stuart with an opportunity for one of his

uncanny imitations of his older brother. "Uncanny" was one of the
words critics had used in praising Stuart's performance.

He was a shrewd, unconfiding boy, four years younger than Deak.
Circumstances or a harder nature had driven him inward, toughened
him and toughened him until his heart shriveled. The years of Stuart's
childhood had been a stormy time for Walker and his wife. They
were both ambitious, jealous of each other, consumed with the Life.
Connie had tried to keep working, rehearsing, studying. There had
been the business with Lu Anne. Probably neither of them was there
enough, in the right ways. They never spoke of it although they both
knew; it was too hard.

Stuart had hidden and survived. Deak, who was loving and sensitive, had been caught in the coils; neither his humor nor his grace had
served when the drugs came like a punishing wind to sweep away all
the unprotected children. Abstemious Stuart did just fine.

So, to please, no doubt unconsciously, as a part of his uncanny
repertoire, Stuart would perform his Deak impression and glow with
a kindly fire not his own. That had been Deak's when Deak was
healthy and favored.

Walker crumpled up the letter and thought of Deak, his passionately loved, his angel.

Faint with anguish, he stood up and walked to the window. If—
perhaps, only to speculate—he went through it and over the balcony,
the pain would stop. He could do it any number of ways.

If he went out he would be killing Deak. Deak would eventually
follow him, in that as in everything. Probably he would be killing
Stuart as well. Stuart would prosper, have his fame and fortune, but
time would bring him down. You could not make his kind of adjust-
ment without paying in the end.

So there could be no question of leaps or lethal measures. The
luxury of abandoning hope was not available to him. Hope might
make a fool of him and compound his grief, but he was bound to it
as much as the next man. For his sons, himself, even his marriage.
He leaned against a cornice beside the balcony window and took deep

hopeful breaths, his eyes closed. It was a matter of inner resources. It was a matter of getting through the day.

When he was ready for the road again, Walker checked himself out of the San Epifanio Beach and drove back to the San Diego Freeway. Within an hour he was at the boat basin north of Rosa Point.

He found a spot in the club parking lot and got out and walked along the dockside. The rain had stopped; pale sunshine was filtering through the low cloud. A party fishing boat rode at anchor off the point but the sea was still rough and there were few sailboats out. A stiff wind from the bay rattled the wire rigging of the boats at moor, banging stays against masts in a ceaseless tintinnabulation.

One of the dozens of powerboats tied up in the basin was a forty-foot Chris-Craft rigged with a pulpit; the legend SAM THE MAN was inscribed on her brightly finished after woodwork. Walker halted beside the boat, braced against a piling and called down into the cabin.

"Quinn?"

A portly sandy-haired man, deeply tanned, came up from the cabin and squinted up at Walker. He was bare-chested and powerfully built, although a slab of gut hung down over the waist of his dungarees. There was a red neckerchief at his throat.

"Hey, Gordo," he said, and wiped his mouth as though he were hiding a smile.

"Hello, Sam."

"You want a drink?"

"I want some cold water," Walker said.

Quinn ducked back into the cabin and emerged with two bottles of clear liquid. One he handed up to Walker; the second he upended and drank from deeply.

"Want to give me a ride, Gordo? Figure you were on your way up to the ranch anyhow, right?"

"Sure," Walker said.

They went back to Walker's car and took off along the coast road. A few miles south of the point they passed a crescent beach tucked between cliffs; offshore twenty or so leonine surfers sat their boards in the chop, waiting for a wave. Walker pulled over and they got out,

walking through ice plant that was littered with beer cans and cello-
phane bags.

"Little fuckers go on forever," Quinn said.

Walker stopped near the edge of the cliff and lit a cigarette.

"I had a fantasy once," Quinn said. "I'd get a net a quarter mile
wide. I'd get a dragger, a galleon with black sails." He turned to
Walker, who had hunkered down in the brush. "Under cover of the
fog I'd come in, see, and I'd play out my net and I'd catch the young
turkeys and haul 'em in. Fill my hold with 'em. Boys. Girls. Don't
matter." He reached into his pants pocket, took out a joint and lit it.
"Work the coast clear from Mendocino to Imperial Beach. Then,
when I had a load, I'd sail the whole mess to Jidda. Sell 'em as slaves
to the Arabs."

Walker declined the joint when it was offered, knowing how strong
it would prove.

"You told Lu Anne about that plan," Walker said. "She told me."

"Sweet thing," Quinn said. "She's working down in B.H."

"I know," Walker said. "I'm going to see her."

Quinn grinned at him with a sidewise glance. One of the caps on
the man's front teeth had a gold death's-head design worked into it.

"Fine woman. You kiss her for me, man."

They got back in the car and drove until the highway was inter-
sected by a dirt road, running between rows of glass commercial
greenhouses. They turned off there. After the last greenhouse there
were rows of avocado trees and then the road began to climb, ascending one side of a canyon. Yellow tule grass grew on the crest of the
hills. On the inland slopes there were live oak and cactus. Their road
crossed and recrossed dry riverbeds and tributary canyons until it
ended at a cattle grid. A wooden ranch fence held a sign that read:
DANGER NERVOUS GUN FREAK. There was another sign that said: TRES-
PASSERS WILL BE VIOLATED. Beyond the fence was a grove of cotton-
woods and beyond the trees an old white frame farmhouse with an
attendant barn and duck pond.

Walker parked in front of the barn, alongside a dusty Bentley which
was missing a wheel.

"Everything pretty much as usual?" he asked Quinn.

"Yes and no," the big man said. "Little of this, little of that. What's up with you?"

Walker told him that his wife had left for London, about the play in Seattle and his plan to visit Lu Anne. Quinn nodded curt approval.

"Connie was always bourgeoise."

"Connie was a fucking hero," Walker said.

The pain of loss he felt when he thought of her quite surprised him. He had only begun to realize that he had seen the last of her heroics and that she would not be coming back to him.

For years he had survived through her calm resolution and good sense; suddenly she had used them in her interest. He had not expected that. It seemed like betrayal to him.

For his part, he had never stopped loving her. Now he would have to force her out of his mind, confine her to the interior white space that held all those elements of his life too painful to consider. He could manage it, he thought; he was tough and selfish enough.

As he grew older, the number of things he sought to banish from his consciousness increased and so did his skill at keeping them in isolation.

"Whatever you think, Gordo."

Behind the house was a small field with a dog pen, a fenced corral and an overgrown garden enclosed by strands of wire. Empty milk jugs were tied at intervals along the wire to stir on the breeze. It was close and warm in the hollow where the ranch was; hills shut out the ocean wind. The sky overhead was clear.

Walker and Quinn took chairs on the back porch.

"Lu Anne," Quinn said reflectively. "She's all right. I was glad to hear she's working again."

"She's a lead," Walker said. "My script."

"Yeah, I heard all that." He rocked slowly back and forth, watching his guest. "How's her head?"

"I haven't seen her much," Walker said. "What else have you heard?"

Quinn shrugged. "Not a lot. That she married a doctor years back. A shrink. Probably handy for her to have one at home."

"Yeah," Walker said.

"Funny her getting an Oscar nomination for playing spacey," Quinn said.

"Yes," Walker agreed. "We all used to kid about that."

"But she's good," Quinn said. "That's the thing. There's no one better than Lu Anne. Not out here. Not in New York."

"What about you, Sam? Working any?"

Quinn smiled, flashing his Jolly Roger.

"Too old and fat," he said. He was leaning back in the rocker looking at the sky. Walker turned to follow his gaze and saw two people hang-gliding high above the next ridge. They were beautiful to watch and, Walker thought, incredibly high. They seemed to command the wind that bore them.

"Shit," Quinn said, "look at that."

"Does it make you paranoid?" Walker asked.

"Nah," Quinn said. "Makes me fucking cry, is what. Think that isn't kicks, man? That's the way to do your life, Gordo. Look the gray rat in the eye."

"I think we all do that anyway."

"We're little worms," Quinn said. "We piss and moan."

"So," Walker said, "I wonder if you can help me out."

Quinn crooned in a black-toned bass. "Got yo' weed, got yo' speed, got yo' everythin'."

"I'm on this fucking thing," Walker explained. "I'm doing a lot of blow and then I'm drinking. I have to dry out. I need downers."

Quinn screwed up his face and sounded a high-pitched comic cry.

"Ai, Gordo. I don't got them. I got blow. Speed. Sinsemilla. No downers. Except, you know, I could get horse but that's not for you in your frame of mind."

"Christ," Walker said. "I was hoping to break the cycle."

"Sorry, man."

"I'll have to wait until I get down there, then. I hope Siriwai's the doctor on this picture."

"Siriwai's got a Laetrile clinic now. I doubt he even works flicks anymore."

"Are you serious?"

"Absolutely. He's got this enormous spread in San Carlos Borromeo. He cures cancer."

Walker sat in silence, looking at the dun boards of the back porch.

"If you're gonna drive," Sam Quinn said, "it's not that much out of your way. I'm sure old man Siriwai could fix you up if he felt like it."

"I suppose," Walker said.

"Hate to send you away disappointed, Gord. Can I offer a drink? A fine line?"

"Oh sure," Walker said.

Quinn got up and went into the kitchen. Walker sat rocking, watching the hang gliders. When he looked down again, he saw a young red-haired woman coming from the barn, leading a little boy of about three by the hand. The young woman's eyes were fixed on Walker as though in recognition. As far as he knew, he had never seen her before. He rocked and watched the two of them approach.

"Hello," he said, when they had reached the porch, and directed a cordial smile at the child.

"You're Gordon Walker," the woman said.

Walker was not used to being recognized by name. The woman before him looked like a great many other women one saw in Los Angeles; she was attractive, youthful a bit beyond her years. She seemed like someone imperfectly recovered from a bad illness.

Her face broke into a sudden, quite marvelous smile.

"You don't remember me," she said. "I'm Lucy Brewer. I played the radical chick in *Stover*." The child, who had Lucy's auburn hair, shouted and pulled against her grip. "Woman, I should say. Of course, they cut a lot of me."

"Sure," Walker said. "Certainly I remember you." He had absolutely no recollection of Lucy Brewer and very little of the character. *Stover* had been the next thing to a doctoring job, done years before. "I have trouble with names," he assured her. "But I don't forget people."

"You had a cute little boy, I remember. You brought him out to the set."

"I have two," Walker said. "They aren't little anymore."

"Well, he was one cute little guy."

"He's an actor now," Walker told her.

"Another one of us, huh?" She was good-humoredly restraining her own little boy with both hands. The child broke away finally and ran off toward the corral.

"Speaking of cute kids," Walker said.

"We were having our nature walk. We saw the animals and the cemetery."

Walker chuckled agreeably. Sam Quinn came out with two drinks on a tray. Beside them was a tiny glass bottle of cocaine with a miniature chain attached to its cap. Seeing Sam, the little boy turned around and came running back toward the porch.

"Sam Sam Sam," the infant shouted.

"What cemetery?" Walker asked. Quinn handed him a drink.

"Ah," Sam Quinn said, "we bury the animals. We have a ceremony."

"And we buried Hexter," the little boy cried.

Quinn sighed. "We gotta talk about this," he said to Lucy. "I mean really."

"We buried our dog," Lucy said merrily. "Hexter."

"Oh," Walker said. A few years before he had known an aspiring screenwriter, a fellow Kentuckian, by the name of Hexter. Hexter had left for New Mexico some time before.

Lucy gathered the child to her loins. She seemed oppressed by Quinn's even stare.

"Well," she said to Walker, "best of luck."

"The same to you, Lucy," Walker said. He waggled his fingers at the little boy. Lucy took the boy by the hand and led him off.

Sam Quinn turned his back on an imaginary breeze, dipped the cap-spoon device into the vial of cocaine and had himself a snort. Done, he screwed the cap on and passed the works to Walker.

"I'm a murderer," Quinn explained. "I murder my enemies. I bury them under my barn and then I drink champagne from their skulls."

"We were talking about a dog," Walker said.

"We were friends," Quinn said. "We were close. He got into fucking nitrous oxide and he was *not* getting it from me. One time he comes up here from Taos and his pickup is loaded with tanks. We have parties, it's great, except he won't stop doing it." Quinn sniffed and wiped his nose with his wrist. "So one morning I go into the john and Hexter's in the tub. He's underwater and he's stone fucking dead and the tank's on the floor next to him. So what am I supposed to do, send for Noguchi? I don't want the damn cops up here. I loved that man, Gordon. He was like a brother."

Walker took a hit off Quinn's coke. It was very fine, better than his own. It dispelled his anxiety and his sorrow about his sons. He watched Quinn with a tolerant smile.

"I welded him into an oil drum and we brought out the Bible and we laid him to rest. He was divorced, didn't have no kids. He's home, man, he's in Abraham's bosom." Quinn shrugged. "All right—it sounds kind of sordid."

"I see," Walker said, and did another tiny spoon.

They sipped their vodka-and-tonics. The hang gliders disappeared beyond the inland ridge.

"I have to get out of this business, Gordo. My nerves are shot. My life is in danger. Then I got Lucy and Eben to think of."

"Funny," Walker said. "I can't remember meeting Lucy."

"*Stover*," Sam Quinn said. "I don't think she's worked since then. She had a speed problem and a couple of crazy boyfriends. I helped her out."

"The kid yours?"

Quinn shook his head. "I can't tell you whose kid that is, Gordo. Very big name. Since deceased."

"You ought to get out," Walker said. "I thought you'd be doing stunts forever."

"Yeah, I was born to die in a burning stagecoach. But I'm too old for it, that's the problem. I tell you, Gordon, this after-forty shit sucks."

"You could coordinate. You been all over. You know a lot about filmmaking."

"I'm associated in the industry with drugs. Once that didn't matter.

But these days it is not so good." Quinn drained his glass and set it
aside. "I ought to move. Maybe up to Newhall—I got a lot of old
buddies up there might get me something. I should get Lucy out of
here, get her straight. I should sell my boat, sell this place—I'd get
ten times what I paid. There's a couple of hundred goddamn things
I should do. But I don't know which, the way things are. I don't want
to be broke no more, Gordon, I ain't used to it."

"Well," Walker said, "if you think of a way I can help you, let me
know." He set his own glass down. "You really think Doc Siriwai
could fix me up if I stopped in Borromeo?"

"I'm sure of it," Quinn said. "I see him once in a while." They
stood up; Quinn yawned and stretched. "Lee Verger," he said. "Good
old Lu Anne. You give her my special love, you hear."

"I will."

They shook hands and Walker got behind the wheel of his car. As
he drove by the cottonwood trees, he passed Lucy and Eben. Lucy
was smiling; she had bent over the child and was encouraging him to
wave. Walker threw them a salute. As soon as he came in sight of the
sea, the fog rose to meet him.

W hen they were gone she sat on the beach in front of her casita.
She had not ridden to the airport, only stood in the driveway
before the main building and waved them away. Lionel and the sun-
ripe children, happy-eyed. Were they also pleased to be quit of her?
They were sensitive children, they had seen a few things they should
not have seen. Driving away, they had not turned to wave or to look
back at her and it had made her feel hurt and afraid. Only their
excitement, she had thought, walking back down the path. But it was
as though their eyes were fixed upon some wholesome future in which
she had no part.

At least there was work. But it was a few hours until her call, so she spent twenty minutes or so doing breathing exercises and then commenced swimming laps in the small patio pool. Lu Anne was a strong swimmer and the pool barely more than an ornament; she coursed the length in two strokes and flipped at ends in a racing turn. She kept at it until her breath came hard and her shoulders ached.

Overhead, the sky was leaden; distant heat lightning flashed. She could hear the men at work beside the lagoon where the Grand Isle set was. For weeks she had been listening to the trailer-truck engines and the roar of articulated loaders. Lines of peons, armed with machetes, had been chopping cactus, beating the brush for scorpions, laying track for the giant Chapman crane. Now it was ready, the ground cleared. A roadway of two-by-twelve boards, stacked three layers deep, stretched from the dunes to the mild surf. Only the odd shout or burst of laughter, the whine of a power drill or the beat of a hammer drifted across the tame surface of their civil bay. From the other direction, where the unchecked Pacific whirled in narrow canyons along the point or thrust itself against the black sand of Playa China, she could make out the crash of surf, muffled by the offshore wind and the guardian mountainside.

That would be the place to swim, she thought, to work the negativity from her frame, to contend. She sat quietly in the sun, eyes closed, imagining the half-heard surf, forcing, as well as she was able, all other thoughts aside.

A rapid knock sounded on the casita door. She rose, thoroughly annoyed, and opened it to find Jack Best, the unit publicist, and a writer named Dongan Lowndes, who was down to do a feature for a prestigious magazine and was not, one was forever being reminded, just another hack.

In Lowndes's company, Jack Best, who was just another flack, assumed an elevated diction.

"Miss Verger," he declared, "I'd like to introduce Mr. Dongan Lowndes. I'm sure you know each other's work and I'm sure you'll have a really interesting conversation."

Lowndes did not seem embarrassed. He was a tall man with a long narrow face; its up-country Scotch-Irish frankness was spoiled slightly by the smallness of his close-set brown eyes.

Lu Anne and Dongan Lowndes shook hands; she gave him a sympathetic smile, which she noticed he did not return.

"Shall we go in?" Jack asked. "I've ordered lunch sent down."

"Gosh, I'm sorry, Jack," Lu Anne said. "I just spaced this interview. I was going to skip lunch and prep." She turned to Lowndes, expecting that he would offer to go. He only stared at her, not unpleasantly, but quite fixedly. His stare might have been taken for one of polite interest had its object been other than human.

Jack Best looked unhappy. In his book Lee Verger was not big enough medicine to space lunch dates with the highbrow press. Mr. Lowndes declined his assistance.

"Well," Jack said nervously to Lowndes, "we've got a bit of a condom here."

"I suppose," Lu Anne said after a moment, "it must have washed up on the beach from town."

Lowndes kept his small eyes fixed on Lu Anne. "I bet you meant to say conundrum, didn't you, Jack?"

"Yeah," Jack said quietly. He looked awestruck. "How could I have said that?"

"There you are, Mr. Lowndes," Lu Anne said. "Your first Hollywood malapropism."

"I've lived among ignorant people most of my life," Lowndes told Lu Anne, "and I've never heard better."

"Well," she said, "come in, guys."

"I'm really sorry," Jack Best said. "I mean, Jesus, it just popped out."

"That's O.K.," Lowndes said. "Miss Verger and I know each other's work and now we're going to have a really interesting conversation."

"Are you going to stay, Jack?" she asked.

The service wagon arrived, propelled by a waiter who wheeled it into the patio. Best stared at the floor, then stood up and helped himself to a glass of tequila. He looked at Lowndes, then at Lu Anne.

"Come here, kid," he said to her. He motioned her toward the door with a toss of his head.

"Me too?" Lowndes asked.

Best ignored him. Lu Anne followed the publicist outside.

"So I look like a jerk," Jack said. "Let him have me fired."

"The hell with him," Lu Anne said kindly. "I mean, where's your sense of humor?"

"I'm supposed to stay with you. You want me to?"

"I believe by now I can hold my own with the Dongan Lowndeses of the world."

"I humiliated myself in front of him," Jack Best said through his teeth. "I'd like to punch his smart mouth."

"For heaven's sake, Jack," Lu Anne said, laughing, "it's just a giggle. Forget it."

"He's a rat, this guy," Jack said. "You watch yourself. He'll use everything you say against you. I know the kind of rat he is. The stupid thing I said—he'll put that in."

"You know they're not going to print that."

"You be careful. I mean, I oughta stay but I can't stand him. I'll kill the son of a bitch. Don't tell him nothing, tell him your hobbies. See, Charlie doesn't know—he's out to screw us. Make us look funny."

"Well," she said, "I'll proceed from there."

Best gave her a dark look and went up the path.

In his patio chair, Lowndes smoked a cigarette, ignoring the food before him.

"You're a wonderful actress," he told Lu Anne.

"Thank you," she said, wondering again what people thought they meant when they said that. "I work hard. I try to get it right."

"And what is *it*?"

"To inhabit them," Lu Anne heard herself say. "To be in the place you're supposed to be." She watched him stare at her. "Don't you take notes?"

He shook his head. "Aren't you going to tape us? So I don't mis-quote you?"

"You'll misquote me anyway. Then your magazine's lawyers will read it and if they say it's O.K. I'll come out the way you like."

"Do you always talk to interviewers like this?"

"Can I tell you something off the record?"

"I don't know yet," Lowndes said, "ask me later."

"I haven't given an interview in years. Not a real one." She thought his eyes seemed somehow soiled. Mud-colored. Shit-colored. "You go to est training or something?"

He laughed but she thought she had embarrassed him.

"Do *you* go to est training?"

"I meditate," Lu Anne said. Lowndes had an aura, she realized. His aura brought forth creatures, like the Long Friends. They were attracted to him. She could hear their prattling from inside the casita. Something about lost things, lost jewelry, old photographs, old-time things. He would not be aware of them, she reminded herself, because they were not there for him.

"You mean like Zen?" Lowndes asked, amused. "Alpha states?"

The Sorrowful Mysteries, she thought. In the casita she could hear the rattle of rosary beads. They were not hers, they belonged to Props but she had appropriated them.

"Everyone meditates," she said. "It's just clearing your mind for concentration."

"What is acting?" Lowndes asked. "How is it like living?"

"Those aren't possible questions," she said. "They don't make sense."

"Yes, they do, Miss Verger. You can answer them."

She laughed. "Mr. Lowndes, you don't ask those questions of a person." He had power over her. The aura that drew the Long Friends gave him great strength. And his contaminated eyes. "If you want to speculate on those things, if you want to hold forth on life and acting and whatnot for your readers, well, do it. But don't ask me to give you the words."

"Do you really know my work?"

"I read your novel, Mr. Lowndes. Some years ago. I admired it."

"The novel? Not a studio synopsis?"

His eyes held her; she knew she must look troubled. His arrogance did not offend her but that he dared to speak so made her fear he knew his own power. Perhaps he was the same with everyone, she thought. He had humiliated poor foolish Jack Best. Considering his cruelty, she examined his stance, the lines of his body. When she felt the first faint thirst of desire, the Long Friends inside sounded a chorus of stern whispers.

"You-all hush," she said softly.

"I'm sorry," Lowndes said, surprised. "I was kidding."

"Yes," Lu Anne said. "Of course."

"You're from Louisiana?"

"Yes," she said, "it's in the handout. From Boulanger."

"I'm from Georgia."

"I know," Lu Anne said. "I know from your name. Lowndes, that's a Georgia name." She was only flattering him now to keep him at bay, starting to tell lies. She saw that he was pleased.

"I love to swim," she told Lowndes. "When I was sixteen I was an Olympic candidate. But I had a fall and broke my leg."

"A fall from a horse?" Lowndes asked.

"Yes," she said, "but I still swim regularly. And I ride occasionally."

Lee had never been an Olympic candidate for anything. At four she had broken her leg being chased by a hog during a Christmas party. If her cousins hadn't rescued her, her father said, she might have been eaten and gone into sausage.

"You went to Newcomb?"

"I went to Newcomb on a Madison Foundation scholarship. Then I went to Yale drama school."

"And you were in that production of *As You Like It* where everybody in it became rich and famous."

"People said it was like John Brown's hanging. I was Rosalind."

"Rosalind," Lowndes mused. "Tell me about that."

She shook her head with a secret smile. "No." She has nothing to do with you, Lu Anne thought. With your bent back and your shitty eyes.

He was studying her refusal to answer when the telephone rang. It was transportation and her call.

"Time for me to go to work," she told him pleasantly, and went into the bedroom to change. The Long Friends had left a smell, like sweet wine and lavender sachet, and Lu Anne was aware of it as she sat by the bedroom mirror.

She chewed a piece of sugarless gum and brushed out her hair, hoping to see Rosalind and not some ugly thing. When she had been married to Robitaille he had accused her of constantly looking in mirrors. Because, she had told him, my face is my fortune.

They had told her to stay out of the sun, to keep the character's genteel pallor. In the end it could not be done without the most rigorous efforts and they had relented and let her tan. It had been a good idea; with the right makeup and in the right colors, she photographed young and golden.

It was Edna in the glass now, not Rosalind. Lu Anne studied herself. Gone, that young Queen of the New Haven night. Sometimes it seemed to Lu Anne that she missed Rosalind the way she missed her children. She turned to study herself in profile.

Years ago in Boulanger, a judge who was one of her ex-husband's relatives had called her "a lousy mother," right out in court, in front of her daughter and in front of her own mother and daddy. Now she was Edna Pontellier. Of Edna, Kate Chopin had written:

She was fond of her children in an uneven impulsive way. She would sometimes gather them passionately to her heart; she would sometimes forget them.

You lost it all anyway, Lu Anne thought. You lost the child inside yourself, then the person that grew there, then the children you never bore and the children you did. The boys, the men, the skin outside, the self inside. Feelings came and went like weather. You could not tell if they were real. You could not tell if they were your own. You could never even be sure that you were there. People pretended.

"She looks fine," Lu Anne told herself in the glass. The unseen Friends buzzed. They were all guilty agitation, old-aunty admonitions.

Don't say she *look* fine, she heard one whisper. Say she *is* fine.

Lu Anne smiled, lowered her head and put a finger across her lips.

"Lee?" It was the voice of the writer, Lowndes. "Your car is here."

She stood up and went out; meeting his eyes, her own gaze faltered and he saw it.

At the door, Billy Bly, the stuntman, was waiting for her with the driver. Seeing each other, they both blushed.

"Hi," he said, and glanced quickly at Lowndes behind her. "They told me to ride over with you. See if there was anything you wanted."

"Just your good company, Brother Bly," she said. She introduced him to Lowndes; they got in the hosed-down Lincoln that would carry them to the set.

Looking out the car window as they approached the sea, she was struck by the uncanny light. The sky seemed to threaten a storm out of season.

"You look fine, Lu Anne," Bill Bly said. She laughed. They had sent him out as her protector, replacing Jack Best. A heavy-handed touch, she thought.

"I *am* fine, Billy," she told him. She was aware of Lowndes, a watching darkness on the seat beside her. "I *am*."

Around twelve, Walker pulled off the freeway in Del Mar and drove to a drugstore on the coast to telephone Shelley.

"Everybody's thrilled," she told him. "They think it would really be great. In other words, they'll put up with you for a day or two but don't push it."

"I will be their guest, will I not?"

"Yes, Gordon. You will."

"That's what you said they'd do."

"People don't always do what I say they'll do. Very often, though."

"Doesn't that make you feel good?"

"No, shitty. It's depressing. How do you want to travel?"

"I'm driving."

"Is that wise?"

"I'll be all right."

"*Buen viaje*, Gord. Don't get sick."

He was about to hang up when Al Keochakian came on.

"Smart guy," Al said.

"Take it easy," Walker said. He was afraid of Keochakian's anger and afraid of his own.

"I'm taking it easy, Gordon. I want to tell you something Shelley said to me. She's off the line."

"Don't get pissed at her. I asked her to set it up."

"Of course you did. And she owes you her job here."

"What are you going to do, fire her, for Christ's sake? Why are you so hysterical about this?"

"I would never fire Shelley, Gordon. She'll grow old in my service. I want to tell you something. I want to tell you what she said about you."

"If it's something I should hear I'll hear it from her."

"She said, 'He's dying, Al.' That's what she said to me this morning. 'He's really going to die.' "

Walker felt the sudden sweat under his arms and on his palm that held the telephone. A charge of fear exploded beneath his heart, like the fear that had seized him at the mirror the morning before.

"You malicious son of a bitch," he said to Keochakian. "You're cursing me."

"You think so?"

"I understand you now. I don't know why I didn't before."

"What I'm trying to make you understand," Keochakian said, "is that you're very sick. Your life is in danger."

"I don't believe that motivation," Walker said. "I heard the satisfaction in your voice."

For a few moments there was silence. When Keochakian spoke again his voice was tremulous.

"You are sick, man. Physically and mentally you're sick. You have me on the phone here . . . in this unprofessional way . . . we are arguing like a couple of faggots here. I won't stand for it."

"Al," Walker said, laughing, "go fuck yourself. You're fired."

He stayed on the line until he heard Keochakian hang up. Then, deliberately, he replaced his own receiver. His insides churning with fear and anger, he pulled recklessly out into the coast road traffic, forcing the southbound lanes to a squealing halt. Pursued by obscenities and shouts of outrage, he headed for I-5 and the border.

I n their oversized custom-built trailer a short distance from the setup, the Drogues, father and son, watched a young woman in turn-of-the-century costume ride a horse-drawn trolley car on a video screen. The woman was Joy McIntyre, Lu Anne's Australian stand-in. The vehicle was moving against a dimly perceived woodland background; Joy held tight to the standee pole, her hands clutching both the pole and her folded parasol.

"Pretty kid," old Drogue said.

"Looka the way she holds the parasol," Walter Drogue the younger said. "She thinks she's on the bus to Kangaroo Springs."

"A proletarian reflex," the old man said. "And a cute ass. I think she's endearing."

"The more I look at her," young Drogue said, "the more I realize we have a true original here. I mean, you get the McIntyre touch. You get McIntyrisms. Like there was Lubitsch, there was Von Sternberg, now there's McIntyre."

"Maybe there's something there, eh? Maybe nature didn't intend her for just an extra."

Young Drogue blew his nose on a Kleenex.

"Nature intended her for a water spaniel. She can't name the days of the week."

They watched pretty Joy, her jaw set, grimly hang on.

"Kind of a phallic pole," Drogue junior said.

"You know," old man Drogue intoned, "we had an extra once—they called him Freddy the Fag. He was six-eight, three hundred pounds, and he had Gloria Swanson's moves. One time we're making a Western—big saloon fight scene, roulette wheels flying, guys crashing through balconies—and Freddy walks up a flight of stairs like he's on his way to get a bouquet from Bert Parks. Next take, the A.D. says, 'Freddy, for Christ's sake, can't you walk up those stairs like a man?' Freddy turns around and says, 'If you want me to play character parts you'll have to pay me for it.' "

On the screen, Joy's trolley swung past a line of wooden structures and rolled on through a grove of live oaks.

"She should sit," the old man croaked. "The stance is passive."

"It's comical," his son said. "It's a comic composition. It won't do."

He kicked open the trailer door and stepped out into the strangely turned Mexican light, calling for his assistant.

"Eric!"

In a few moments Eric Hueffer, the A.D., rounded the edge of the trailer.

"Yeah, boss."

"Let's take her around again sitting down. I mean, Christ, she's holding the parasol wrong. It doesn't feel right."

"Right," Hueffer said. "Toby was wondering about the light on her face under that hat. She had her head down."

They were walking toward the camera setup, Hueffer and young Drogue in step, the old man a few steps behind. As they approached, they heard Joy McIntyre begin to sing.

"And it was grand," she sang in an antipodean quaver,

"Just to stand

With his hand holding mine

To the end of the li-i-i-ne."

"How come you let her hold the parasol like that?" young Drogue asked Hueffer.

"I thought it was natural."

"I want to watch her go around again on the tape. I want her sitting up straight, with her head up. I want the parasol in one hand, touching the floor. With her other hand she can hold the pole. Maybe. We'll see."

"Lee's here," Hueffer told his director.

"Well, I'll talk to her now. We'll watch the shot again while she gets into costume." He watched his assistant walk back toward the setup. "Eric!"

The A.D. turned, squinting.

"Anybody heard anything about Walker?"

"He's supposed to be coming down," Hueffer said, "but he wasn't on the plane with Charlie."

"Good," Walter said. "The guy's bad luck," he told his father.

"He's a contentious drunk and that's never *good* luck. Charlie—with his reporters and writers—he doesn't know what's good for his picture. In my day we'd have either kept a guy like Walker off the set or we'd have kept him busy with rewrites. Don't you think he might upset Verger?"

"I think Lu Anne might extend with him around," the younger Drogue said. "It's a calculated risk. Anyway, I don't want to fight with Charlie over it."

"Give him to Lowndes," old Drogue said. "Give them each other."

Lu Anne sat in front with the driver, Lowndes and Bill Bly in the back seat. The big stuntman's presence had a subduing effect on Lowndes. It was a presence that was straightforward and physical and created about itself an atmosphere unsympathetic to leading questions and intimidation. Lu Anne was glad to have him along. They drove in silence over a dusty road lined with giant eucalyptus. On the way they passed Jack Best trudging flat-footed through the dust. When the driver slowed for him, he waved them on. Best's face was red and he appeared to be talking to himself.

"Is he all right?" Lowndes asked Lu Anne.

"He's fine," Bill Bly told him.

At the end of the road was the great laager of trailers and light trucks that marked the borders of the Grand Isle set.

In the center of an enormous clearing stood a grove of live oaks that had been trucked in from the Tamaulipas coast. They stood beside this alien shore looking as natural, as firmly rooted and grave in authority as the ancient trees of her home place, garlanded, like those, in beards of Spanish moss. The open ground between the grove and the beach was covered in anthemis vines that seemed to bear the same white and yellow flowers as Lu Anne's native camomile but lacked the apple fragrance. This air was too thin, she thought, to bear the scents of home.

Getting out of the car, she stood and looked over the scene. In the strange light it had a sinister magic. Dongan Lowndes came and stood beside her. Bly stayed in the car with the door open.

"Thanks, Billy," she said. He closed the door and was driven away.

"Weird, isn't it?"

"Yes," she said.

"Make you feel funny?"

"They always do," she said, "these tricks. I think I like it. I think it puts me in the working vein."

In the center of it all, beside the thickest oak, stood a small antique trolley, looking a bit like a San Francisco cable car. The trolley rested on a narrow-gauge track that ran a long parabolic route between the oak grove and a row of bathhouses at the edge of the dunes. Two handsome chestnut horses were harnessed to the car. An elderly, ebony-skinned man, wearing a period derby and a faded, collarless striped cotton shirt, sat on the driver's platform. Joy McIntyre swung loosely from the trolley bar, grasping it one-handed. She was wearing an exact replica of the Gibson girl costume that Lu Anne herself would wear for the scene.

"Hi, Joy," Lu Anne called. "Hi, Joe Gates."

"I'm Judy Garland," Joy said happily. She leaned forward from the bar, balancing on the edge of the trolley, waved and displayed the eagerest and most brightly toothed of Judy Garland smiles. "When you have a costume, you can be Judy Garland too."

Joe Gates half turned in his buckboard and tugged on the bell cord beside him.

"Zing, zing, zing went my heartstrings," he sang to them, in flatted hipster tones.

"Joe Gates was actually in *Meet Me in St. Louis*," Joy said. "Right, Joe?"

"Naw," Joe Gates said. "That was another man."

Camera crew were struggling to mount the Panaflex aboard the trolley and keep it fixed in place. Joe Gates climbed down from his perch and one of the Mexican grips took up the team's bridle. Lu Anne turned and saw young Walter Drogue approaching.

Lowndes, standing next to her, was holding her copy of the script. She took it from him quickly but not before Drogue saw.

"Don't read the script, Lowndes," Drogue said. "You'll spoil the end for yourself. I mean, give us a chance, huh?"

"I want to see what one looks like," Lowndes told the director. "I wanted to read what she wrote in it."

"I understand," Drogue said smoothly. "Now if you'd like to watch—and I'm sure you would—you could get a fine view from the back of that pickup behind the camera."

He directed Lowndes's attention to a red Ford truck near the clearing.

Lowndes ignored him.

"Work well," he told Lu Anne. She smiled at him as he walked away, a smile she knew would encourage his quickening attentions. She had no particular idea why she had done it.

"Work well?" Drogue demanded. "Who the fuck does he think he is?"

Lu Anne helped herself to another stick of sugarless gum.

"I know his type, Walter. He's what a former husband of mine would call a moldy fig."

"And you have a weakness for that type?"

She shrugged. "I'm indifferent. I believe that type has a weakness for me."

Drogue stared at her. "What former husband?"

"Oh," Lu Anne said, "the clarinet player."

He took her by the arm and they walked together toward the trolley.

"Look at this light," he said. "What does it do for you?"

"It makes me sad," she said.

"Come on," he told her, affecting an excited tremolo, "this is El Greco light. It's holy."

She looked at the sky, hoping to catch his excitement. It looked to her like late-summer weather at home. Edna, she thought, would know the oppression of that yellow-gray dog end of summer light. But the air was different where they were. It was the West, and not old Pierre Pelican land. Even in famished Baja there was an edge of hope to the air.

"We've just done Joe Gates on his buckboard," Drogue said. "Atmospheric, sinister as shit. I mean," he said, "the dude's been a millionaire half his life. Give him his cue and he'll give you three hundred years of servitude and lonesome roads."

Lu Anne smiled for him.

"Joe was in *Salt of the Earth,* you know that? Dad brought him in. He played the Black Worker, or as they used to say, the Negro Worker, and let me tell you, the Negro Worker was bad! This big young hulk of a guy—huge pecs, chest like a fucking draft horse. He didn't give a shit about blacklists, he was rich in real estate."

Toby Blakely, the cinematographer, walked up to join them.

"Turned out," Drogue went on, "they never even noticed him in *Salt.* He worked through the whole decade. He played weepy singing convicts on death row, he played old wimpy butlers, the whole shtick. But you should have seen him as the Negro Worker."

Blakely took off his baseball cap, a half-servile gesture.

"If we're gonna use this light we'd best be doing it, boss. It'll be hell to match and I'm afraid there's a storm coming."

"That's not possible," Drogue said. "I'm assured it's not possible."

"Well," Blakely drawled cautiously, "they do have these out-of-season storms, Walter. They're called *chubascos*."

"Well, fuck that," Drogue said. " 'Cause I gotta match that light. And I'm gonna personally piss on the Virgin of Guadalupe if it rains on my picture."

"That's not helping, Walter," Lu Anne said. Lowndes had put his glasses on; he was watching them from beside the truck.

"Now listen," Walter said to her. He walked in step with her and they performed a wide paseo around the sweating figure of Toby Blakely. "We're going to do great things with this trolley ride to the beach. We have a wonderful spooky light and we know how to use it. Then if the light holds—if we have any kind of sunset at all—she gets to walk on water."

Lu Anne said nothing. She had been hoping to save Edna's walk down the beach for a special day, even perhaps for the last day of location. But they were shooting out of sequence for reasons of economy. There were at least ten days of filming on the Grand Isle set.

"Do you mind doing both those scenes today?"

"I can do them both," Lu Anne said. "They go together."

Drogue stopped, facing the trolley, arresting Lu Anne in mid-stride, clutching her arm.

"Look at that light, kid."

"Yeah," Lu Anne said. The light frightened her.

"So tell me—if you were taking your last trolley ride, how would you do it? I mean, would you do it standing up holding the bar like Joy or would you sit?"

Lu Anne thought about it.

"Maybe I should try it both ways. I sort of think sitting. You know, a little stunned. Standing, it's like *Queen Christina*."

Drogue smiled. "What's wrong with that?"

"I think what you want is an anti–Judy Garland, right, Walter? I'll take care of that for you."

"The question is sitting or standing and for me it's a question of composition," Drogue said. "I'll get another tape of Joy on the trolley while you sit up here. I'll watch the tapes, you think about it."

"When the time comes," Lu Anne said, "we'll know."

"Hey, I like the way you think, kid."

Lu Anne watched him walk off in his crouched, bent-backed scurry. His movements were always startling. He was given to sudden violent gestures that continually caught her off guard and made her feel like cringing.

As she watched, he pivoted without warning, as though he were dodging the swoop of a predatory bird.

"Tell Frank you love it," he said. With a limp outstretched arm he indicated the faked trees and the trolley, the whole artificial world they had made there. Frank Carnahan was the production designer. "Tell him you feel like you're back in the bayou." She nodded. On the way to her trailer she saw Carnahan headed toward the beach that would be their next location.

"Frank!" Going up to him, she tried a little variation on Walter's walk. "Hey, I love it," she told the designer. "I feel like I'm back in the bayou."

Carnahan looked pleased. His breath smelled strongly of rum. All designers were alcoholic Irishmen; it seemed to be traditional. The smell of liquor made her want a drink. Or something. Carnahan smiled with pleasure.

"Don't think there isn't a story behind it, Lee."

As Carnahan unfolded the story behind it Lu Anne's eye roamed the location in search of people from whom she might score. She had already solicited Joy and Jack Glenn, the young actor who played Robert Lebrun; both had disclaimed possession. Bill Bly, who stood stroking one of the trolley horses, was always a prospect. But Bly and Lu Anne had a past which she did not care at that moment to re-examine; and she knew he had been appointed to oversee her secretly. George Buchanan, a middle-aged actor who played Alcée Robin, was not in sight. A few years earlier George had been able to produce anything conceivable at an hour's notice but he had become a family man and joined A.A.

"So, Christ, I thought," Carnahan was telling her in his broad Pawtucket accent, "jeez, Spanish moss, it's a goddamn tree disease. They'll never let me get away with it. I thought we'd have to fake it . . ."

Lowndes kept watching her. He had opened his shirt to the sun, thrust out his pale chest and assumed a somewhat fascistoid stance. This, Lu Anne thought, might be a modified variation of the Country Come-on, which she had seen performed quite often enough. Cocaine, est conditioning, childhood trauma—who could tell what such a posture reflected? In any case, there was no chance of asking him for drugs. He was the enemy.

"So I sez," Carnahan said, "don't shit me, I sez. I seen this shit growing on trees at Rosarita Beach. Of course," he said with a burst of emphysemic laughter, "I ain't never even been to Rosarita Beach."

She came right in on the laugh. "That's too much, Frank," she giggled. "Hey, is it true that Gordon Walker is coming down?" She squared her shoulders, straightened up and leaned her fists on her hips, having a short shot at Lowndes's stance to see what it would feel like on her.

"I dunno," Carnahan said. "Who is he?"

"The writer."

"Aw," Carnahan said, "I dunno. He didn't fly in with Charlie and the dailies."

She felt relief. Ever since the call she had been waiting for him with combined joy and anxiety. Better that I rest, she thought. That evening, she decided, she would take a little of her medicine as prescribed and sleep. That was the purpose of the operation after all. That her scenes be played with clarity and the right moves and the right timing.

Things were under control. The landscape was a bit overbright, that was all. She was not saying inappropriate things, and the only voices she heard were concealed under the wind or in the sound of the sea and she knew them for illusion and paid them no mind.

Vera Ricutti, the wardrobe mistress, overtook her on the way to the trailer.

"I just been looking at these seals," she said excitedly. "There must have been dozens. These darling little seals," she exclaimed, "with their little faces sticking up out of the water."

"Oh, I would love to see them," Lu Anne enthused. "I hope they come back."

"So cute!" Vera said as they went into Lu Anne's trailer. "You gotta see them."

The assistant director's voice sounded across the laager. "Joy, please? Driver? Everybody ready? I want quiet, the director wants to hear the sound on this. Right," Hueffer shouted. His voice was turning hoarse. "Quiet! Roll! Action!"

Vera closed the door of Lu Anne's air-conditioned trailer. Lu Anne herself sat down before her mirror, wiping her brow with Kleenex. Everything in the mirror was shipshape. She felt ready to work.

As she undressed, Vera held up a light-colored corset for her inspection.

"See what we got for you? This goes on first."

"My God," Lu Anne said, lifting her arms for the fit, "is this thing wool?"

"It's a synthetic. This is the same one you had on at the fittings except we made it out of lighter stuff and put a zipper on it. But the real ones, the ones they wore then—they were real wool. This one was for tennis and jumping around in."

"I can't believe they went around in wool corsets in Louisiana in summer."

"So they shouldn't see your bod sweat, that was why they had it. No underarm stain and your dress couldn't stick. We tried this number out on Joy and it photographs O.K. Anyway, we got another dozen white dresses if you do sweat it up."

"I'm a sweater," Lu Anne said when she was zipped in. "But I mean, how could they play tennis in woolen corsets?"

"India," Vera said. "Africa. The white ladies wore woolen corsets. The locals, I guess they got to let their jugs dangle."

The door opened and Josette Darré, the hairdresser, came in. There was a thin film of frost between Lu Anne and Josette; they never spoke except about the business at hand. Josette was a sullen Parisian hippie. She had rebuffed Lu Anne's French with a pout and an uncomprehending shrug and that, for Lu Anne, had been that.

Josette stood by while Lu Anne got into her dress and stood before the mirror, letting Vera tie her loops behind and straighten her hem. Then she sat down to let Josette work on her hair, making faces at herself in the glass.

"Lucky locals," she said, wiping her forehead again.

There was a knock at the door and Joe Ricutti, who was the makeup man, came into the trailer. He was laughing.

"That McIntyre kid is a barrel of laughs," he rasped. "She's in her own musical."

"I don't know," Vera said in a weary tone. Vera was Joe's wife; they worked together most of the time. "Where do they find them?"

Josette stepped aside; Joe Ricutti stepped in behind Lu Anne's chair. Lu Anne raised an upturned hand and the makeup man squeezed it. They made small talk and gossiped while Joe gently held her chin and turned her face from side to side, examining her profile in the mirror. His fingertips delicately probed beneath her bones; in his free hand he held a makeup brush. Lu Anne sat, a prisoner, listening to the trolley outside and watching as Joe found the soft spots around her jaw, the lines to be disguised. She examined the stringiness at the base of her throat and it made her think of a dry creek bottom— cracks, dry sticks, desiccation where it had been serene, smooth and cool and pleasing.

There was a Friend in the room. I don't like her, it said, the way she look. Lu Anne hushed it silently.

"I think," she told Ricutti, "I think the kid's a little long in the tooth for this one."

Joe sang a few bars of protest. "Whaddaya talkin' about? You look good! Look at yourself!"

He turned her head to reflect her profile and ran his finger from her forehead to the tip of her chin. "I mean look at that! That's terrific."

Gazing sidewise, she saw in the mirror Josette's expressionless eyes.

Made-up, she sat for Josette's last applications. Vera Ricutti brought forth a straw boater from one of several identical boxes and ceremoniously placed it on Lu Anne's head. The Ricuttis drew back in admiration. Josette stood to one side, arms folded. Lu Anne caught a scent of lavender sachet. She saw the inhabited mask of Edna Pontellier before her.

The Drogues were watching Joy McIntyre ride her trolley on their tape monitor. Now, instead of standing and clinging to the pole, she sat on the car's wooden bench. Her back was ramrod straight, her chin raised so that the weird light, refracted through overhanging tree boughs, played dramatically on her face, which was partly shadowed by her straw hat.

"The speed is perfect," old Drogue said. "Make sure they keep it."

"That kid," young Drogue said of Joy McIntyre, "everything you put her in looks overdone."

"Use her," the old man said.

"Use her for what? She can't act. Her diction's a joke. She's so flamboyant you can't tell what your scene is gonna look like if you use her to light."

"If you throw away that face," old Drogue said, " . . . a face like that, a body like that—you have no business in the industry."

After a moment, the younger Drogue smiled. "You want to fuck her, Dad?"

"That's my business."

"Say the word."

"I'll manage my own sex life, thanks a whole lot."

"Patty will flip. I can't wait to tell her."

"I told you," the old man said, raising his voice, "mind your fucking business."

In a humorous mood, young Drogue opened the trailer door to find Hueffer and Toby Blakely awaiting him.

"So," he asked them, "is it gonna rain or what?"

"I honestly don't think so," Hueffer said.

Drogue studied his assistant for a long moment. "Hey," he said to all present, "how about this guy?"

Hueffer blushed.

"Well," Toby Blakely said, "obviously we can't intercut with the trolley footage if it rains."

"We'll keep shooting if it rains," young Drogue told them. "If it stops we'll make rain to match."

"Yessir," Blakely said. "That'd be the thing to do. These *chubascos* can last an hour or they can last for three days."

"The next scene is all that concerns me," Drogue said. "I'll be goddamned if I'm going to shoot the last scene of the picture in rain. If it rains for a week we'll wait for a week."

Hueffer and Blakely nodded soberly.

Young Drogue charged toward the setup in his loping stride. Hueffer and Blakely accompanied him. His father ambled along behind.

"So we're home free, right? Rain or not."

"Unless it rains tomorrow and not today," Blakely said delicately. "And we still have the last scene to shoot."

"Go away, Toby," young Drogue said.

Hueffer and Blakely went back to the camera setup. Drogue had caught sight of the producer, Charlie Freitag, who was standing with his production manager in the eucalyptus grove beside the trolley tracks.

"He has to show up now," young Drogue said bitterly. "Freak weather, there's no cover set—Charlie arrives. You can show him four hours of magnificent dailies and he'll give you five hours of handwringing because an extra stepped on a nail."

"Well," old Drogue said, "that's his function."

Lu Anne, sitting outside on her folding chair for Ricutti's last ministrations, became aware of young Drogue's spidery approach. She looked up at him and he offered his arm, parodying antique chivalry.

When she rose to take it, she saw that the writer named Lowndes had not moved from the spot where they had left him. Charlie Freitag was speaking to him but he was watching her.

"Is that guy bothering you?" Walter Drogue asked. "That Lowndes?"

She told him that it was all right. But although it was her business to be watched, the concentrated scrutiny oppressed her. There were too many eyes.

"My ride?" she asked.

Drogue nodded. "I think you're right about her sitting. It looks good. Would you like a rehearsal? I was thinking we might steal a jump on time if we shot it. If you were ready."

"Yes," she said, "let's do it."

Drogue looked her up and down. "Can you walk in the skirt? Are the shoes O.K. on this ground?"

"Costume's fine. If you like the colors."

Vera Ricutti hurried up and bent to Lu Anne's hem, judging its evenness.

"The hatband to match the parasol," she told Drogue. "That's how they did it."

"It's pale green," Drogue said. "Is pale green the color of death?"

"*Bien sûr*," Lu Anne said.

"No rehearsal?"

"Just let me prep, Walter."

"All right. Take care of it for me, kid." As she was walking off, he called after her. "The old nothingness-and-grief routine."

She gave him a smile. Under the huge gum trees she paced up and down. "If I must choose between nothingness and grief," she recited, "I will choose grief." The words were only sounds. Voices on the wind that stirred the trees took them up. Wild palms. Nothingness. Grief.

Joe Ricutti was weighting the elements of his portable makeup table against the breeze. Drogue stood beside him watching Lu Anne.

"How is she?" he asked the makeup man.

"Fine, Mr. Drogue. She talks normal. Pretty much."

Drogue turned to Vera, who nodded silent assent.

Hueffer came up to them earnest and sweating.

"I had a thought, Walter."

Drogue said nothing.

"What would happen if we used a sixteen-millimeter lens on her ride. Maybe even a fourteen?"

"Nothing would happen," Drogue told him. "It would look like shit, that's all."

Hueffer pressed him. "Seriously?"

"If you like," Drogue said pleasantly, "we'll talk about it later. Let's get everyone standing by."

Hueffer went back to the setup.

"Standing by in two minutes," he shouted. "Everybody out of the set."

"He's an asshole," Drogue told the Ricuttis. "A gold-plated shit-head."

The Ricuttis made no reply. Joe Ricutti shrugged.

"If I must choose between nothingness and grief," Lu Anne recited as she paced the dry ground, "I'll have the biscuits and gravy. I'll have the jambalaya and the oyster stew."

It was Edna choosing. Lu Anne's path took her toward the trolley and she saw them all watching her. Lowndes. Bly. Walker was coming down. But Edna was the one in trouble here. The pretty woman in the mirror.

"Hush," said Lu Anne. Edna would be at home among the Long Friends.

Edna was independent and courageous. Whereas, Lu Anne thought, I'm just chickenshit and crazy. Edna would die for her children but never let them possess her. Lu Anne was a lousy mother, certified and certifiable. Who the hell did she think she was, Edna? Too good for her own kids? But then she thought: It comes to the same thing, her way and mine. You want more, you want to be Queen, you want to be Rosalind.

Edna walking into death was conscious only of the sun's warmth. So it was written. Walker's notes had her dying for life more abundant. All suicides died for life more abundant, Walker's notes said.

She walked on through the light and shadow of the huge trees. It was, she thought, such a disturbing light. She could see it when she closed her eyes.

The woods were filled with phantoms and she was looking for Edna. Only her children came to mind, as though they were lost and she was looking for them. As though she were lost.

In such a light, she had knocked on the door of their first house in town. It was the first time, so far as she could remember, that she had ever knocked on a door in the manner of grown-ups. For a long time—she remembered it as a long time—the door stood closed above and before her. Then, as she remembered, it had opened and her father loomed enormous in the doorway, his blank gaze fixed at the far and beyond.

So she had said: I'm down here, Daddy.

His swollen drunk face turned down to hers after a while. His eyes were red and lifeless.

I thought it was somebody real, he had said. Someone had laughed. Maybe he had laughed.

I'm real, Daddy.

Life more abundant, Lu Anne thought, that's the ticket. That's what we need.

Then they were ready and Ricutti was wiping her down.

"You been crying," he said. He started to daub under her eyes. "Your eyes are all red." When she stared at him he lowered the cloth.

I'm real, she thought.

"Let's go with it."

"I don't know," Joe Ricutti said. "Maybe he don't want that, Lee."

"Leave it," she said. "Just get the damn sweat off me."

When they were ready to roll she sat in her marks on the trolley bench. Drogue called for action, the trolley bore her along, and she saw that the field around her was filled with fake camomile. In that moment she found Edna. Edna knew what living was worth to her and the terms on which she would accept it. She knew the difference between living and not living and what happiness was.

It occurred to Lu Anne that she knew none of these things. Too bad, she thought, because I'm the one that's real, not her. It's me out here.

When they had pulled the trolley around for another take, she saw Walter looking at her through the viewfinder. Who does he think he's looking at? she wondered. Or is he just seeing movies? Across the reflectors, she saw Bly and Lowndes and Charlie Freitag, all looking. She began to cry again.

"How about it, Edna?" Walter Drogue asked. He spoke without taking his eye from the viewfinder. "What's it gonna be?" He was just chattering to keep their spirits up. "Nothingness or grief?"

"Beats me," Lu Anne said.

A few hours south of the border, Walker sat in a vast cool room whose upper walls disappeared into darkness. Four columns of light descended from an unseen source in the ceiling to form rectangles of light beneath them like campfires on a plain. One column lit a reception station where a young oriental woman in nurse's whites attended a bone-white desk. Another fell upon an altar-like two-tiered platform arranged with desert plants, Indian ceramics and feathered rattles. The contrast between the sun-drenched barrens outside and the deep, almost submarine gloom within was very striking.

The room's combination of primitive sanctity and futurism was a bit stagey, Walker thought, which was hardly surprising in the establishment of Dr. Er Siriwai. There were no devices of therapy or prosthesis in sight; nothing visible in the great room was suggestive of sickness. Yet it seemed to Walker that something in the refrigerated air was subtly foul. This was almost certainly, he decided, imagination.

Presently his name was called by the young woman at the white desk. Smiling, she handed him a shiny brochure and directed him through a dark doorway that opened at his approach. He found himself following a barefoot Mayan servant along a corridor of cool brown tiles.

The Mayan led him to a garden with a fountain in the center, a pleasant and restrained reproduction of an old Spanish cloister garden. There were herbs of all kinds and orange and lemon trees. An entire section of the garden was given over to the cultivation of red and yellow poppies. The air was fragrant and pure as sound doctrine.

Taking a stone bench in the shade, Walker had a glance at the brochure the smiling young woman had given him. It told the story of Er Siriwai, M.D., Ph.D., who, born on the roof of the world and reading, Mulligan-like, at the Royal College of Surgeons, Dublin, arrived in America to discover his preternatural curative gifts and become Physician to the Stars. The brochure went on to describe the doctor's renunciation of self-serving, his carefully documented researches, his traduction by medical pharisees and finally his withdrawal to the wilderness in which his healing visions had taken shape and blossomed forth like the fig, the date, the almond and other such evocative trees.

After a few minutes of reading, Walker looked up to see his old friend come into the garden.

"Hello, Doc," Walker said. "I guess you're doing well, huh?"

Dr. Siriwai, a tiny man, who in his medical whites complete with reflector and band resembled a child's doctor doll, struck an attitude.

"Come," quoth Dr. Siriwai, "let's away to prison;
  We two alone will sing like birds i' the cage:
  When thou dost ask me blessing, I'll kneel down,
  And ask of thee forgiveness: so we'll live,
  And pray, and sing, and tell old tales, and laugh
  At gilded butterflies . . ."

The doctor seemed so moved by his own recitation that he was unable to continue. Walker was impressed by the facility with which he was able to quote poetry about prison, since he had only escaped its humiliations by a matter of minutes. At one time, Dr. Siriwai had been the film colony's most eminent writing doctor and on two or three occasions something very like a medical hit man.

"And take upon's," the little doctor said, recovering, "the mystery of things,

As if we were God's spies."

Dr. Siriwai spoke an English that combined traces of his cloud-capped homeland and sporting Dublin.

"I'd love to have seen you, Gordon," he said. "Bigod, it's many years since I've seen *Lear*. I think it was Donald Wolfit I saw. Sir Donald Wolfit."

"Well," Walker said, "too bad you couldn't make it."

"I saw it in *Variety*," Dr. Siriwai said. He sat on the end of Walker's stone bench with his legs folded beneath him. "My immediate thought was this: Is he old enough for Lear? Does he know enough—from chasing skirt and bending his elbow—to essay a tragedy of that dimension?"

"Yes," Walker said.

"Can it be, Gordon?"

"Remember how it is up there, Doc. You hang around, people tell you you're terrific. You make a few big mistakes. People aren't as nice. You know enough before you know it."

"Still hacking away at the lingo, are you? On your way to B.H., I suppose? *The Awakening?*"

"I guess that was in *Variety* too."

"You'll never learn, Gordon. No hope for you."

"I suppose you're right."

"Downers, is it?"

"It is. If you'd be so kind, Doc."

"Righto," Dr. Siriwai said. He unwound from his posture, disappeared among the dwarf citrus and presently returned with three small cardboard boxes marked in Spanish.

"This is the only genuine Quaalude in the state," he told Walker. "The rest of it's counterfeit. Made from mannite, foot powder, God knows what."

"I appreciate it, Doc," Walker said, and reached for his wallet.

"Keep your money, man. A tiny favor. Pass it along. The favor, I mean, not the downers necessarily."

"When I get down to B.H.," Walker said, "down to the location, I'll tell them hello. Lots of people down there remember you fondly."

Dr. Siriwai settled Western-wise on the edge of the bench.

"No doubt," he said, "they remember my little bag fondly. My uppers and my downers and my come-into-the-garden-Mauds."

Walker saw that there was still dew on the trilliums in one shaded corner of the garden.

"You were much in demand at poker games, I recall."

"Right," the doctor said. "I was a wanton player, a desperate case. Lost. Always. Heavily." He was watching Walker. "You're not well," he said after a moment. "You look very badly off indeed."

"I thought I might put myself away for a while after B.H.," Walker said. "Clean up my act."

"If you want my advice," Siriwai said, "you'll do it now. Leave the coke and the 'ludes alone. You're doing coke, I can tell you are. You'd better stop the lot, Gordon. You're not a boy, you know."

"My life's a little out of hand," Walker explained. "I'd like to make one stop before I rest."

"In peace, Gordon. That's how you'll bloody rest. Christ's sake, man, when I first saw you I thought you were one of the customers."

"Well, I don't feel that bad. I'm going down to B.H. to see them shoot my movie. By the way," he asked Dr. Siriwai, "why do you call them customers? I mean instead of patients or something more . . . agreeable."

"I call them as I feel them to be," Dr. Siriwai explained. "I don't call them squeals, or marks or tricks. I call them customers. I'm their dealer."

"I see."

"You're going to see that schizophrenic poppet, eh? That little southern creature with the booby eyes? Lee Verger?"

"She always liked you, Doc. I think she'd hope you might always speak well of her."

"Don't give her cocaine, Gordon. No coke for her. You want to see fair Heebiejeebieville, my lad, give one of them cocaine. Mark my words. Hide it. Throw it away before you let her have any."

"I'll bear that in mind," Walker said.

"And for God's sake take care of yourself. Alcohol especially—it's such rubbish. And when your liver goes, well . . ." Dr. Siriwai shuddered with distaste. "It's a jolly unpleasant way to die, Gordon. Almost as bad as . . . what we treat here."

"I know what it's like," Walker said. "My father died of it."

"Do you remember what W. C. Fields said about death?"

"He said he'd rather be in Philadelphia."

"I don't mean that. He called death the Man in the Bright Nightgown. Do you see? It has the originality of delirium. Fields was in total bibacious dementia. So when he went out, his death probably looked to him like a man in a bright nightgown." Dr. Siriwai giggled.

"I like your poppies," Walker said. "I always think of them as wildflowers. I don't associate them with gardens."

Dr. Siriwai smiled at the fine blue sky.

"Poppies, yes. Sweet forgetfulness." He closed his eyes.

"If ye break faith with us who die
   We shall not sleep, though poppies grow
   In Flanders fields."

"This stuff you give your . . . customers, does it work?"

"Work? My dear man, assuredly it works. It cures cancer."

"Really?"

"I wish I had a tanner for every abandoned life we've saved here, Gordon. I myself have been awestruck with some of our turnabouts. It gives you a mighty respect for nature's capacity to heal, I'll tell you."

"Is it what you give them or is it attitude?"

Dr. Siriwai seemed to find the subject trying.

"There are no miracles, Gordon. I mean to say, old chap, I don't believe in miracles, do you? There is attitude, yes. Also herbal therapy, diet, exercise, the lot. Holism. The holistic method."

"Anyway," Walker said. "It's a pleasant place."

Dr. Siriwai looked grim.

"You learn to conserve your spiritual energy here. There's a lot of negativity about. I instruct my staff to keep a positive attitude. Hang on to the handrails, I tell my people, or they'll drag you down with them."

"So you do lose a few. Customers."

"Some of them, Gordon. It's their time and they've no right to be here. But one doesn't turn down a contract. Hope is the anchor when all is said and done."

"Too bad," Walker said, "you can't save them all."

"Well," Dr. Siriwai said, "it would be wonderful for business. I mean, are we talking philosophy or what?"

"I was just curious," Walker said, "about whether you believed in it or not."

"I believe in hope," Dr. Siriwai said.

"The anchor."

"Indeed," said Dr. Siriwai. "Exactly so."

"I should be on my way," Walker said. "I have a few hours of driving."

"Tell them at reception to give you one of our decals. It'll ease your passage on our highways and byways. We're not without influence in this part of the world."

They shook hands and Walker offered his thanks for the Quaaludes.

"I remember you, Gordon. I remember some fine evenings of drink and jaw under the palm trees. I always thought you were a clever fellow and a great wit. But the thing is, I don't remember your work at all. Nothing you ever did quite maintained itself in my memory."

"I'm sorry to hear that, Doc. I thought you liked the things I did."

"Ah," said the doctor, "no doubt I did, no doubt I did, Gordon. But your work—I'd have to say it—sat lightly on my recollection."

"Work in movies can be ephemeral."

Dr. Siriwai patted Gordon's forearm.

"That's it, you see. Ephemeral. Sure, it's the nature of the medium." Siriwai's eyes came alight. He took Gordon by the arm and walked him around the garden. "I had a list once, Gordon—not a written list, of course, but a private mental list—of people I thought were supremely talented. Or good at certain things. Or clever but spurious. Or talented but lost or wasted it. I wasn't just a sawbones, y'see, indifferent to the artistic aspects of the motion picture. I cared"—he touched his heart—"and I loved, I appreciated the work of the people I met in practice. But in your case, Gordon, though I love you dearly, old son, I can't for the life of me remember the things you did. Or where on me little list you figured."

"As one who loved his fellow man," Walker said.

"Oh ho." Siriwai gave a little clap with his soft hands. "Well said."

"I was all right. I started as a kid. I had no training and I never took acting as seriously as I should. Never learned my craft until it was too late. As for writing—the kind I did was always the kind anyone can do. I never tried another kind. Except, of course, for that show. The opera."

"Never got to direct?"

"No."

"Pity," Siriwai said. When they had completed their garden round, he released Walker's arm.

"Perhaps you gave in too much. The immediate rewards were impressive to a young fellow—I remember well. And in my day there was the glamour of it all. One can't give in too much to immediate reward, you know. You lose something, eh? Have to pay off on one end or the other."

"That was it, I suppose."

"Look at me," Dr. Siriwai said. "You'd think I was well situated. I might envy myself from the outside looking in but little I'd know about it. I'm more than sixty-five, Gordon. According to the Vedas I should be free. I should return to the mountains, free as a mountain bird to meditate, and think about it all from morning till night. But I can't, you see."

"How's that?"

Dr. Siriwai laughed merrily.

"Because I failed where you failed, Gordon. Failed to do the job. When I was studying in Great Denmark Street, now, I thought I'd go home to practice. Up the valleys. Into the starving villages. Over the rope bridges I'd go, risking fever and dacoits, only my books for company. In the end—not a bit of it." He shook his head and uttered a series of reflective grunts. "I had an odd experience on my way from Dublin back up to London. Doubtless you know the Indian expression 'karma'?"

"It's widely used, Doc. You hear it all the time."

"Well," the doctor continued, "there I was, years ago and I'm just off the ferry from Dun Laoghaire on the Holyhead–Euston train. Somewhere—Bangor it must have been—the guard comes through first class, shouting his head off for a doctor. Well, I thought, who's that excellent thing if not myself? So I went with the man and what do I find a few cars back but a lad in an empty compartment who's stinking of Jameson's and going cyanotic before our eyes. There's an empty tube of Nembutal in his fist.

" 'Stop the train,' I cried, and they did and off I went with this chap, my very first patient, to the nearest hospital and they pumped him out and he awoke to the light of day. Now, I later learned, Gordon, that the fellow recovered completely. In hospital he chanced to meet a beautiful young Welsh nurse with whom he fell madly in love—as she with him—and whom he subsequently strangled. Naturally they hanged him. I was a bit put off by it. First patient, value of life and all that. I daresay I'd have been sued today. In any case, finally, I went for the big bucks and the bright lights just as you did."

"First you think it's the money," Walker said. "Then you're not so sure."

"Well, there's no going back to the mountains for me now, Gordon. I have to stay here and die. With my customers."

"I guess," Walker said, "I'd better be rolling. To get down there before dark."

"Do get yourself straight, old fellow. Hope the anchor, eh? Who knows but you may do something worthwhile one day. Only remember what the holy book says, Gordon: 'We are not promised tomorrow.' "

"Thanks, Doc. I hope you continue to prosper."

"Gordon, as long as there's . . . well"—he smiled broadly and, as Gordon had remembered, some of his teeth were indeed of gold— "you know what I mean. I'll be in business for a while."

As Gordon went out the doctor's hands were pressed together in benediction.

I n the air-conditioned gloom of their trailer, the Drogues, father and son, watched a videotape of the last take. It was Lu Anne on the trolley, a continuous medium-close shot. Eric Hueffer and Lise Rennberg, Drogue's Swedish cutter, watched with them. They sat in a semicircle on folding metal chairs.

"We have some very nice cutaways for this if you need them," she told the director.

"Neat," young Walter Drogue said, and switched on an indirect light over his desk.

"Walter," Eric Hueffer said good-humoredly, "just so you don't think I'm a complete nut, could I offer my arguments for a fourteen-millimeter lens in that scene? Or the next one?"

"Interesting idea, Eric."

"Well, jeez," Hueffer said, "you dismissed it out of hand an hour ago."

"Did I?" Walter asked. "How rash of me. Of course we could use a fourteen there, Eric. But we'd need painted backdrops instead of the trees. Do you think we could work that out?"

"Come on, Walter," Eric said.

Lise Rennberg smiled sedately.

"Maybe we could use footage from *Caligari*, huh, Eric? To show that the character's at the end of her tether?"

"Obviously I was wrong," Hueffer said, and got out of his chair. He was a tall young man, almost a head taller than Walter Drogue junior, and his height compelled him to stoop when he stood in the trailer.

"Don't even think about it," young Drogue said.

When they were alone the Drogues ran the videotape over again.

"Man," young Drogue said, watching the screen, "that's what I call inhabited space."

Old Drogue reached out and stopped the tape, freezing the frame.

"You had her crying?"

"She cried. I thought I'd keep it." He turned to his father. "You don't like it?"

"I like it but something bothers me."

He started the tape over again, stopping it about where he had before, on very nearly the same frame.

"Something," old Drogue said softly, and shook his head.

"What's the trouble?" young Walter asked. "You want it shot through a fourteen too?"

"You're very hard on that young man," Drogue senior told his son. "He's efficient. He's enthusiastic. I mean . . . a fourteen-millimeter —it's off the wall but you can see how he's thinking. He comes out of the schools."

"So do I," Drogue junior said.

"Maybe if your name was Hueffer you'd be his A.D., huh? Then he could be sarcastic to you."

"You don't know what you're talking about," his son told him. "You don't know what it was like. You can't."

"If your name was such a burden," old Drogue said, "you should have changed it."

"I was Walter Drogue the Less."

"Tough shit," the old man said.

"And I was never allowed to be as much of a fool as fucking Hueffer."

"Stop picking on him," old Drogue said. "You're lucky to have him. He could go all the way, that kid."

"His day will come," young Drogue said.

"Will that be good news for him?"

"He'll get his own picture. Little by little things will get out of hand. He'll try weird shit—like spooky lenses. He'll try to do everything himself. Presently they'll smell his blood. They'll sabotage him and laugh at him behind his back. His actors will panic. His big opportunity will turn to shit before his eyes. He'll be afraid to show his nose on his own set."

"Well," the old man said, "that's how movies get made. Myself, I'm too superstitious to wish disaster on my own assistants."

"It's not my wish. It's inevitable. It's the kind of guy he is."

Drogue senior started the tape again. He and his son watched Lu Anne take her ride.

"I could watch that for twenty seconds, couldn't you?" young Drogue asked. "Do most of the ride in one continuous medium-close, then maybe cut away to her point of view?"

"Why did you have her cry?"

"Hell, she was crying. Why not?"

"It looks out of character."

"Only to us."

"What do you mean?" old Drogue demanded. "It's her cracking up."

"For Christ's sake, Dad, don't you think I know that? It'll play just fine."

"Ever try to edit around somebody going bananas? You end up as crazy as them."

"Well, I have two options, don't I? I can make her not be crazy. Or I can get the picture completed with her as she is. Which do you recommend?"

"She has a way of being crazy," old Drogue said, "that photographs pretty well."

"Right," his son said.

"Some do, some don't."

"She does. Ever since her old man started packing, her energy level out there has been a hundred and twenty percent."

"She could do a complete flip. She has before."

"Then I guess I fly in Kurlander or nourish her with my blood or
something."

"You don't have too far to go."

"I have some of Walker's literary scenes to do up in L.A. Some
important interiors. I need her coherent for that." They watched the
trolley tape run to its completion. "I'll have Walker down here. I've
got that peckerhead novelist to keep amused. If I can get her through
this weekend, I can get her the rest of the way."

"Good luck," the old man said.

They went out into the afternoon; young Drogue looked at the sky.
Overhead the sky had cleared and the wind had slackened. The storm
hung on the horizon out to sea, a distant menace.

Hueffer and Toby Blakely had discovered a tarantula hiding in the
shade of the trolley's undercarriage and were tormenting it with a stick.

"They can jump really well," Drogue told his men. Hueffer got to
his feet.

"I was raised with tarantulas," Blakely said. "Learned to love 'em."

"I think maybe you're right about the rain, Eric."

"You thinking about shooting Lee's walk tonight?" Blakely said.

"I'm thinking if it doesn't rain we better do it. We'll never get a
better match and it could be pissing buckets tomorrow."

"I'll go on record," Hueffer said. "Beautiful sunset tonight. Indicating *chubasco* in the morning. A day and a half of solid rain."

"You predict weather on my set, you better be right," Drogue said.
"I have vast powers of evil. I don't like bad predictions."

"I think he's right," Blakely said. "If it was my money I'd pay the
overtime and keep everybody out. Be better than looking at the rain
tomorrow."

"I'll talk to Lu Anne," Drogue said to Hueffer. "And since we have
the producer here we can consult with him. Which is always fun."

He looked down and discovered the tarantula approaching the tip
of his Tony Lama boot. "You fuckers better be right," he told them.
He raised his foot, brought it down on the creature and mashed it
into the sandy ground. "Or else."

Blakely looked at him evenly. "That'll just make it rain, boss."

He and Drogue watched the young assistant director set out purposefully in search of Axelrod, the unit manager.

"You like that kid?" Drogue asked his photographer.

"Yeah," Blakely said. "I kind of like him. Don't you?"

Drogue had begun to scrape the hairy remnants of spider leg and thorax from the bottom of his boot and onto the edge of the trolley.

"Don't you think he has a certain assholish quality?"

Blakely stood looking into the director's eyes for several seconds.

"Maybe," he said at length.

Drogue nodded affably. "I kind of like him too."

L u Anne was having her hair combed out as Vera Ricutti folded the last of Edna Pontellier's cotton dresses, putting the pins in a cardboard box.

"God," Lu Anne said, "they did you up like a celestial. Then they turned you loose with more spikes and prongs than a bass lure. There must have been young boys cut to ribbons."

"That taught them respect," Joe Ricutti said. "They should bring it back."

Shortly afterward young Drogue appeared at the trailer; Josette and the Ricuttis took their equipment and left, unbidden.

"How are you?" young Drogue asked. She told him that she was fine. The pins on the dress made her think of defense and escape. Thorns. If I could, she thought, I would emit the darkness inside me like a squid and blind them all and run.

"Let's go for a walk," Drogue said.

They walked in a wide circle among the trees, hand in hand, Lu Anne wearing the thin white beach robe over her underwear.

"The most important question to me," Drogue told her, "is whether you want to do it tonight. If you don't, we'll wrap."

She said, after all, it was just walking in the water. She told him she would do it and that was what he wanted to hear.

Back at the trailer Vera Ricutti asked her if there was anything she wanted. Darkness was what she thought she wanted. Cool and darkness.

"Just to put my feet up awhile," she told Vera.

When she was in the cool and dark the Long Friends emerged and began to whisper. She lay stiff, her eyes wide, listening.

Malheureuse, a Friend whispered to her. The creature was inside her dresser mirror. Its face was concealed beneath black cloth. Only the venous, blue-baby-colored forehead showed and part of the skull, shaven like a long-ago nun's. Its frail dragonfly wings rested against its sides. They always had bags with them that they kept out of sight, tucked under their wings or beneath the nunnish homespun. The bags were like translucent sacs, filled with old things. Asked what the things were, their answer was always the same.

Les choses démodées.

She turned to see it, to see if it would raise its face for her. Their faces were childlike and absurd. Sometimes they liked to be caressed and they would chew the tips of her fingers with their soft infant's teeth. The thing in the mirror hid its face. Lu Anne lay back down and crossed her forearms over her breasts.

Tu tombes malade, the creature whispered. They were motherly.

"No, I'm dead," she told it. "Mourn me."

In the next moment she found herself fighting for breath, as though an invisible bar were being pressed down against her. She turned on the light and the Long Friends vanished into shadows like insects into cracks in the walls; their whispers withdrew into the hum of the cooler. Delirium was a disease of darkness.

Her pills were on a shelf in the trailer lavatory. She went in and picked up the tube. Her body convulsed with loathing at the sight of the stuff.

Outside, the sun was declining, almost touching the uppermost layer of gray-blue storm cloud over the ocean. Wrapping the beach robe around her, she stood for a moment close to panic. She had no idea where to go, what to do. In the end she went to the nearest trailer, which was George Buchanan's.

Buchanan rose in answer to her knock; he had set his John D. MacDonald mystery on the makeup counter.

"George," she said breathlessly. "Hi."

"Hi, Lu Anne." He looked concerned and cross. He was a stern-faced man, a professional villain since his youth in the fifties. "I'm not here, you know. I'm hiding out."

"Are you, George?"

"My son is with his girlfriend back at the bungalow. I came out here to give them a little . . . what shall we call it?"

"George," she said in a girlish whine, "do you have a downer? Please? Do you?"

He looked stricken. He was so shocked by her request that he tried to make a joke of it.

"For you, Lu Anne, anything. But not that."

"It was just a shot," she said.

"Hey," Buchanan said, "this is me, Buchanan. I'm into staying alive. I mean, Christ's sake, Lu Anne, you know I don't use that stuff. It tried to kill me."

She shook her head in confusion.

"I mean, I can't believe you asked me."

She slammed his door shut, turned and saw Dongan Lowndes, the writer, apparently on the way to her trailer. He had seen her coming out of Buchanan's quarters. He did a little double take to let her know that he had seen it.

"Mr. Lowndes," she said. "I'm sorry but I can't remember your first name." She bit her lip; she could not seem to lose the whininess in her manner.

"Forget it," Lowndes said. "Call me Skip."

"Skip," she said, "Skip, you wouldn't have a downer on you? Or maybe back at your room?"

OF LIGHT

He stared at her. Had he taken the reference to his room for a proposition?

"No," Lowndes said. "Or uppers or anything else."

"Oh dear," Lu Anne said. She smiled disarmingly for Lowndes. "I was hoping for a little something."

"Sorry," Lowndes said, looking as though he were. She saw that he was anxious to please her.

"Even liquor would do," she said. "I don't usually drink when I work, but now and then a small amount can prime a person."

"Right," Lowndes said, "well, I don't drink anymore myself. I can't. But can't you send out to the hotel for it?"

She shifted her eyes from side to side broadly in a comic parody of guilt.

"I don't want people to know." She paused and sighed. "Dongan, could you?"

"Skip," Lowndes said.

She looked at him impatiently.

"Skip," he repeated. "Call me Skip."

"Oh, that's nice," she said. "I can just see why your folks called you that. Could you get us a bottle, Skip, so we can sneak a slug down here?"

"I have trouble handling it," Lowndes said. "I'm off the stuff."

For a little while he looked at her, a faint fond smile playing about his thick lips.

"I guess I could, though."

She opened her eyes wide and swallowed bravely. So go and do it, she was telling him, you shit-eating bird. The Long Friends cackled admonition.

"Scotch?" he asked. His gaze was sad. Whether he was begging for her favors or simply disillusioned, she could not tell and did not care.

"Yes," she said, sounding absurdly eager, "that'd be nice."

"I'll go up and get a bottle," he said. His voice wavered as he said it, like an adolescent's.

Lu Anne did not feel particularly like drinking liquor but it seemed important that there be something to take.

"Oh great, Skip," she said. "Now, you remember the car we came in, huh? Well, you just go back to that car and get him to take you up the hill and you can get us a jug. Only carry it in something, will you, because I don't want people to think we're a couple of old drunks."

"Right," Lowndes said. "I'll brown-bag it."

"And when you're up there," she said as he started for the car, "you ask them if a Mr. Walker has arrived, O.K.?"

"Mr. Walker," Lowndes repeated. "And a plain brown wrapper."

Across the clearing, Lu Anne saw Jack Glenn, the actor playing Robert Lebrun, in conversation with Joe Ricutti. She went over to them. A few years before, she had heard an agent describe Glenn— a natural who could fence, juggle, swing from vines and play comedy—as too small to be big. Whenever she repeated the story she got her laugh and people said it was a voice from Vanished Holly- wood. But the agent had not vanished and Jack Glenn, at five feet nine inches, worked irregularly. Someone had told her it was because he was fair-skinned; a fair-skinned actor had to be taller. It was a matter of semiotics, the person had said.

He turned to her approach. "Ah," he said with his hand over his heart, "*Les Douleurs d'amour*." He kissed her hand, correctly, with the appearance of a kiss. Glenn was nice-looking and bisexual but for whatever reason she had never been attracted to him. Perhaps because he was fair and short.

"I don't suppose," Lu Anne said, "that since we talked you've come into any . . . you know, into possession of . . ."

"What a coincidence that you should ask."

"You have!" she exclaimed joyfully.

"No," Jack Glenn said. "But I was just thinking about it myself. I was thinking of asking that guy."

He pointed to a middle-aged Mexican in a safari jacket who was holding one of the trolley horses with a twitch, examining its leg. As he worked, he was humming "The Trolley Song" from *Meet Me in St. Louis*.

"Who is he?" she asked.

"The vet," Glenn said.

"What?" she said.

"The vet," Joe Ricutti told her. "For the horses. So they shouldn't get sick."

Lu Anne turned to watch him work.

"I never thought of Mexican locations as having vets."

"I always thought they shot the horses," Jack Glenn said archly. "Don't they?"

"This is No Help City," Lu Anne said. "I mean, it's a very bad situation."

"This unit doctor," Glenn said, "you tell him you can't sleep, he tells you how many gringos are locked up in Baja Norte. 'One hundred twenty U.S. citizens in jail.' That's the only English sentence he knows. So I was just thinking, like hmm—there's the vet. Maybe he has something nice for us."

"Oh God," Lu Anne cried in exasperation, "like horse tranques? How about an STP trip? Or some angel dust?"

"Get him to give you a shot," Joe Ricutti said. "You'll go off on the rail at Caliente and finish first at Del Mar."

"Well," Lu Anne said, "we'll have to tough it out, won't we? Everything will have a clear black line around it, like a death notice."

Jack Glenn laughed. "You're so weird, Lu Anne."

"That's why we're all here," she told him. "You included."

"I don't know how people can joke about drugs," Glenn said in mock sadness. In fact, as Lu Anne well knew, Glenn was mainly indifferent to drugs. He was only trying to amuse. "We should get someone to score for us in L.A.," he said. "Bring shit down with the dailies."

"Maybe Joy got hold of some," Lu Anne suggested.

Glenn shook his head.

"Well," she said, "I'm going to lie down and die again."

She went back across the field to her trailer and there was Lowndes, sitting on the three little metal steps with a brown bag beside him. He stood up and presented the bag.

"Got any ice?"

But of course she did not want Lowndes, only the liquor. Or something. She opened the trailer door, trying to think how she might get rid of him. He followed her into the trailer and closed the door behind them.

She had some weeks-old ice in the trailer. She smashed the tray repeatedly against the miniature sink to get the cubes free, brushing aside Lowndes's gestures of assistance. There were two plastic glasses on her makeup table; she filled them with ice and whiskey and passed one to Lowndes.

"We'll have to make this a quick one, Skip, O.K.? Because I'm not really through working, you see." She could not keep her words from running together, so intensely did she want the drink and Lowndes out. "I just wanted something . . . you know, when I get out of the water to dry me out. Well," she said, "I guess dry's the wrong word, isn't it? I just wanted something to keep me wet between takes, aha."

He was a magazine writer, she reminded herself, an important one, and he was there to write about the picture. With fascinated horror, she watched his upper lip draw back to expose a line of unhealthy red gum. "Not," she laughed gaily, "that I'm planning to play the scene loaded, because that's not how I work. Hell no, why . . ." She broke off. The man in front of her seemed to grow more and more grotesque and she was no longer confident about the reality of what she was seeing. There was something familiar about him, familiar in a most unpleasant way. It might be that he reminded her of someone. Or it might be worse.

"It's been a very long time since I had a drink," Lowndes told her.

"Is that right?" she asked. "Well, here's how."

When they drank, Lowndes's features puckered with distaste. His eyes watered.

"I'll tell you what," she said to Dongan Lowndes, "when I'm through this evening we'll have a proper drink. We'll set around and drink and talk. How's that?"

"I thought it would be all gnomes and agents and flacks," Lowndes said. "I'd love to see you later." He finished what was in his glass in a swallow and turned pale. "Shall we have dinner?"

"Yes, yes," Lu Anne said, standing up. "Dinner it is."

She gave him the one-hundred-and-eighty-degree smile. He was a starfucker, she thought, a cheap starfucker who wanted to get her in bed and then brag to all his colleagues about it and then, without fear or favor, humiliate her before all of with-it, literate America. Not, she thought, that it hadn't been done before.

"Yeah, that's great," Lu Anne told him. "After work." She put a hand on his arm to shove him toward the door. Then she realized that she must not shove, so the hand on his arm was transformed into something like an affectionate gesture. She plucked an imaginary thread from his shirt. After work—it was just like waiting tables again, only they knew where you lived.

"Are you working late?"

"Sundown. After six."

"Well," Lowndes said, "I'll be in the bar around seven-thirty. I'll see you there."

"Is he here?"

"Who?"

"Gordon. Gordon Walker."

"Gosh, I'm sorry. I forgot to ask. He's the screenwriter, isn't he? Is he a friend of yours?"

"Yes. Yes, an old friend. Hey, thanks for the scotch," she called as he went out. "Skip."

He had brought a full bottle of Dewar's. The only problem was that it was whiskey and it would smell up her breath and the trailer, so she would have to rinse her mouth and spray evil-smelling deodorants around.

She sipped her first drink slowly. It changed things for her; changed the trailer from a ratty piece of aluminum machinery into a cool, well-appointed refuge. She turned the overhead lamps down a few degrees of intensity and found that she had created a happy kind of light. It was all so much nicer.

When she had finished her first drink, she poured a second into her plastic glass, half filling it. She wet her face with a cool towel, turned the air conditioning up and shivered comfortably.

Her copy of the script was on the makeup counter beside her chair, face down, open to the scene that was to follow. After a moment's hesitation she picked it up, not at all sure if she was in the mood for work or Edna, Kate Chopin or Gordon Walker's take on things in general. She had read it many times before.

The scene was the novel's climax, her walk into the sea; if she opened her trailer door she would be able to hear the grips at work on the setup for it.

She moves like Cleopatra, Walker had written, *as though impelled by immortal longings*. The lines of direction were addressed only to her, a part of their game of relentless Shakespearianizing, half purely romantic, half higher bullshit. He meant he wanted Edna going out like the Queen in *Antony and Cleo*, Act V, scene 2.

She senses a freedom the scope of which she has never known. She has come beyond despair to a kind of exaltation.

Well, Lu Anne thought. Well, now. She had a little scotch and put the script face down in her lap.

"Really, now, Gordon," she said.

Of course, that was the spirit of the book and its ending. But exaltation beyond despair? She had never found anything beyond despair except more despair.

There were some questions to take up, some questions for the writer here. Did Walker really believe in exaltation beyond despair? Did that mean she had to? Would she be able to play it? For that she had an answer which was: absolutely, you betcha. We play them whether they're there or not. And once we've played them they're there and there they stay, just like Marcel Herrand's Larcenaire, Henry Fonda's Wyatt Earp, Jimmy Dean's Jimmy Dean. Exaltation beyond despair, she thought. Christ, I can stand that out in the middle of the floor and tap-dance on the son of a bitch.

It was wearying to have to think about despair, to have to think about Edna and Walker and what was there and what not. About the last especially, she wasn't sure she had the right to an opinion. Who knew what was there and what wasn't? The liquor made her head ache. Who could say what exaltations there were?

What if walking by the water one day you broke through it?

You're walking into the water like our Edna and bam! Life more abundant.

That's a trick, she thought suddenly. That's a mean trick, because Walker was right about the lure of life more abundant. To go for it was dying. That kind of abundance, going for that was dying.

That was what he had meant. That, and *Antony and Cleopatra*, Act V, scene 2.

Very clever, Walker, she thought, but a pretty tough one to lay on your old pal. He had rewritten the ending over the past year, not the action but the emotional tone in his descriptions. It occurred to her that he might think he was about to die. Or be wishing himself dead, or her.

There was, she decided, no point in getting upset about it. It was only the script, and the script an adaptation from what was only a book. *Beyond despair to a kind of exaltation* as far as she knew was nothing more than a theatrical convention, just as walking into the drink at sunset was only movies. Her trouble with Walker was that, down deep, she thought he knew everything. The past, the present and future, all the answers. But he was just a writer, as she was what she was.

She drank a little more; a confusion of emotions assailed her, her head ached. She took a couple of aspirin, turned out the lights and slumped into a chair with her legs up on the lounger, the glass in her hand.

What's going on, Walker? she thought. What's happening here? Who are we and what are we playing at? Where does one thing leave off and the other stuff commence?

"I'm real," she said aloud. Having so declared, she had to have a drink and think about it. I know that I am. I know what's me and what's not me. That's all I know. She finished what was in her plastic glass and threw it gently onto the makeup counter.

It was not quite dark inside the trailer. The late-afternoon sunlight hurled itself against every hatch, every weld and seam in the big metal compartment. The Long Friends came out to gossip and brush her with their wings. They were always there when it was dark and reality in question. Their lavender sachet breath was cloying, narcotic.

"Hush now," she told them.

They prattled on about secrets. Much of their talk was about things that must never be known, ruinous scandals, undetected crimes.

The incessant undercurrent of noise drove her to rise and turn on the overhead lamps. Only one of the Long Friends remained with the light, curled up in the darkest corner, smiling vacantly.

The ones born aren't enough for you, the Friend said. The ones unborn, they're too many.

"Don't *unborn* me," Lee said. "Really," she said, "really, you have a nerve giving that abortion crap to me. I gave life to four and you took one back." She turned to the corpse-like creature in the corner. "Want me to lie awake nights? No, thanks." She cursed it in Creole French until it raised chalk-white splayed fingers to stop its ears. Watching it do so, she raised her own hands to the side of her head.

"You're a sickness," she said without looking at it, "that I breathed in from a graveyard."

She had an inward vision of a hot September day that sometimes came to her in dreams. She was small, always a child in her dreams, and walking a sandy road down home. On one side of the road, government pines were planted in rows and beyond them tupelos grew beside the motionless river. She crossed herself walking beside a cemetery wall; the oven graves on the far side were invisible to her. She held her breath as long as she could but she could hold it only so long. It was before the hurricane and the high water, just before they'd moved to town, the same summer she remembered her father huge and drunk in the doorway, looking past her for somebody real. Sometimes it pleased her to imagine she had breathed in the Long Friends that day, although it was years before she began to hear and finally to see them.

She turned and looked at the one in the corner. The rough cloth in which it had wrapped itself, the colorless god's-eye pattern of its wing seemed as vividly present as anything in the trailer.

"Do you love me?" she asked. She began to laugh and cut herself off. Her prescription pills were in the pill case in her carry bag. She took them out, poured them into her hand and mentally counted them. There were enough to put her out forever. That was what she had wanted to see. All right, she thought. There were enough—there would be enough tomorrow. Next year and the year after that. It was always there. She put the pills back into their plastic capsule.

Resting her brow on her hand, she tried to think about the scene she was about to play. Cleopatra. Immortal longings and exaltation beyond despair. She clenched her teeth and shook her head violently, wrapping the beach robe closer about her shoulders. Then she began to sing.

Her song was a wordless prayerful hum. Years before, she had sung in convincing imitation of the saintly folk sopranos of her youth; she had no training but she liked to sing. As she sang, she relaxed, closed her eyes and let her arms go limp beside her. The song located her to that September day when walking beside the burial ovens she had breathed in some evil fateful thing.

Save me, she sang. That was what the song was about. Somebody, save me.

She leaned her head back, clasped her hands and let her voice rise in a strong tremolo. The song summoned up such a wave of sadness, of recollected hopes, old loves and losses that she thought she would die.

Where's my exaltation beyond despair? she thought. There's nothing here but this dreaming child, all unhappy.

She let her song rise again and spread out her arms. In Louisiana the old black people called that kind of singing a *bajo* or a *banjo* song, a homesick blues for where you've never been, which for them was Africa but for her was God only knows.

Be there, Lu Anne sang. Be there, Sweet Jesus. Be there.

She leaned back in the lounger, exhausted. When she turned to the mirror she saw her own secret eyes. No other person except her children and the Long Friends had ever seen them. She had used them for Rosalind, but so disguised that no one looking, however closely, could know what it was they were seeing in her face. None of her children had secret eyes.

She got to her feet, transfixed by what she saw in the mirror. The shock made her see stars as though she had been struck in the face. She watched the secret-eyed image in the glass open its mouth; she tried to look away.

Clusters of hallucination lilacs sprang up everywhere, making a second frame for the mirror, sprouting from between her legs. In her terror she called on God.

Suddenly the place was filled with ugly light, sunlight at once dingy and harsh. Trash light. Josette was standing in the open doorway, wide-eyed and pale. She took a step backward, her lip was trembling. It was the first time Lu Anne had ever seen the Frenchwoman show anything other than unsmiling composure.

Look, you little bitch! Lu Anne thought. Then she was not sure whether she had not said it aloud. Look at my secret eyes!

Vera Ricutti and her husband were behind Josette; Vera had a costume over her arm, a gray cotton garment and a blue bandana. The Ricuttis looked up at Lu Anne with something that might be reverence.

"What's wrong, kid?" Vera Ricutti asked.

"I was prepping," Lu Anne said. The accusatory malice and disgust she saw in Josette's eyes made her feel sick.

"You were screaming!" the girl cried. She turned to the Ricuttis for confirmation. "She was screaming in there!"

"I was singing," Lu Anne said quietly.

Josette looked up at her with a twisted triumphant smile; Vera Ricutti was holding her by the arm.

"Don't tell me!" she shouted at Lu Anne. "You were screaming."

"I was prepping."

The woman shrugged and grunted.

Joe Ricutti came forward and spoke quietly to her and she walked away.

"We'll take care of it," Joe said in his gravelly voice. "We'll talk to Eric. I mean, you don't have to take that from her."

Lu Anne stood in the trailer doorway, her beach robe undone, leaning one elbow on her wrist and chewing her little finger.

"Shit," she said.

Vera stepped up and gently urged her back inside.

"So you were screaming. You got a right."

"Absolutely," Joe Ricutti said.

Walter Drogue and his father were walking from their trailer to the beach. The old man wore a blue bathing suit that scarcely concealed his privates and a gondolier's striped shirt.

"You think you have to be smart to direct pictures?" the old man asked his son. "Bullshit. Some of the biggest assholes you ever met are immortal."

"I never said you had to be smart," his son replied. "I said it was useful. I was thinking of my own case."

"Ford," the old man said. "A born political director. An Irishman with the eye of a German Romantic. Peasant slyness. He never got in trouble here and he wouldn't have got in trouble over there like Eisenstein."

"You're lucky it was here you got in trouble," young Drogue told his father. "Over there they would have just shot your ass and no fancy speeches."

At the beach Blakely and Hueffer were waiting for them. The Chapman Titan had been driven onto its track.

"Check out the sky," Blakely said.

Old Drogue went off to settle himself in a folding chair beneath a beach umbrella. Drogue junior, Blakely and Eric Hueffer looked at the horizon.

The line of storm cloud seemed to have risen some thirty degrees, so that the horizon line was a convergence of two gold-flecked tones of blue. The sun's intensity was just beginning to fade.

"If those clouds will stay where they are when the sun sets," Blakely said, "we're gonna have us one fuckin' humdinger of a sunset."

"I'm God," Walter Drogue told his assistants. "I still the restless wave. I command the sun. Where's Joy?"

"Joy," Eric Hueffer called, and Joy McIntyre stepped out from inside the nearest bathhouse door. She wore a form-fitting gray cotton bathing suit. A blue bandana was tied around her head.

"Want to watch a tape?" Hueffer asked.

"No," Drogue said. "I want to watch her walk."

A pair of grips were summoned to lower the arm of the crane; Drogue climbed aboard the camera turret and was weighted in.

"Joy!" Hueffer shouted. "Got your marks?"

"Yeah," Joy said.

They weighted Toby Blakely in beside his leader.

"Action!" Drogue shouted, and the mounted camera retreated before Joy's advance down the beach, hauled along by the grips at their guide ropes. Young Drogue peered through the camera's eye, his baseball cap reversed like a catcher's.

"O.K.," he said, when he was satisfied.

The grips swung the Chapman's arm to its original position and brought Blakely and young Drogue to earth. Joy leaned on one extended arm against the side of the bathhouse. Drogue, Hueffer and Blakely hunkered down near the water's edge.

"She's so fucking beautiful it's gross," Drogue said. "She comes out of there and you just think: I want to fuck her. You lose your sense of proportion." He glanced over toward where his father sat and saw the old man's glance fixed on the comely stand-in.

"Lee has a lot more dignity," Blakely said. "And a pretty sexy frame for a woman with two or three kids. Or even more."

The three of them walked over to where Joy was standing and looked her up and down.

"I like this bathing suit," Hueffer said.

Drogue patted Joy's shoulder, and seized a piece of her bathing suit between his thumb and forefinger. "It's cotton. To be accurate, it should be wool, but we figured fuck it. So," he said, pointing to Joy, "as not to cause unnecessary discomfort to our personnel."

Joy smiled gratefully.

"Actually," Drogue told his associates, "we're cheating a lot with this suit. This thing is circa 1912. If we gave 'em the real Gay Nineties article this scene would look like Mack Sennett."

"I should think this 'un might be good for a few laughs," Joy said. The three men looked at her sternly.

"When you take it off, doll," Drogue told her, "no one will be laughing."

"Crikey," Joy said. "Take it off?"

"Don't you look at the script?" Drogue asked her. "Of course you take it off."

"Crikey," Joy said.

"Miss Verger is taking her suit off. It's in the script. If she can do it, you can do it."

"I suppose," Joy said doubtfully.

Drogue turned to Hueffer and drew him aside. Blakely went along with them.

"What I need to know here is how it's going to look when she takes that suit off. It's tight, she'll have to wriggle—O.K., we don't want a striptease. We'll probably cut to the suit falling away but I'm not sure how far into the disrobing we want to go. So let's roll tape on this shot—have her come down the beach to her marks, take the bandana off and toss it. Then let her get out of that suit as gracefully as she can and drop it aside. See if she can start by raising her right arm and baring her right breast."

"Good," Hueffer said. Drogue reacted to his approval with a slow double take. "Do you want her to go into the water?"

"No time for that. We're shooting for sunset and that means three takes if we're lucky. Otherwise we have to do it again tomorrow."

"If it doesn't rain," Hueffer said.

"Yeah, yeah," Drogue said. "Hurry up. Go tell her what she has to do."

"I'm thinking eroticism," Drogue said to Blakely. "I'm thinking sacrifice. Motherhood. Yes?"

"Right," Blakely said.

"I'm thinking human sacrifice. Madonnahood."

"Tithood?"

"Tithood too."

They watched Eric discuss the situation with Joy McIntyre. Eric was speaking enthusiastically and at some length. Joy was pouting.

"Look at the ass on the little bitch," Drogue said angrily. "Christ almighty."

"Well," Blakely said, "don't get pissed, boss."

L ate in the afternoon, as the highway curved down from the Cerro Encantada, Walker found himself driving within sight of the sea. He pulled over at the next turnoff, got out of the car and walked to the end of a promontory from which he could see the ocean and the trail that lay ahead of him. The sun was low and losing its fire, the ocean a cool darkening blue that made him shiver in the desert heat. Between the ridge on which he stood and the sea lay the Honda Valley. It was every variety of green—delicate pastel in the circular irrigated cotton fields, silver-green in the stands of eucalyptus, a sinister reptilian emerald along the base of its canyon walls. Miles away, perhaps as much as an hour of cautious driving over the tortuous highway, a paved road descended in figure-of-eight switchbacks to the valley. He could make out the hotel buildings. From where he stood they seemed to rest precariously in the folds of a red table rock that commanded the coastal plain.

As his gaze swept the valley, he saw sharp glints of reflected sunlight from the seaside edge of one of the eucalyptus groves. Before a line of wooden structures, tiny human figures went to and fro along the shore. The sunlight was striking silver-paper reflectors, metal and glass. It took him a moment to understand that he was seeing *The Awakening* unit at work.

There was a copy of Peterson's *Western Birds* and a pair of binoculars behind the rear seat of the Buick; Walker's wife was a birdwatcher and he had driven her car to Seattle. He took the glasses, walked back to the edge of the ridge and picked out the unit. He saw a woman in an old-fashioned gray bathing suit walking toward the water. As he watched, the woman stopped short and sauntered back to the spot from which she had begun.

Walker watched her start again, noted the camera crane on its track and the figures on the turret. A sound man attended the woman like an acolyte, carrying his boom aloft. He saw the woman remove a bandana from around her head and toss it to the sand. He saw her walk on, remove her bathing suit and stand naked and golden in the sun. He was seeing, he supposed, what he had come to see.

It was very strange to see them as he did—tiny distant figures at the edge of an ocean, acting out a vision compounded of his obsessions and emotions. He had never been so in love, he thought, as he was with the woman who stood naked on the beach in front of that camera and several dozen cold-eyed souls. It was as though she were there for him, for something that was theirs. He felt at the point of understanding the process in which his life was bound, as though the height on which he stood was the perspective he had always lacked. Will I understand it all now, he wondered, understand it with the eye, like a painting?

The sense of discovery, of imminent insight excited him. He was dizzy; he checked his footing on the uneven ground, his closeness to the edge. Her down there, himself on a rock miles away—that's poetry, he thought. The thing was to get it straight, to understand.

He saw them dress her again, saw her walk, lose the bandana, then the bathing suit in what, from where he stood, read as a series of effortless moves. Tears came to his eyes. But perhaps it was not poetry, he thought. Only movies.

The seed of meaning he had touched between his teeth began to slip away. He was struck by the silence between their place and his; he strained for the director's voice, the sound of the sea. Gulls were what he heard, and wind in the mesquite.

What had it been? Almost joy, he thought, a long-lost thing, something pleasurable for its own sake. It had slipped away.

Fuck it, he thought. I got something almost as good.

He went back to his car, looked up and down the road to see that he would not be surprised and managed with some difficulty to do a few lines. Some of his cocaine blew onto the car seat and he had to brush it away and see it scatter on the wind.

It had been just like a dream, he thought, the same disappearing resolution, the same awakening to the same old shit. It wasn't there. Or was hardly there—a moment's poetry, a moment's movies. Hardly enough there to count, not for the likes of him.

The coke was no help. It had been something like a daydream, provoked by the smell of the wind and the dizzying height and his impatience to see her; no drug would bring it back. Rather, the drugs gave him the jitters—made him feel exposed, out there in the open beside the road, pursued and out of breath. When he went out to the ridge again and fixed his binoculars on the naked figure he saw it was not Lu Anne but a younger woman who somewhat resembled her. There's your poetry, he thought. Your movies.

The Drogues, Blakely and Hueffer crowded into the director's trailer to watch tapes of Joy's undressing.

When the screen showed her stripping, a reverent silence fell over the group.

"What was the big fuss?" old Drogue asked.

"She bitched. She didn't want to show her ass."

"Did you tell her that Lu Anne would?"

"I told her. She had the nerve to tell me her problem was the Mexicans. She said, 'They take it wrong.' " He mimicked her accent and demeanor. " 'They take it wrong,' she said."

A murmur of disapproval arose in the dark trailer. They all sat quite still, watching Joy naked on the screen.

"A frame like that," the old man said, "and she never took off her pants for a camera? Hard to believe."

Young Drogue froze the frame.

"That's going to be broken up," he said. "It *does* turn out to be a striptease."

"Remember," Hueffer said, "with Lee it won't be as flamboyant."

Drogue was thoughtful for a moment.

"I think the opposite," young Drogue said. "Joy's so built and busty and dumb that you kind of . . . the thing gets this wild unpredictable quality. You don't know what the hell's happening but it's weird and it turns you on. With Joy I might use it."

"The kid does something for a camera," Blakely said. "No question."

"She'll be my angel," old Drogue said.

"With Lu Anne, you might have her bare her breast and it's tragic. You don't want to see her undress. She'll look humiliated and an-orexic and crazy. The whole ending goes limp and we're dead."

"He's right for once," old Drogue told Hueffer. "You're wrong."

"Let's do this in one take, guys!" young Drogue shouted. He mo-tioned Eric to his side. "When you get Lu Anne on her mark, Eric, clear the set."

"Why?" Heuffer asked.

"The Mexicans," young Drogue told him. "They take it wrong."

J oe Ricutti had set up shop under a beach umbrella beside the bath-house. He sponged and powdered Lu Anne's face and gave her a neck rub. Josette worked on her hair, no more sulkily distant than was usual. The gaffer and best boy were winding cable for an arc. Lu Anne had a look at the sun and picked up her worn copy of Kate Chopin's novel. The wording was a solo *Liebestodt*, death as liberation.

Edna had found her old bathing suit still hanging, faded upon its accustomed peg, Chopin had written.

When Josette finished with her hair, Lu Anne stood up.

"I'm going to walk it through," she told Ricutti, and reading as she walked, set out for the bathhouse.

She put it on, leaving her clothing in the bathhouse. But when she was beside the sea, absolutely alone, she cast the unpleasant prickling garments from her, and for the first time in her life, she stood naked in the open air, at the mercy of the sun, the breeze that beat upon her, and the waves that invited it.

"Clear the set, please," Eric Hueffer intoned through his megaphone. "If you're not working, we don't want you on the set. Clear the set, everybody, please." The Peruvian continuity girl made the announcement in Spanish, for the Mexicans.

Lu Anne leaned her head against the side of the bathhouse and thought of Edna naked in the open air for the first time. How sad it was, she thought. There was no way to film it. She had never thought of herself like Edna, but some things, she thought, they're the same for everyone. A little Edna in all of us.

Naked for the first time, the open air. In the heat of the day it should be. A beach on the Gulf, midday, the water just cool, the sun hot on your body, the wind so still you can smell your own skin.

She finds out who she is and it's too much and she dies. Yes, Lu Anne thought, I know about that. I can do that, me.

Too bad about the sunset, because it was clichéd and banal. Low-rent theatrics. Middle-income. Middlebrow theatrics.

She strolled at the water's edge, reading. No one had called for quiet but the gaffer and the best boy spoke in low voices.

How strange and awful it seemed to stand under the sky! how delicious.

She felt like some newborn creature, opening its eyes in a familiar world that she had never known.

The touch of the sea is sensuous, enfolding the body, in its soft close embrace.

The cosmic fuck. Well, Lu Anne thought, who better than me? But the drowned people she had seen in the church hall after the hurricane down home had not looked particularly fulfilled.

She read the line again aloud: *"The touch of the sea is sensuous, enfolding the body, in its soft close embrace."* She looked out to sea. That's how it would seem to Edna. Something out there for me. Life more abundant. You let it go and you lie back and you let it happen. You don't have to keep your clothes on or your mouth shut, your legs crossed or your hair up or your asshole tight. You don't have to worry. You don't have to do a goddamn thing but . . .

"Miss Verger, please," Eric Hueffer called into his megaphone. Mechanically, she turned back toward her chair and the makeup table. Ricutti put a dry sponge to her temples. Josette ran a comb through her hair.

"Please, everyone," Hueffer was telling the stragglers, "if we don't need you, we don't want you here."

Lu Anne read on about Edna Pontellier's last swim.

She thought of Leonce and the children. They were a part of her life. But they need not have thought that they could possess her body and soul.

Well, Lu Anne thought, nothing is free, Edna. Her life had not afforded her the opportunity to experience that sentiment. No doubt it was dreadful. *A Doll's House.* Empty days. Childbirth. Massa having his nights out with the boys, his quadroon sweetie. The kids night and day. She decided it did not do for her to think about children.

They were waiting for her. She put the book down and stood up and Drogue came up to her, guiding her toward the bathhouse, telling her about the shot, how to come out, where to take the suit off, when to go into the water.

The mercy of the sun, Lu Anne thought. The informing words. *Awful. Naked. Delicious. Sensuous. Soft close embrace.* Dying was always fun. *Immortal longings. Exaltation beyond despair.* So much popcorn, she thought. To get the character you had to go down and inside to where your grief was. The place your truest self inhabited was the place you could not bear.

She stopped and leaned against Drogue. They were at the door of the bathhouse, and the camera was advancing on her. Two Mexican grips waited beside the Titan, privileged characters who were expected not to take it wrong when she undressed.

"O.K., partner?" Drogue asked.

"I'm fucked, honey," she told him. "Life's a condom."

She looked into his panic-stricken face. He's seeing it, she thought. Yes, she thought, behold the glory, Jim. Look at me shining, I'm the Queen of Lights.

"How about a half-moon on the bathhouse door, Walter? I could come out and do Judy Canova." She bared her front teeth at him.

"Great," Walter Drogue the younger said. "Only—some other time, maybe?"

"Have no fear," she told the director. She stepped inside the bathhouse, closing the door behind her. There was only one of them inside.

How can you dare speak so to them? it asked gently in the old language. They don't understand you. It's we alone who do.

"Which one are you?" she asked it wearily. It was Marie Ange, she knew.

"Marie Ange," she sighed. "Monkey-face. Go away, eh? *Va-t'en.*"

Eric was calling for quiet.

She raised her eyes into the darkness. "Oh, darkness above," she prayed, "help your sister darkness below."

She crossed herself quickly. She hadn't meant such a terrible prayer. She thought that she might go to church in town that evening.

Drogue's voice cut through the silence on the other side of the door. "Action!"

She opened the door and walked out into the golden sunlight and caught a quick glimpse of Charlie Freitag, the producer. She fixed her gaze on a point above the reddening horizon where the sun's fading glare might light her eyes yet not dazzle her. At the appointed mark, she stopped and lowered the shoulder straps of her one-piece gray bathing suit. It was not, she thought, of any thwarted love that Edna died. The suit peeled away easily as she eased her torso free. She kept her eyes on their quarter of the sky.

It was dangerous to probe one's inward places. The chemistry was volatile, fires might start and burn out of control. What if I, Lu Anne thought, who cannot see past mirrors, should confront myself there? My self.

If I, who see everything in mirrors, who cannot approach the glass without some apprehension, were to see my inward self there, I would not die. But Edna might.

Medusa, she thought. That's what that's about. It's your own face that turns you to stone, your own secret eyes.

Poor Edna. Poor Edna gets a sight of herself, she explodes, crashes, burns. Never knew she was there. Catches fire like the feckless child of family legend, little Great-Aunt Catastrophe in her going-to-mass dress on Christmas morning, alight from the Christmas candles, a torch-child spinning around the parlor.

Poor old Edna, little Dixie honey, sees her own self on the shield of hot blue sky and dies. Sees all that freedom, that great black immensity of righteous freedom and swoons, Oh My. And dies.

Stepping out of the suit, Lu Anne tossed it aside and walked on toward the water. All at once she was reminded of Walker, but whether it was of something he had told her or something in the script, she could not recall. Something of him had come to her mind for a moment and gone. She stepped into the warm water; two brawny men in swimming trunks stood waist deep just outside the shot, a third waited thirty or so feet out, resting on a float with a coiled length of line.

Shoulders back, head high, she walked along the inclining sandy bottom. The camera tracked with her, eye to eye, and when she lost her footing and pushed off, she was aware of it pulling back and hovering overhead as she swam out from shore.

When Drogue called cut, the man with the float advanced toward her but she turned back. Wading out of the water she heard a little clatter of applause.

"Where's the crew?" Lu Anne asked, shaking her hair. Vera Ricutti brought her a beach robe.

"We cleared the set," Drogue told her. "We thought it would be friendlier just us."

"Well, Walter," she said happily, "if you-all are going to applaud I would like a lot of applause rather than a little."

"Shall we bring them back?" he asked. "Want a claque?" He strode away from her, calling for his soldiers.

"O.K., *muchachos*! Once more for protection."

"Arcs ready if you want it," Hueffer told him.

"I don't want it. I want reflectors in place."

Lu Anne went to the trailer to have her hair dried and combed.

Light was fading; the sun seemed to hang suspended above a thin curl of purple cirrus cloud. They were running out of clear sky. A gray wall of rain was approaching from the northwest; the wind carried a few fat drops to spatter on the beach and people looked at the sky in alarm. In the end, the rain held off and they had time for two more takes of Lu Anne going to the water.

"I'll give it to you two ways, Walter," Lu Anne said.

Drogue was on the crane with Blakely and the camera operator. Eric Hueffer stood beside the truck watching the sky.

"Anything you want, babe," Drogue told her.

Action was called, Lu Anne flung her suit aside and went in.

Vera brought her the robe and they started back to her trailer.

"That was the James Mason 'think I'll do a few laps around Catalina between Old-Fashioneds' one," she called to Drogue as she went by.

As they set up for the sky and ocean shot, Drogue looked grim.

"Watch this," he told his assistant. "We're gonna have the Lu Anne Happy Hour."

"Is that a bad sign?" Hueffer asked him.

"Fuckin' right. But it's the up side."

She came out again for their last take of the day and repeated the scene. The bathing suit was tossed aside. Numb with self-recognition, Edna went to her death.

"Hey, Lee," Hueffer asked her as she came out of the water, "what was that called?"

"That," she told him, clutching the robe about her shoulders, "is called Lupe Velez Takes a Dunk."

Hueffer broke up. Drogue, Blakely, even the operator chortled as they clung to their uneasy perches.

When Lu Anne had passed, the laughter froze on Drogue's face. He looked at Blakely and shrugged.

"She's funny," he said.

It had been dark for over half an hour when Walker's road began its snaking descent from high desert to the canyon floor. His headlights were focused on a wall of deepening green that seemed to spin before him; the indifferently banked road felt as though it were falling away beneath his tires, threatening to send him out of control. At last, to his relief, the road ran flat and straight. He kept to the center, wary of animals, riders, pedestrians—and in less than a mile he saw the hotel sign.

Its entrance was tree-lined; a fountain played in front of the foyer. Its buildings were of white stucco that glowed under decorative lamps. To Walker after his weary drive it seemed all compounded of inviting sounds, liquefactive shadow and soft light.

An attendant took his bags and at the desk he found himself expected. The room to which he was conducted was as tasteful as its elegant extravagance could bear, a showy red-and-black room that suggested Spanish melodrama, theatrical sex and violence. *Carmen.* He overtipped the bellman with a ten from his winning roll.

He felt anxious and weary. On a whim, he had come to a place where he was without friends to see a woman whom he had no business to see. There were no other motives of consequence behind his journey.

In the shower he hummed an old number:

You take Sally, I'll take Sue.

Makes no difference what you do.

Cocaine.

The breeze that came through his open balcony window was fragrant with sage, jasmine, eucalyptus. At Santa Anita his winner had been called O.K. So Far.

Among his supplies he found a packet of cologne-soaked towels, part of a first-class flight kit issued him on a flight that someone else had paid for. Not the Shakespeare people; there was no first class with them. Television. He dressed and brought out his works. He was preparing a snort, thinking O.K. So Far, when there sounded a knock on his door. He put the drugs away and went and opened it.

His visitor was Jon Axelrod, the unit manager.

"Hey, Gordon. Our house is"—he gave his hand a flip—"you know?"

"Thank you, Jon. I'm glad to be here. May I offer you some blow?"

Axelrod took a chair.

"I have to tell you the unit has very strict rules regarding the use of drugs. We report narcotics to the police. Otherwise we can't get insurance."

Walker spread a few lines out on his mirror.

"Stop at Siriwai's?" Axelrod asked.

"Mexico's not Mexico without the doctor."

"Did you tell him we all miss him?"

"He knows."

Axelrod removed a crisp U.S. twenty from his wallet, rolled it and took a snort. He was a slightly built man with an ageless fey face. He

138

regarded Walker from the corners of his eyes, which were blue and bright with fractured whimsy. Walker took a line for himself and they sat in reflective silence for a moment.

"Lu Anne is good," Axelrod said. "What I seen. Not a whole lot. But good stuff."

"How's her head?"

"She seems cheerful."

"I can't imagine," Walker said, "what you mean by that."

"She's working well. We're watching her. See, her husband just took their kids off on a trip. We weren't expecting that. We thought —the guy's a shrink, he's her shrink. We put them all up on the budget. Then he leaves."

"Where is she now?"

Axelrod smiled.

"Take a guess."

Lu Anne, Walker thought, would be either screwing in a Jacuzzi or in church.

"In church?"

"Pretty good, fella. She went to church in town. Billy Bly took her down."

Walker was not too pleased to hear about Bly.

"Billy's keeping an eye on her," Axelrod told him. "We're trying not to leave her alone too much."

"How come he's here? What do you call him on the budget?"

"Stunt coordinator. Hey, we made some changes in the shooting script, Gordon. We have a lot of falls."

Walker was not amused.

"We got him down for special effects. He supervises the guys in the water, the guys with the horses. Lu Anne likes him."

"They keeping company?"

Axelrod looked puzzled. "No," he said. "I mean, her old man just left."

"It's a bad sign," Walker said, "when she goes to church."

They finished what was on the pocket mirror.

"How's Walter?" Walker asked.

"Walter's the same. What a talent, huh, Gordon?"

"Fuckin' A. Will he be happy to see me?"

"Maybe he's scared you might get to Lu Anne. Maybe not."

Walker said nothing.

"You know Walter, Gordo. He doesn't care if people like him. He thinks most people are wienies."

"What does he think I came down here for?"

"He knows, Gordon. Everybody does."

"Do they really?" Walker said. "Isn't that something?"

"Wipe your nose good," Axelrod said. "We should go see Charlie."

The hotel restaurant had a terrace overlooking the bay. Adjoining it was a blue-tiled lounge with a service bar and a few candlelit tables. Two graying men sat at a table near the door. One was Charlie Freitag, esteemed gentleman producer. Charlie rose when Axelrod and Walker came in.

"Hello, Gordon," Charlie called. He looked quite surprised. "How was your drive?" He turned to his companion. "This man *drove* down from L.A. He insisted!"

Walker was always happy to see Charlie Freitag, a pleasant, friendly man, possessed of a fatuous manner and many well-laid plans.

Charlie introduced the man he was drinking with as Howard Robinson. Robinson had the best suntan of anyone there; he wore checkered slacks and white loafers.

"Don't care to fly?" he asked Walker.

"I like driving in Mexico," Walker said.

"I could keep you in that for life," Howard said, "if that's what you like."

Walker decided he represented Las Vegas investors, and it developed after a brief exchange that he did. He and Axelrod proved to be old acquaintances and Axelrod was the son of an IATSE enforcer from the days of the labor wars. There were always a lot of hoods around on Walter Drogue's pictures and Walker had never determined the reason for it.

"Walter told me to greet you on his behalf," Charlie said to Walker. "He bids you welcome."

"Ah," Walker said.

"You know who I think you should meet?" Charlie Freitag asked Walker. "You should meet Dongan Lowndes. Know his work?"

Walker knew it. It was a single novel of great force.

"I'm glad," Freitag said. "He's doing a piece on us for *New York Arts*. It can do us a lot of good where it counts."

They went toward a dark corner where another party of two were sitting. Walker recognized one as Jack Best, the unit publicity man. Best hated him relentlessly over some drunken misadventure he could not recall.

"Mr. Lowndes," Charlie said, with the air of a man opening first one expensive cigar and then another, "let me introduce Gordon Walker, who adapted *The Awakening* for the screen. You know Mr. Axelrod, I think."

Lowndes when he leaned forward turned out to be a bulky man with a pitted face and aviator spectacles. The hand he offered Walker was big and thick-fingered like a countryman's.

"How're you?" Lowndes said. Walker saw that he was drunk and so was Best.

"This is Dongan Lowndes, Gordon," Freitag said. "Our guest from New York." He clapped Walker on the shoulder. "Listen," he said, "we finished the late work today, so tomorrow we can drink and be merry. People are coming for a cookout at eight o'clock. *Carne asada* under the stars. We'll talk."

"Great," Walker said.

"Claire would have loved to make it, but—you know, she's busy with groups. She sends her best."

"And mine to her," Walker said.

Freitag took a quick rueful glance at his publicity man and went back to his table.

Walker smiled and murmured and made himself small. He was exhausted, propped upright by cocaine; he wanted people to be agreeable.

"We've been waiting for your girlfriend," Jack Best said to Walker. "She just stood us up for dinner."

"It was very informally arranged," Lowndes said. He spoke in a quiet lowland southern accent. His diction was just ever so slightly blurred about the edges. "I probably misunderstood."

"No," Jack Best said. "She's like that. A lot of them are. They don't care about the public anymore."

Studying Best across the table, Walker blundered into eye contact and suffered the full weight of his gratuitous hatred.

"I figured she was probably with him," the publicist said, indicating Walker and staring him down.

"C'mon, Jack," Axelrod said. "Be nice." He put a friendly arm around Best's shoulder and squeezed him.

"I liked your novel," Walker told Lowndes, still wanting to please. "I mean your most recent one."

Lowndes raised his glass. "My one and only," he said.

Walker saw that he had said the wrong thing. He had intended to be polite and Lowndes was offended.

"Walker," Jack Best intoned. "Gordon Walker." He rose gravely and staggered off toward the toilets.

"I don't know what he's got against me," Walker said to Axelrod when Best was gone. "What's his problem?"

"His problem is you humiliated him in front of about a hundred people in Colorado two years ago. You don't remember?"

Walker tried remembering. "No," he said.

"Too bad," Lowndes said. "It must make a funny story."

"I think I'll have a drink," Walker said. He had decided that he was not among friends and that there would probably be some kind of trouble. He supposed that had been in the cards all along. "Have they closed the bar?"

The bar was still open; Axelrod found a waiter and they ordered another round. Lowndes ordered for Jack Best.

"He's so amusing," Lowndes said. "I thought we should keep him greased."

When Best returned, he drank a full half of his drink and settled his gaze on Walker again.

"Jack's been telling us the history of film," Lowndes explained. "I've learned a lot too."

Lowndes's tone held a warning for the unwary but Walker decided the hell with it. He wondered if Charlie Freitag really thought that an article about a Mexican location in *New York Arts* would do any good where it counted. He concluded that the reference was to where it counted for Charlie Freitag.

"For instance," he asked Lowndes.

"Jack believes," Lowndes told them, "that *Marty* was the beginning of the end. It was all down thereafter."

"Marty who?" Axelrod asked.

"The picture," Lowndes explained. "The film of that name."

Jack Best half rose to his feet.

"You," he shouted at Walker. He turned to Lowndes and Jon Axelrod. "Him!"

"Yeah, Jack?" Axelrod asked softly. "That's Gordon, Jack. What you wanna tell us?"

"I saw him years ago. I saw you years ago, Walker. I saw you and I was talking to King and I says"—he heaved a sigh and drew breath—"I says looka that guy. I says look. Because the guy—him. Walker. The guy has this stupid shirt on. A fuckin' hippie shirt on. Hippie shirt. And his hair. And I says—King. King, I says. Is that a boy? Or a girl? And King says." A mask of bewilderment closed over his features.

"We must infer what King says," Lowndes declared.

Walker finished his own drink. "No," he told them. "King says— fuck you, you disgusting little pissant of a flack. You're not fit to lick the chickenshit off that talented young man's shoes. You're a drunken contemptible cipher, a dirty little hole in the world. A crepuscular fool, King says. A homunculus, King says. Go over to Oblath's and cut your weasely little rat throat, King says. Anyway," Walker told them, "that's the way I remember it."

"Hey, Gordon," Axelrod said, "you're doing it again, man."

"King?" Lowndes asked. "Vidor?"

"Kong," Walker said. "Dennis King. Dolores King. Jack knew them all."

Best appeared to have gone to sleep. Axelrod nudged him and he sat upright.

"The choreographer at the Sands is dead!" he told the people at the table. Everyone watched him. "That's it," he shouted. "The choreographer at the Sands is dead!" He choked and his head fell forward. Just before his nose hit the table he retrieved his posture and his face rose up at Walker like a creature from a black lagoon. He was shaken by spasms of what appeared to be laughter. He reached over and seized Walker's arm and held it hard. "The choreographer at the Sands is dead!" he shrieked. Freitag and Robinson, the restaurant staff all turned to see him. His voice became a croak. "And the Sands . . . the Sands doesn't . . ." He seemed too shaken by his fit of peculiar laughter to continue. "The Sands doesn't even have a line!"

Having said so much, he uttered an explosive cry and fell face forward, still clutching Walker's arm.

"What do you call that?" Axelrod asked.

Walker detached his arm from the old man's grip.

"The riddle of the Sands," he said.

T he plaza of Bahía Honda town was not much to look at but it took on a little ragged charm at night. There was a raised pavement of whitewashed brick in the center, set around a single pink tile on which glitter-covered seashells had been pasted to form the numeral *1969*. Under a row of naked bulbs at the edge of the sere football field, a few vendors were selling tortillas, ices, plastic sandals. The town's few fishing boats were in port and there was laughter and music from one of the square's two cafes. The other, opposite, stood empty, gloomy and ill lit. Before the town's cinema, people of all ages and conditions stood in line for the evening showing of *Dr. Zhivago*. At the eastern end of the square, the town's single church, an unimposing box of white masonry surmounted with a little bell tower, stood open for the Friday-night service of benediction.

As Bill Bly, with Lu Anne on his arm, walked past the queue, people fell silent to look after them. One or two of the free spirits in the crowd felt emboldened to whistle; it was Bly who provoked them. He was a man something less than six feet tall, he wore white slacks, a black tee shirt and a white baseball cap with the word SHAKESPEARE over the visor. His hair, spilling out from under his hat brim, was curly and seemed more golden blond than any number of tropical locations' suns could bleach it. But Bly drew catcalls only from behind his back and only from innocents. The street-wise, the hustler or the desperado had only to check out the way in which he carried himself to know caution. He moved with the balance of a wire walker, as thoughtlessly well centered as an animal. The artisan class of the film industry cherished its Bill Bly stories: the amok knifer in the Philippines spun three hundred and sixty degrees on his own wrist; the bar louts laid out unconscious before they had stopped smiling. Bly worked as a bodyguard quite as often as he did as a stuntman and sometimes informally undertook both jobs at once. In his middle thirties now, he looked younger. He had been a stuntman since the age of fifteen.

Lu Anne walked, as it were, in the lee of him. She wore as her church clothes a beige skirt and blouse and a Spanish mantilla. As they walked up the church steps she clutched his elbow. At the door she smiled up at him. When she went in he lingered outside on the top step, watching the faithful as they passed, playing with a straw finger trap he had picked up in the market.

Benediction had not begun and there were only a few people inside the little church. Lu Anne walked across the stone floor to a crucifix that stood beyond two rows of votive candles to the right of the main altar. The crucifix was as old as anything in that empty quarter of the country, recovered from a fire on the mainland. Its crossbars were burned black, the seared Christus figure was tortured into a shape that made it look stylized and somehow modern. Its charred condition served to enhance the sense of martyrdom and elevated suffering it conveyed. Half a dozen worshippers stood or knelt rapt before it. Lu Anne took her place among them.

My God, she prayed, be there for me. So there is something there for me. So I am not just out in this shit lonely, deluded and lost.

The day's work, the walk through the town among strangers had made her anxious, and the drink made her head ache. Strange sounds, echoes, toneless music rang in her inward ear. There was an incessant low chatter of inaudible, half-recognized voices. The voices bore some secret inference that made her afraid.

For a moment she thought she might be alarming the people around her. When she saw that they took no notice of her, she bowed her head.

Help me, Lu Anne prayed, You who are more real than I am. My only One, my Reality.

When she looked up at the crucifix she saw that the hanged Christ nailed to the beams had become a cat. It was burned black as the figure had been, its fur turned to ash, its face burned away to show the grinning fanged teeth. She looked away and with her face averted walked to the doorway of the church where Bly was waiting for her. When she was outside she leaned against the building wall, taking deep breaths, avoiding the gazes of the people who were coming in.

"Ain't you gonna stay for the service?" Bly asked her.

She shook her head. As he stood watching her, she took hold of his arm about the biceps and with the nail of her right hand drew an invisible line around it. Bly stood by in confusion and embarrassment.

In the worst of times, Lu Anne thought, there's meat.

On the terrace, Jack Best was coming to himself again. His eyes were filled with tears.

"The Sands," he sputtered, "it doesn't . . ."

Axelrod helpfully interrupted him. "It doesn't have a line, am I right, Jack?" He turned to Lowndes. "I'm hoping this isn't where you find your story."

Lowndes stared at him for a moment without answering, then smiled.

"Certainly not," he said.

In the garden outside, Walker suddenly saw the figure of a woman leaning against the terrace wall. The sight brought him to his feet. As he started toward her she moved away. He went faster, trying to get to her side before she was lost in the shadows. It was as though she were running away from him.

She was wearing her hair as she had worn it fifteen years before, he thought. He knew her silhouette, her moves, her aura.

"Lu Anne," he called.

"I'm not her," said a small antipodean voice.

Walker halted in confusion. When he came nearer he saw that it was Joy McIntyre, a stand-in and body double who had once spent time with Quinn. Her husband was a stills photographer, Walker's acquaintance and sometime connection. The photographer had initiated Joy's career by spreading her frame across two pages of a slick nudie book.

"That's twice today you fooled me," Walker said.

"Gordon, is it? They won't be happy to see you about."

"You mean Drogue won't. Where's Lu Anne?"

"She's in church," Joy sniffed. "That's what I heard."

"Are you crying?" Walker asked. "What's the matter?"

"Hoi," Joy snorted. "I mean wow!"

"Are you all right?"

"Yeah," she said. "I'm all right." Her eyes in the darkness appeared wide and wondering.

"How's Lu Anne?" Walker asked.

"Just fine," Joy said. "Outside of being in church. Know where I've been?"

Walker considered his answer. "With someone?"

"I shouldn't say."

"O.K."

"I've been up with Mr. Drogue."

"Ah," Walker said.

"Balling, like."

"Well," Walker said, "whatever turns you on, we used to say."

"Not the younger Mr. Drogue," Joy said unsteadily. "His dad."

"Ah," Walker said. "Well . . ." He broke off. Troubles enough of his own.

"I mean, I had to tell someone, didn't I?"

"Strictly speaking," Walker said, "no."

"I said to him—'Mr. Drogue, I'm shocked. It's my turn to be shocked now,' I said."

"It's probably for the best. He can help you. I think you probably did the right thing. Careerwise."

"I'm not talking about it," Joy said. "I'm going to forget it ever happened."

"I will too," Walker said. "I mean, I'll forget everything you told me."

"What have I told you?" Joy demanded. "I haven't told you anything."

"Right."

"Old Ryder," she said, "he's your pal, isn't he?" Ryder was the photographer, Joy's husband.

"I don't see him much anymore."

"We split up, you know. Love lost its luster for us."

"I'm sorry," Walker said.

"Boring, like."

"That's life, isn't it?" Walker said. "I mean," he said, "when it's there it's there. And when it's not it's not."

"Oh yeah," Joy said. "Well, we tried getting the old moonlight and roses back. No way." She shook her head. "He used to get me into trouble like tonight," she told Walker. "I mean, he put me forward like that. It must be second nature to me now."

"Don't blame yourself."

"Well, I'm not," she told Walker. "I'm blaming him. He's the one had me out doing that sleazy phornpone," she said.

"Right," Walker said.

He recalled that Ryder had coerced Joy into accepting a position as a lewd telephonist for a pack of Melrose Avenue fatsos who rejoiced in her cultured British accent. She had stayed with the job until the owner of the shop was murdered.

"Waste of time, that was," Joy said.

"A waste of something."

"See, we took a holiday up in Mendocino, Ryder and me did. Bloody rained. He was piss paranoid. Didn't bloody speak. The television set was screwed. I spent the whole bloody time walking in the bloody rain."

"It can be so pretty up there," Walker said. "Are you sure you're O.K.?"

"Yeah." Joy shook her head, took a deep breath and looked at Walker once more as though she had discovered him that moment before her. "One thing," she told him, "I saw two animals there. Two animals fighting on the beach."

Walker brightened. "That must have been exciting," he said. "What sort of animals?"

Joy sighed deeply. "I think they were winkles."

"The choreographer at the Sands is dead!" Jack Best shrieked. One of the cooks had come out of the kitchen and was crossing herself. Axelrod and a waiter were struggling to get Best out the inner door. At the table where he had been sitting, Walker saw Lu Anne seated next to Dongan Lowndes.

"Well," Joy said. "Another bloody night, eh, sport?"

"Right," Walker said.

He walked into the bar, his heart beating faster. Once she seemed to look his way but her eyes never settled on him. He took the chair that Best had been sitting in.

"Hello, Gordon," she said calmly.

Her casual greeting stung him like a blow.

"Hello, Lu Anne."

"We're having a wonderful time filming your script."

"That's great," he said.

"We have quite a famous author down here to write a piece on us, Gordon. Mr. Dongan Lowndes. From *New York Arts*. Have you all met?"

"Yes," Walker said. "We've met."

"You know, Mr. Lowndes," Lu Anne said, "there are whole passages from *Naming of Parts* that I can remember just by heart."

"Lu Anne used to be the president of the Good Old Girls' Good Old Book Club," Walker told Lowndes.

He watched Lowndes's slack mouth tighten. Walker's hands were trembling and he kept them out of sight.

"You know," Lowndes said, "a lot of times when Hollywood people tell you they like a book it turns out they're referring to the studio synopsis." He laughed rather loudly at his own observation.

"That's not true of Lu Anne," Walker assured him. "She's a great reader."

"I wasn't thinking of Miss Verger. It's just something I began to run into."

"Was your book ever optioned?" Walker asked.

"Yes," Lowndes said. "There was something up. I don't know what became of it."

"It would have been difficult to film," Walker said.

"In those days I suppose I would have been thrilled to have it made. Now I realize that the world can get on quite well without a film version of that book."

From where he sat it seemed to Walker that Lowndes had moved his chair very close to Lu Anne's, that their bodies must be touching at some point and Lu Anne had made no move to draw away. She seemed to hang on his words.

"If we get into what the world can do without," Walker said to Lowndes, "God knows where we'll end."

Lowndes smiled. His left hand was below the table; Walker could not escape the thought that he was fondling Lu Anne. Yet, he thought, it might all be pure paranoia. As for her, he had imagined every reaction to his arrival except the smiley indifference he was experiencing. He ordered another round of drinks.

"So," he asked Lowndes when the drinks arrived, "how long have you been down?"

"Just a day," Lowndes said. "I think."

Lu Anne nodded enthusiastically. "Yes. A day."

"Let me tell you a little about what I want to accomplish down here," Lowndes told Walker. "You may find it interesting."

Walker saw Lu Anne and Lowndes join hands behind their chairs.

"Why not?" he said to Dongan Lowndes. "Why not do that?"

"I really don't think anyone's ever written a good piece on the making of a film until after the fact." Lowndes disengaged his hand from Lu Anne's and went into his pocket for cigarillos. Walker declined; Lowndes lighted one for himself. "My thinking is—if I hang around here, see a little of it all going on—I can get an insight into the process. So I did a little boning up on who everybody was. Now I can watch them do their thing. Then I can analyze the final product in terms of what I've seen."

Walker looked at Lu Anne to see if what the man was saying made sense to her. So far as he could tell it did and she seemed profoundly interested.

"I don't really understand," he told Lowndes. "That sounds very complicated and ambitious." He tried to imitate their smug amiable demeanor. "It's a nice place to spend a couple of weeks. I'm sure it'll turn out fine."

"You decline to take me seriously, Mr. Walker," Lowndes said.

"I don't get it, that's all. I don't know what you're trying to prove."

"I have all your scripts," Lowndes told him. "Every one you ever wrote."

Jon Axelrod, red and sweating, returned to the table and sat down wearily. "Holy shit," he said. "Sorry."

Walker stared across the table at Lowndes. The idea of this soft-spoken, pockmarked man poring over the hundreds and hundreds of scenes that he had written made him feel violated and ashamed. All those scripts, he thought—the record of petty arguments lost or won, half-assed stratagems and desperate compromises. A graph of meaningless motion like the tube-worm trails in a prehistoric seabed. Here and there some shining secret as withered and barren as a stone pearl in a fossil oyster.

He thought of the things written that he ought not to have written. They were like the things done that should not have been done. The things not written were worse.

"How'd you like them?"

Lowndes smiled.

"They're really very good."

"Gordo's very good," Axelrod said. "Ask anybody." Axelrod was in the process of discovering an unwholesome stain on his sleeve. He touched his finger to the stain, brought it away, looked at his finger and excused himself again.

"Some things about your writing make me wonder," Lowndes said.

"Ah," Walker said. "Wonder about what?"

Walker took a quick look at Lu Anne. There was a fond smile on her lips. In the shadowy light her face was porcelain, as pale and witchy as a Crivelli madonna's.

"Well, I'm a Georgia boy," Lowndes said with suitably bucolic languor, "and maybe I'm just simpleminded. But it seems to me— goddamn—you guys got a magic lantern out here. Being simple-minded makes me think of all the things I'd like to try doing if I had the chance."

Walker stirred his drink.

"You aren't simpleminded, Mr. Lowndes. You know the secrets of the heart. I know you do because I read your book. It's a true article, your book. It made me cry, what do you think of that?"

"With envy?" Lu Anne asked.

"I hadn't thought of that," Walker said, looking into her fixed smile. He saw that she was off her head and in some character of her own construction. He rejoiced; he had thought it was really she there—cold, mocking and lost to him. "I don't think envy makes you cry. It was for the usual reasons. For love of it."

"Shit," Lowndes said. "Love my dog, love me."

He extended his hand. Walker looked at it, paused and shook it briefly.

"I see what you mean," Walker said. "My compliments. But even if you were country-simple, as you plainly aren't, even if you were Pogo's great-grandpuppy, I'd have trouble believing you were as naive as you claim to be. I think you're trying to make me feel bad about what I do."

"Say that again?" Lowndes asked.

"I said that even if your grandfather was a fucking alligator you ought to know more about the movie business than that. Do you really need it all explained to you, or are you just trying to give me a hard time?"

"You got me wrong, man. You're touchy."

"I'm sorry. I had a long drive."

"Don't be sorry. Bein' touchy's good. It indicates you have your pride. Where'd you say you were from?"

"Kentucky," Walker told him. "Lexington."

"I wouldn't have thought that," Lowndes said. "But you know, I have relatives in Kentucky named Walker. I wonder if you're one of those Walkers?"

"No," Walker said.

"Well, let's pretend my granddaddy was an alligator. How would you explain to me the screenwriter's role?"

"Oh Christ," Walker said, "the screenwriter's role?"

"Is that the wrong terminology?"

"You have to believe that it's worthwhile," Walker told him, "and you have to accept the rules. You can't be a solitary or an obsessive. You can't despise your audience. It requires humility and it requires strength of character."

Lowndes turned to Lu Anne.

"Now that's a very eloquent defense of an often derided trade, don't you think?"

"Oh yes," Lu Anne said brightly.

"Very eloquent, Mr. Walker, and I believe every word of it. Only tell me this: isn't it true that on the screen what you and I might call a cheap shot works infinitely better than on the page?"

Walker thought about it.

"Yeah, O.K. That may be so."

"Doesn't it follow then that an instinct for the cheap shot is an advantage to a screenwriter?"

"There are rules, Lowndes, I told you that. You usually work within the terms of genre. Your flights of fancy are reduced to technical possibility because on one level you're moving machinery. If you're heavy-handed your characters will flatten out very badly. You have to be good at it."

"Suppose I say," Lowndes said, "that as a movie writer you're restricted to a literal-minded so-called *realism* that changes its nature every five years or so. Would I be wrong?"

"I have a feeling we're going to read that in *New York Arts* whether I think it's true or not."

Lowndes laughed.

"I don't think it's true," Walker said. "Nor do I think I have an affinity for the cheap shot."

"Well," Lowndes told him, "maybe that's why you haven't been as successful as you should."

"How successful should I be, Mr. Lowndes?"

"Secrets are forbidden," Lu Anne said helpfully. "There's a clause."

"There's also," Walker observed, "a sanity clause."

When Axelrod arrived back from the gents' a wet spot had replaced the stain on his shirt.

O   F   L   I   G   H   T

"G'wan," he said as he resumed his seat, "you no foola me. There ain't no Sanity Claus."

Walker and Lu Anne looked blankly into his fading smile. Lowndes kept his eyes on Walker.

"Nobody makes you do it," Walker told Lowndes. "You're usually well paid if you don't get cheated, and you usually don't. There are things you can do. You can have your moments."

"I know that's true," Lowndes said. "I just wanted to make sure you felt as bad as you should." He punched Walker on the arm. "Hey, I'm only foolin' with you, man. I know you're a serious guy."

"How bad do you feel, Gordon?" Lu Anne asked.

"Medium," Walker said.

Jack Glenn came in with some production people and the Peruvian script girl. They waved, hesitated for a moment and took a different table inside the bar. Charlie Freitag and his Las Vegas pal had gone off into the night.

"I'm going to turn in," Walker said. "I enjoyed our talk. I hope it was helpful."

"You bet," Lowndes told him. As he got up he saw Lowndes put his hand over Lu Anne's.

"Me too," Axelrod said. He wandered over to the other table.

As he went down the corridor toward the opposite wing he heard running steps on the carpet behind him. For an instant he thought himself pursued by Dongan Lowndes but before he turned he knew it was Lu Anne. Her face was contorted with terror. As she crowded into his arms, she held her hands protectively over her temples as if to ward off a blow. He had to untangle her from her cringing stance to kiss her.

"Gordon," she said, "you have to help me. That man's been put over me."

"Put over you? I thought you were going to let him climb on top of you. I've been high on you for five hundred miles and when I get here you're playing footsie with that big swamp rat."

"Gordon, you just don't understand anything at all. I'm really scared, Gordon."

"It's all right, Lu. Everybody says you're doing fine. You look very beautiful."

"I went to church tonight," Lu Anne said, "and there was a thing on the cross that wasn't Jesus at all."

He experienced a brief surge of panic. The panic was compounded of several fears—his fear of her madness and of his own folly, his fear of death and of life. It was too late for panic to do him any good. He did not propose to let her go.

"You're alone, aren't you, Lu Anne? Your husband's gone and the kids?"

"I'm alone," she said. "With that man over me. Don't you think he looks like the winner of a flaming-cat race?"

"Absolutely," Walker said. "Are the . . . are you seeing those people you see?"

She put a finger across his lips and nodded.

"What about your pills?"

"I tried," she said. "I can't work with them."

He let her rest her head against his shoulder and stroked her hair. He had no idea what to do.

"That man," Lu Anne said, "he saw me run out after you. I left him and he'll take it out on us."

"I thought you were making it with him."

"I was fooling him," she said. "They said I had to. They said he'd write about me."

"Who said?"

"Well, Charlie. And Jack and Walter."

"Forget about him. I don't think it matters what he writes."

Standing with Lu Anne in his arms, he saw Lowndes appear at the far end of the corridor. Lowndes stood watching them with an expression that appeared vaguely benign. He was uglier upright, slope-shouldered and paunchy, a poor soul. After a moment he went his way.

"Is he there?" she asked without turning around. The perception of schizophrenics was unnatural, Walker thought.

"He's gone."

"There's always someone to be afraid of," Lu Anne said.

"We don't have to play their games, Lu."

"But we do," she said.

He stepped back, holding her.

"Come with me tonight."

She shook her head.

"There's tonight," he said. "I don't know what else there is. It's touch and go."

"Touch," she repeated dully, "and go." She shook her head. "I can't," she said. "I'm afraid. I don't know why you want me."

"I think we settled that," he said, "a long time ago."

"And you never learned better?"

"I never learn, Lu Anne."

"The geisha and the samurai," she said. "You're the geisha," she told him. She fingered his cheek with a long unpainted nail. "I'm the samurai."

"That's so," Walker said.

People passed at the end of the corridor but he never turned to look. Lu Anne took his hands in hers and they stood with their fingers twined like old friends at some family ceremony.

"I'm so fucked up, Gordon. I mean, I think I love you—it's been so long. It was always someone and I think it was always you. I'm sick and I'm scared. I have to hide."

"Hide with me."

When she eased away from him he followed and took her in his arms again.

"Don't make me," she told him. "Wait for me. Wait for tomorrow."

We are not promised tomorrow, Walker thought. He would wait for her, for that unmerited, far-off day.

"Yes," he said. "All right."

Then she was off, barefoot, down the hall. She had left her going-to-church shoes where she stood. As he bent to pick them up he heard an insistent pounding from the wing of the hotel to which she had retreated. He walked to the end of the passage and saw her rapping against the door of an apartment on the court three stories below. The condominiums here faced the mountainside; they were less expensive and less elaborately appointed. Teamsters lived here and technical assistants and people who liked to be where the serious card games were.

Walker stepped to the metal rail and saw the apartment door open and Billy Bly appear in the lighted doorway. He watched as they spoke, saw Bly close the door to her. Waiting, she leaned her forehead against it until Bly came to open it again. This time she went inside and, though Walker waited for almost ten minutes on the upper landing, holding her shoes under his arm, she did not reappear.

P lease, Pig," Lu Anne pleaded. "Honestly, honey, I don't want to be alone. I'm afraid I'll die."

Bly was looking down at her bare feet on his plastic doormat. He worked his jaws in embarrassment.

"I figured you were waiting for Gordon Walker."

"I was," she said. "I am."

"Well," Bly said, "he's here."

She shook her head.

"But I'm not, Pig. Just suddenly I can't handle it. I told him—wait for tomorrow. He's so nice, you know. He said he would."

"You scared?"

"I am deathly afraid," Lu Anne said. "I have to hide. I must."

"Well," Bly said, "this is the thing. I ain't alone tonight."

She stared at him and, without a sound, mouthed the words.

"Please. Pig."

He watched her as though he were trying to gauge the measure of her fear. "You want to wait," he said. She made a move to rush past him but he blocked her with half a step.

"Honey," she whispered urgently, "I'll talk to the boy. I'll explain."

"I told you to wait, Lu Anne. Now you wait."

He closed the door and she leaned her head against it. When she heard the Mexican boy's angry incredulous voice, she raised her hands to stop her ears.

After a minute or two, Bly opened the door and stepped aside. As she went into the large bedroom suite, she thought she caught a glimpse of a moving figure on the mountainside balcony. A pot broke on the tiles outside.

"Was he real mad?" Lu Anne asked.

"Yes, he was," Bly said.

"He broke a pot, didn't he?"

"Probably just knocked it over. Climbin' down."

"Honestly, Pig, I'd do it for you. I'll make it up to you. You know there's always a day and there's always a way."

"Just so you know, Lu Anne. It's the same as if . . ."

"Pig," she said earnestly, "I realize that, you know. I'm not so insensitive. Gosh, I hope you were . . . like . . . done."

Bly shrugged. He was standing by the mirror taking his shirt off, checking his pecs.

"I never really feel done," he said.

He was a serious man and not given to humor. It was Lu Anne's delight to make him laugh. She rushed to him.

"I'm so happy now," she said, "and I was so scared before." On the counter she saw a cluster of amyl nitrate caps. She went over and stirred them affectionately with her forefinger as though they were a litter of pet mice.

"You want a Quaalude?" Bly asked.

"I can't think of anything nicer," she said brightly.

Bly's tanned face reddened, he pursed his lips. It took Lu Anne a moment to realize that he was laughing. She hugged him.

"You smell so nice," she said.

As he went into the bathroom for some Quaaludes, she realized that in the moment of their embrace she had felt him tense very slightly and that the moment of resistance to her body's pressure constituted a discreet discouragement of any notions she might be cultivating of fun and games. It would not have been unconscious. Bly was as free of involuntary physical responses as a person could be.

They lay down on the unmade bed together and had their Quaaludes with ice water from a pitcher that sat on a silver salver on the floor.

"I could give that boy some money," Lu Anne suggested. "I feel so bad about it."

"He don't want money. You know," Bly added after a moment, "we get the wrong idea. Lots of these Mexican people—they don't want money."

"Forgive me," she said.

"No problem. This time."

The room was chill with air conditioning and the windows were closed. No breezes came from the mountainside. She snuggled next to Bly, put her hands on his muscular shoulders, then guiltily withdrew them.

"You know how it gets."

"Yes, I do."

"Now don't think I have it mixed up, Pig. I mean, I always understood that you and me was a one-time thing. It wasn't going to go on and all. Because of how we both were."

"One of them bells," Bill said, "that now and then rings."

"How nice Quaaludes are," she said. "The world is possible with art."

He turned over, looked at her eyes and lay back on his pillow.

"What'd you tell Drogue about me?" she asked him. "You tell him I was O.K.?"

"You are as far as he's concerned, Lu Anne. He doesn't care how you really are. He's just worried about his ass. Like Charlie's worried about budget and insurance and all that."

"How do you think I really am?"

"I don't know. I can't always tell because I ain't as smart as you."

"I was a quiz kid, Pig. Did you know that?"

Bly yawned.

"Lu Anne," he said, "if you was half the things you claim you been you'd have to be seventy-five years old."

"I'm older than people think," she said sadly.

"I mean," Bly told her, "I don't know why you lie. I don't understand it. You're a great star, what more do you want? What are you trying to prove?"

She bit her finger and looked at him. Billy Bly believed in never borrowing money to gamble with, that it cost a fortune to erase tattoos, in reincarnation and in Great Stars. The Greater they were, he believed, the easier they were to get on with. Lu Anne was not really a Great Star in Bly's order of precedence but he afforded her an honorary inclusion.

"I want you to tell me location stories," she said. "Then I'll tell you some."

Bill Bly loved location stories about high-rolling, monster fuck-ups and partying with Great Stars. He loved show business stories of all sorts. So did Lu Anne. Who didn't?

"Hell," Bly told her, "I told you all my good location stories a couple of times."

It was a stylized demurrer. He told her about the Western director, mortally behind in a heavy poker game, who had heaved the once-in-a-lifetime pot into a bunkhouse fireplace. About the actor who had started shooting lights out from his Vegas hotel room. About misassignations, absurd love affairs, fights, comedians and local goodwives. Suits of armor pissed in, motel rooms filled with dirigible-sized polka-dotted water bags, child actors poisoned, chimpanzees released.

Lu Anne told Bill about Werner, the stunt bunny. The concept of Werner evoked his silent laughter.

"We had a stunt mule one time in Durango," Bill said. "We had to pull his legs out from under him every time he got shot."

"Werner was a European hare," Lu Anne told Bill. "He was always wonderfully dressed and he had perfect manners. We met him at the airport and showed him his fall. It was down the south face of the Jungfrau. He looked that old mountain up and down. 'Zo,' he says.

'Ach, zo.' You'd a been scared, Pig. We said, 'Can we get you anything, Werner?' 'Chust show me my marks,' said Werner."

Bly laughed again, his eyes closed. Lu Anne made a little man with her fingers and walked them along Bill's chest.

"Werner had the nicest luggage you ever did see," she told Bly. "He knew how to fold his napkin. You could take him anywhere. You could take him to Le Cirque."

"Where the fuck's that?"

She fingered a circle on his chest.

"Ever turn a trick, Pig?"

The sleepy smile on his face vanished. He opened his eyes but did not look at her.

"I guess you know the way I come up, Lu Anne. I guess you know the answer to that."

"I'm sorry," Lu Anne said, and shivered. "I was thinking about something. I was wondering about something. Hey, Pig, could I have another half a Quaalude?"

Bly stirred himself and put his feet on the floor.

"How come you asked me that?"

"I wanted to hear about it."

"Well, it's ugly as catshit," he said. "It's dirty and scary. It smells. Sometimes you dig it. You know yourself there's plenty of people around here can tell you more about it than me."

He staggered as he walked and turned on her.

"I mean," he asked in a foggy voice, "you want to hear about the men's room in the Albuquerque bus station? What you wanna hear?"

"I'm sorry, Pig."

He brought her her half pill and she took it and he climbed into bed with her. They both got under a decorative Mexican quilt to shelter from the air conditioning.

"I did once," Lu Anne said. "In New Haven. After the show. It was winter. We were doing *As You Like It*. I played Rosalind."

"You told me a thousand times about that night, Lu Anne, and you never told me that. I think that's foolishness."

"No," she said. "No, it's true. A man offered me two thousand dollars. He was a depraved Shakespeare scholar. He would stop at nothing to have me and I suspect he was a Jesuit. 'Top it off with harlotry,' he said, 'you'll feel like a million and you'll make an old man very happy.' "

"Bullshit, man," Bly murmured. His eyes, half open, stared into his pillow.

"He took me down Stoddard Street," Lu Anne told Bill. "The cast was holding one of those Communist-inspired parties we used to have in those days with drugs and promiscuity but I didn't stay for it. I snuck right out of that green room. I was wearing my fake rat fur coat and he took me down Stoddard Street. I remember the Valle's steak house with all the red snowflakes. He said, 'It's Ganymede I'm after'—I said no foolin'? Because they always are, I assure you. I mean, he wasn't telling me a thing I didn't know myself."

"So," Bly struggled to ask, "did he buy you a steak?"

"He took me to a house on a hill. Greek revival. It belonged to another century. The furnishings were exquisite and all the walls were glass. Old glass. From every room you could see all the others, you could see rainbows and tropical fish, everything crystal, Pig, and firelight in the mirrors and outside the glass walls the red snow was falling. In every room there were little glass bells, they shined and they tinkled. Of all the rooms, Pig, there was one into which a body could not see. And do you know why that was?"

"Well, sure," Bly said. His eyes closed. "Why?" he asked.

"Because it was curtained off in furs. And that was where we went. And the man said, 'You are the finest Rosalind that ever was, my dear child.' He says, 'I've traveled the world,' he says, 'I've seen them all, Stratford and the Aldwych, forget 'em all,' he says. 'Your voice is dulcet and you know your blocking and your moves are neat.' "

Bly roused himself slightly. "Hot shit for you, Lu Anne. Did he give you two thou?"

"Better," Lu Anne said. Bly smiled and she stroked his neck.

"Better than two? Three?"

"Better," she whispered. His eyes closed but the happy smile lit his lean face.

She leaned her head on his shoulder. Great silly Quaalude tears like Disney raindrops were rolling down her cheeks.

"If you can hustle, Billy," she whispered to Bly, "you don't have to go home. You need never. You can't ever.

"Pig?" she asked. "You hear my little 'lude poem, home?"

His smile had drained away into sleep. It looked to her like dying. "You get to have a few laughs," she told the aging boy asleep beside her, "but your head will fucking kill you."

E arly the next morning, Walker was treading water in the luke-warm Pacific. He felt less driven after his sedated sleep. His face was turned toward the beach and the dry mountains that rose above the coastal cliffs. The peaks outlined against the morning sky formed a contrast of surfaces so pure and unambiguous that it was literally joy to behold. As he basked in the day's matutinal innocence, his hangover salved with cocaine, he became aware of a disharmony. On the beach itself, still half in shadow, he saw a small man in the resort's livery struggling with a second man twice his size. Walker set out toward shore and as he swam he recalled Joy McIntyre's story of rained-out romance. Two animals fighting on the beach.

He picked up his towel, threw it over his shoulders and walked toward the scene of conflict. Winkles.

One of the hotel's bellmen was attempting to bring a drunken man to consciousness by standing him upright. Having attempted several mechanical strategies to accomplish this, he had fallen back on the old heave-ho and was pulling on the man's arm.

"You'll dislocate his shoulder," Walker told the bellman. Together they took the drunken man by his underarms and balanced him on his heels. Walker saw that it was Dongan Lowndes.

"I never seen him," the bellman said. "I don't think he's from the movies."

Walker saw Jon Axelrod descending a coral stairway toward the beach. A black-haired girl of singular beauty whom Walker had never seen before stood watching from the lowest turreted landing, a princess in a tower.

"Lookit the fucking guy," Axelrod said. "Mr. Class. His first drink in three years, he says. Then has about twenty of them."

"In the sun," the bellman told them, "he can die."

"Listen," Axelrod told the servant, "this isn't your job. Go get Mr. Bly—you know who I mean?"

The youth nodded.

Axelrod, gripping Lowndes by the one arm, took a loose bill from his pocket.

"Go get him. Wake him up if you have to."

The bellman pocketed his bill and ran off up the stairway. As he passed the girl on the landing he paused to bow and smile deferentially before bolting on up the higher stairways.

"In the sun," Axelrod said in imitation of the bellman, "he can die. Because he already fuckin' dead. And he no make it home to his coffin."

"What are you looking for?" Walker asked. "A weapon?"

"I wanna see if he's wired. Some of these fucks, you say something dumb and they write it down. You sue them and next thing you find out they were wired. I'm gonna get Billy to go through his room for a video camera."

"You think he'd do that?" Walker asked. "He's the correspondent of *New York Arts*, not *Confidential*."

"Some of these writers are the lowest scum that ever walked the earth," Axelrod explained. He looked thoughtfully at Walker. "Then there's some that are O.K."

The smell of Lowndes's sweating body was making Walker sick. He turned his face to the wind.

"Who's the lady?" he asked Axelrod.

"That's Helena," Axelrod told him. "She's our valued assistant. She's going to show you around. Come down, doll," he called up to Helena. "Help us hold up this guy."

Helena descended the last flight of steps. She was blue-eyed and lightly freckled. The expression of condescending concern with which she regarded Lowndes made Walker feel like a zookeeper displaying a sick seal.

"Is he drunk?" Helena asked in the British interrogative.

"He's in deep alpha state," Axelrod said, "from trying to meditate with his clothes on. Helena, this is Gordon Walker."

"Ah," Helena said brightly.

Walker braced his legs to adjust his leverage on Lowndes and reached out to take her hand.

"Helena will show you around," Axelrod told Walker. "She's been wanting to meet you."

"Oh," Walker said. "Well." He looked at the young woman to see if such a thing might be true and saw quickly that it was not.

"Your script is wonderful," Helena said. "It's going to be a marvelous film."

Lowndes pulled himself free of their hold and immediately lost consciousness again. Walker and Axelrod just managed to catch him.

"You know what I think?" Axelrod said after a moment. "I think fuck this." He let go of Lowndes and Walker did the same. The author collapsed in a heap at their feet.

"We should bury him in sand up to his neck," Axelrod said, "as a warning to assholes."

Bly came jogging along the beach toward them. When he saw Walker he drew up short and approached at his stealthy, carefully centered amble. He looked down at the crumpled form of Dongan Lowndes, then at Walker.

"Come on, Bill," Axelrod told Bly, "let's get this turkey on ice."

Bly with very little seeming effort drew Lowndes from the sand and shouldered him. Axelrod steadied the burden with his right hand.

Walker saw that Bly was smiling at him. The smile seemed friendly enough, not triumphant or malicious. In any case, Walker looked away. When Bly and Axelrod went off with the prostrate Lowndes, he found himself alone with Helena.

"Had breakfast?" she asked him. He had been on his way to Lu Anne's cabana, hoping somehow that she had not spent the night with Bly after all. The notion to swim had seduced him en route.

"No. Have you?"

"I haven't, actually. Shall we get some coffee?"

"Yes," Walker said. "Yes, of course." Helena's beauty, her youth and her lightly pretended interest in him made Walker suddenly quite sad. The sadness and the thought of Lu Anne with Bly hit him with the force of his rallying hangover and fatigue. He required a line but the cocaine was hidden away in his suitcase in his room.

"We'll walk up, shall we?" he proposed to Helena. "Then I'll just have to get something from my room."

Helena threw him a stagey smile and they walked up the coral steps together. He was tense, unhappy, out of breath. Helena seemed at the point of song.

Breakfast was being served on the terrace that adjoined the bar. Walker took a table with Helena, ordered them coffee with Mexican sweet rolls and excused himself.

He reached his room just ahead of the chambermaid, hung up his *No Molestar* sign and hurriedly prepared himself a measure. In his haste he had more than he intended; the effect was neither exhilaration nor the horrors but a confused enthusiasm without object. He felt for the moment as if he had replaced his true emotions, whatever they might have been, with artificial ones, artificially flavored. When he went out this time he brought a paper fold of cocaine in his beach bag, wrapped in foil to keep it from melting in the heat.

Jon Axelrod and Jack Glenn had joined Helena at the breakfast table.

Glenn and Walker, who had not seen each other for a year or so, shook hands.

"This is the only man I know who *likes* Mexican locations," Jack Glenn told the people at the table. "I hope you didn't come to make changes."

"I am death," Walker said, "destroyer of worlds. I've come to write people out of the script."

"Jesus Christ," Jack Glenn said.

Walker picked up his coffee and drained half of it at a swallow. It was really liquor he wanted, something to slow him down now that he was speeded up.

"To some people," he declared, "Mexican locations are just dollar-ante poker and centipedes. I'm not like that."

"Really?" Helena asked.

"I come," Walker said, "to see the elephants."

"Well," Helena said. "This is all very tame stuff, if you ask me. Outside of the usual drunks. It's so tranquil and businesslike it's almost boring."

Walker saw that she was pitching Jack Glenn. He found himself liking Helena a little less each moment.

"That could change overnight," he told her.

"The last thing I did yesterday," Axelrod said, "was put a drunk to bed. And what was the first thing I did this morning?"

"It's psychodrama," Glenn said. "All location shows are psychodrama."

"Some of us get a little more psycho than others," Axelrod said.

There was a brief tense silence.

"A friend of mine was down here making a movie a couple of years ago," Glenn told them. "It was over by San Miguel. They were all staying at a hotel there and the restaurant cashier fell madly in love with him."

"I do hope this has a happy ending," Helena said.

"The thing was, he never even noticed her. So she went home to her village warlock and got a love potion. Like condor wattles and iguana testicles—she had the cook slip them into his *huevos rancheros*."

"Did it work?" Axelrod asked.

"It worked fine. They had to fly him out in a helicopter. I mean, it was Mexico and everybody was sick, but this guy was ready for El Morgue-o. He sent for a priest."

"What about the girl?" Helena asked.

Axelrod lit a cigar. "She married the cook."

"Those were the days," Glenn said, "when the movies spelled *romance*."

Walker stood up and as he did so Helena and Axelrod exchanged quick glances.

"I'm coming with you," she told Walker gaily. "I'm to show you around."

"She'll show you the location," Axelrod told him. "You can go to the beach. Tonight Charlie's giving a party for you."

"Good," Walker said. "Then you get to carry *me* home."

"Writers sleep on the beach, Gordon."

In the moment before they left the table, Walker noticed Helena try without success to catch Jack Glenn's eye. She was out of luck, he thought with malicious satisfaction. Jack worked harder at sex than anyone Walker knew and did not miss his moments.

Walker went with Helena to the production offices, which were deep in early morning silence. One of Axelrod's *pistoleros* was summoned to drive them to the setup. The drive was accomplished in silence. Helena's good humor was turning steely. When they were at the setup, their driver got out and waited in the shade of a live oak tree. Walker and Helena sauntered along the trolley tracks toward the bay.

The trolley was parked at the end of the line. Walker climbed aboard, felt the brasswork and the varnished benches.

"Frank found that one in Texas," Helena told Walker briskly. "He worked from the old Grand Isle photographs. Piece by piece, he found it all fairly close by."

"How about Frank," Walker said.

From the trolley, they walked across the waving fields of mock camomile to the dunes. Walker looked over the bathhouse and then walked along the beach to the camera track where Drogue's Titan had rolled the night before. A couple of Mexican watchmen hunkered by the trolley, watching.

"It must be a kick," Helena said, "seeing all this. I mean, all of it coming out of something you wrote."

"Definitely," Walker said. "A kick." He was looking out over the bay toward a raft on pontoons that was anchored some forty feet offshore. It was secured by cables to pulleys on the shore to keep it steady in the chop. "Once they built a house I used to live in. Reproduced it in every detail inside and out. It probably cost them more to do it than it cost to build the actual house."

"You must have been thrilled."

"As I recall, I was thrilled. It was a long time ago and I've done a lot of shows since."

"And now you take it all in stride? Or find it boring? Or what?"

"What's that raft out there for?" he asked Helena.

"Walter thought he might want a reverse angle on Edna's walk. There would have been a bloke on it with a Steadicam."

"Dr. Zoom," Walker said. The patches of troubling weather he had seen earlier were still hovering offshore.

"I mean," Helena said, "I don't see how you can be so superior about it."

Walker looked at her. "You're a film student?"

"No," she said. "I . . . just like films. I respect them. I respect the people who make them."

"Why are you trying to pick a fight with me?"

"I'm not," she said, protesting. "Maybe I think more highly of cinema than you do. I'm sure I know less about it."

"How do you come to be here?"

"Through friends."

"Your friends?"

"Yes, why not? Is that your last question?"

"Let me guess," Walker said. "You're here through business connections of your father's. Your father is something like a bookmaker-turned-mogul and he doesn't sound like you at all. You're doing the world, a little slumming, a little high life . . ."

"And you're a fucking burned-out mediocre film writer with a whiskey face and no manners."

"And here we are beside the Pacific. Just the two of us, more or less. As a film buff, do you think there's a scenario here?"

"You're not very highly regarded on this set. I was warned about you."

"Well," Walker said, "next time you're warned pay attention. What were you supposed to do, keep me dangling with smiles and compliments?"

Helena turned away. "Keep you away from her. So you wouldn't get her drinking or give her drugs."

"When your old man turned you loose on the wide world, Helena, didn't he warn you about pimps? Ponces? You let the people who sicked you on me—Drogue, Jon, whoever it was—turn you out. You pretended to like me. I could have gotten the wrong idea. I was supposed to."

The young woman looked at him strangely for a moment.

"You're a tenderhearted soul," she said.

"Goddamn right," Walker said.

"Flirtatiousness is fair, you know. It's a legitimate device."

"Of course it is."

"I suppose you'll go and see her."

"I'll go to her bungalow, yes. And you'll report me."

"Why shouldn't I? I owe them hospitality. I don't owe anything to you."

"Helena," Walker said. "If I find her—give us a while. You don't have to go straight back to Axelrod."

"It's not right," the woman said, "to give her drugs. You'll harm her."

"I'm not going there to give her drugs."

"All right," Helena said. "We'll go back."

They went back to the limousine; the driver left them near the beach at the base of the cliff.

"I'm sorry I was rude," Walker said when they were out of the car. "I get angry all the time."

"I really don't mind exchanging insults," Helena told him. "I was trained to it from an early age. Anyway, you're the first person here who's talked to me as though I were human." She pointed down the beach toward a point beyond the curve of the cliff. "That's where the bungalows are."

"I know," Walker said. "Give my best to the gang in Katmandu."

She turned for the water's edge. Walker trudged along the beach toward the row of bungalows.

A moment after his knock, through the closed door, he heard her startled motion; a shifting step on the tiles, the rustling of cloth. When she opened and saw it was he, she closed her eyes and opened them again.

"Thank God," she said, and leaned her head against his breast.

"Amen," Walker said.

She stepped aside to let him come in.

"Have you anything to drink, Gordon?"

"No," he said. "And you shouldn't."

"Last night. I was so demented. I was out of my gourd. I couldn't handle seeing you."

"You went to Bly's."

She looked at him in alarm and shook her head.

"I went to Billy's place to sleep because I didn't want to sleep alone. I mean, he's gay, Gordon. He's my pal."

"You had an affair with him once, Lu, I know you did. When I saw you creep off to him I was a little put out."

"Gordon, you know I bend the truth from time to time."

"We all forgive you, Lu. As best we can."

"But I'm not lying now, Gordon. I went to Billy's and he gave me a 'lude and we talked. I swear it. I'd just seen you—how could I make it with Billy? I may tell stories, Gordon, but I'm not capable of pushing that many buttons."

"It's funny," Walker said. "I started out being jealous of that Lowndes guy."

"He's a piece of shit," Lu Anne said. She stated it so positively and unemotionally that it sounded like a considered analysis.

"He wrote a good novel," Walker said. "Of course," he added with some slight satisfaction, "he only wrote one and that was a while ago."

"I read his novel," Lu Anne said. "I don't care how many he wrote. He's a piece of shit and he's after me."

"Why?"

"Because he knows I'm crazy and he wants to write about it in *New York Arts*. He's always watching me."

"Lu," Walker said patiently, "he digs you."

"Do you think," Lu Anne asked brightly, "that if I called the room service people they'd send down a bottle of tequila?"

"Not if they've been told not to." He paused a moment. "You can always try," he heard himself say.

"*Mezcal,*" Lu Anne said wickedly, "that's what we want." She put her arm around Walker's neck and buried her face in his shoulder. In an instant, as though she had been posing for a quick snapshot, she leaped to the telephone. "We'll have ourselves an alcoholic picnic. As we were wont."

"We were wont to lose the odd weekend with our alcoholic picnics."

Lu Anne ordered her *mezcal* without objection from the house. The prospect seemed to cheer her; she sat on the edge of the sofa with her hands clasped between her thighs watching Walker.

"Funny about last night," he said to her. "You're with Lowndes, you go off with me. You're with me, you go off with Bly. Lots of *La Ronde,* entrances and exits, bedrooms and closed doors and nobody really gets any. Very Hollywood."

"We used to think we were too late," Lu Anne said. "That we had missed out on Hollywood."

"How wrong we were."

Within a few minutes, two waiters wheeled in a rolling table with a liter bottle of *mezcal con gusano* attended by bottles of mineral water, glasses, lemon wedges and an ice bucket.

Walker poured them out two glasses of straight liquor.

"How about you, Lu Anne?"

She took the drink and drank it down unflinching with a childlike greediness and poured herself another.

"You want to know, Gordon? How it is with me? Is it really your business?"

"Yes, I think so."

"That I bend my eye on vacancy and with the incorporeal air do hold discourse?"

"Sure. And why. And if you want to, you'll get to hear how it is with me."

"You played Lear," she said.

"Yes."

"How was it?"

"It was like life but easier to take. I could spend the rest of my time on earth playing Lear."

"I wish I could play Lear," Lu Anne said. "Maybe I can. Beard up and play Lear."

"You could play the Fool."

Their eyes met. Lu Anne poured them more *mezcal*.

"That's good," Lu Anne said. "Because I could. We could do it together."

"When this is over," Walker said. "We'll talk it up. I'll talk to Al."

"The hell with agents. We'll do it on campuses. We'll do it in church halls for free."

"Yes."

She took the bottle of *mezcal* and examined the little embalmed creature at the bottom of the bottle.

"The worm's an odd worm."

"I wish you the joy of it," Walker said.

"I want to be Cleo too, Gordon. I'm tired of Edna. I'm glad she's dead." She sipped her drink and laughed. "I mean, I just can't die too many times. I can't get enough of it."

"You're such a ham, Lu Anne. You're lucky you can act."

"And you're such a ham," she said to him, "it's a crying shame you aren't any better."

"What's happening with Lionel? Where's he gone?"

"He's gone visiting with the kids. But I don't think he's coming back."

Walker poured himself some *mezcal*.

"He can't just not come . . ."

"No," she said, "he can't just not come back. I mean he's going to leave me. He was aching to get away from me. It was horrible."

"He can't take your kids from you."

"Sweetie," Lu Anne said, "with the right lawyer in the right state he could get me put to sleep."

"Things have changed, you know. You don't have to let him get away with it."

"No," she said. "I can kill him. But I don't think I'd be able."

They sat in silence drinking. Walker went to the window and saw the sky blighted with thick dark yellowing clouds, as though there were a dust storm over the ocean.

"Connie left me, you know."

Lu Anne lay on the bed with her eyes closed.

"I never understood why she stayed," Lu Anne said.

"I was very upset," Walker said. "I think I still am."

"Poor baby," Lu Anne said. "Is that why you came down here?"

"No," Walker said.

"Then," Lu Anne asked him, "why did you?"

"I have a lot of excuses," Walker said, "but I guess I came to see you."

"Ah," Lu Anne said briskly. "Yesterdays. Golden sweet sequestered days."

"Of mad romance and love. Yes, I was moved by the prospect."

"A reunion."

"Just so."

"Well, Gordon," Lu Anne said, inventing a character for herself as she went along, "I too am moved . . ." She stopped and put her fist to her forehead, letting the character fall like a shed skin. "I too am moved." She went to him and reached out, gently touched his cheek and leaned her head against his shoulder. Walker thought he felt an infinite weariness there. "I too."

He held her and he was thinking that this was his golden girl and that she was in his arms and that they could never have peace or a quiet moment or a half hour's happiness.

"It was so foolish of you to come, Gordon. Good heavens, man, no wonder Connie left you."

He said nothing. She broke away from him.

"Connie and I, Gordon mine, we're confronting hollow-eyed forty-odd. We've been screwed, blued and tattooed. We've been put with child and aborted, hosed down ripped open chewed and spat out seven ways from sundown! We've been burned by lovers, pissed on by our kids, shit on by mothers-in-law, punched out for laughing and punched out for crying and you expect us to sit still for your romantic peregrinations? Foolish man!"

"I don't believe Connie had lovers," Walker said.

She stuck out her lower lip and thrust a curved pinky toward him, the gesture of a child's wager. He put his hand over his face; they both began to laugh.

"Foolish man!" she cried. "Stay home and fuck your fecund imagination!"

"I could do that in my garage," he said. "When I had a garage."

"I know all the things one can do in garages," she said.

He kept smiling but her words gave him a vague chill. The picture they brought to his mind's eye was not agreeable.

"The girls get all shriveled and the boys get soft and sentimental. That's how the damn world goes." She went back and put her arms around him again. "What do you want from me, fool? You want us to be kids again?"

"I wouldn't have put it that way."

"Indeed you wouldn't, sweetheart, but that's what you want."

"Who knows?" Walker said.

"Jamais, mon amour. Jamais encore."

They sat down together on the sofa and he kissed her. She pulled back to see his face.

"You closed your eyes," she said, "you still do it."

He shrugged.

"We'll never be kids again, Gordon." He felt her arms encircle him, he put his around her and kissed her.

"We'll have to be spirits of another sort," she said. After he had kissed her again, she whispered in his ear. "We're not alone here."

It brought him up short; then he realized she must be speaking of her Long Friends. They lay together for a moment, then she got to her feet. He stood up and took her in his arms again. The liquor, he supposed, had been a bad idea. It seemed not to matter any longer.

"No more romances for us, Gordon."

When he started to answer, she covered his lips with her fingertips.

"There's only work now. That's all that's left, it's all that matters. That's why I had to stop my pills."

"If there's only work," Walker said, "where does that leave me?"

"You should have made provision," she told him. "You should have lived like other people."

"I always thought I could deliver. You know. Eventually."

"When we do our Lear," she told him, "and I'm your Fool, you'll deliver."

"I wasn't bad, you know," Walker said. "I was all right."

She took his hands in hers. He gently disengaged and kissed her again.

"If I'm the Fool," she told him when they caught their breath, "I've got to be Cordelia. They're the same."

"Yes," Walker said.

"But I'm too old."

"You aren't," Walker told her. "Anyway, I think it's as much a question of weight."

"That *is* what they say. Isn't it, Gordon?"

"Yes, it is. Absolutely true."

She let him pick her up, clasping her hands around his neck. She was not at all hard to lift, thinner than he had ever seen her and as quick.

"That's the way they do it at the ice show," she told him. "Did I tell you, Gordon, about when I was with the ice show?"

"Of course," Walker said. "Of course you did." He walked toward the bed carrying her.

"Howl!" she half cried. Clinging, she looked up at him. "Howl," she whispered. "Howl."

He swung her gently around once.

"See," she said. "I can be a light Cordelia. And I can be a shy Cordelia. Warlike, on-the-march Cordelia." She let go her grip on the back of his neck and sank down across his outstretched arms with a sigh. "And I can be a dead Cordelia."

He placed her on the bed and sat down beside her. When they were both naked he rolled over to face her and found himself beside dead Cordelia.

"Hey," he said. "Come back."

They made love over a daylight hour or so. Once she told him that she had joy in his arrival; her words, while their spell lasted, swept away his weariness and fear and anger. Later they slept awhile.

When he awoke the sun was low in the sky. A blade of sunlight was edging across the bed where they had been, threatening the shadows in which Lu Anne lay sleeping.

That she had taken joy in his arrival, he thought, that she had spoken those words to him should be all that mattered. He wanted more than anything to stay in a time where her words and his love were all that mattered. When it began to slip away, he had a drink of *mezcal* and quietly went to his stash for more cocaine. He brought the drug and his works into the bathroom.

As he was chopping the crystalline powder, he happened to glance in the cabinet mirror. He saw the bathroom doorknob slowly turn. It was too late to hide anything; he steadied the stuff on the ledge in front of him so as not to spill it. In the next moment, as he expected, the door flew open and she was standing in the bathroom doorway, laughing.

"Aha," she cried. "Gotcha."

I n a pink palazzo at the top of the hill, the Drogues and their womenfolk were whiling away the afternoon watching films in which people walked into the sea and disappeared forever. They had watched Bruce Dern in *Coming Home*, Joan Crawford in *Humoresque*, James Mason in the second *A Star Is Born* and Lee Verger in *The Awakening*. Now Fredric March and Janet Gaynor were on the out-sized screen before them. March stood clad in his bathrobe in the character of Norman Mayne.

"Hey," he called to Janet Gaynor. *"Mind if I take just one more look?"*

Old Drogue picked up the remote-control panel and stopped the frame. His eyes were filled with tears.

"Listen to me," he told the others, "this guy was the greatest screen actor of all time. That line—the emotion under it—controlled—played exactly to movie scale. There was never anyone greater."

Joy McIntyre lay on some heaped cushions beside him, weeping unashamedly.

"Wellman was good," the younger Drogue said.

"The vulnerability," old Drogue said, "the gentleness, the class of the man. Never again a Fredric March. What a guy!" He let the film proceed and settled back with head on Joy's bare belly. "You see what I mean, sweetheart?" the old man asked his young friend. But Joy was too overcome to reply.

"Look at the nostrils on Gaynor," young Drogue said. "She acted with her nose."

"Do I have to remind you that she started before sound?"

"I love it," Patty Drogue said. *"Before sound."*

"She was ultra-feminine," old Drogue said.

The younger Drogue studied the images on the screen.

"Her face suggests a cunt," he said.

The old man sighed.

"I don't know why it does," young Drogue said. "It just does."

"You're a guttersnipe," Drogue senior said.

"Something about the woman's face, Dad. It makes a crude but obvious reference to her genitals."

"Some people are brought up in poverty," the old man said, "and they become cultivated people. Others grow up spoiled rotten with luxury and become guttersnipes."

"You look at her face," young Drogue declared, "and you think of her pussy." His brows were knotted in concentration. "Can that be the primal element in female sexual attraction? Can it explain Janet Gaynor?"

"People are surprised," Drogue senior said quietly, "when they find out you can get sex education lectures at the morgue. They're not in touch with the modern sensibility."

Joy was glaring sullenly at young Drogue. The old man shifted his position, the better to fondle her.

"What does he mean," Patty Drogue asked her husband, "sex education lectures at the morgue?"

"In San Francisco," young Drogue said absently. "The coroner explains about bondage. Pops got fixated on this."

On the screen, Fredric March's body double was wading toward the setting sun. This time it was Drogue junior who stopped the frame.

"This one was the best," his father said smugly. "Of all the walk-into-the-ocean movies this one was it."

"In the Mason and Judy Garland," his son told him, "the Cukor version, the scene's exactly the same. Frame for frame."

"The scene is conditioned by what's around it. The other one is a Judy Garland film. Entirely different thing."

Young Drogue went pensive.

"Well," he said, "with Judy Garland now, see, she . . ."

"Stop," his father said sternly. "I don't want to hear it. Whatever idiotic obscenities you were about to utter—keep them to yourself. I don't want to hear your sexual theories about Judy Garland. I want to go to my grave without hearing them."

"Some of us want to remember Judy the way she was," Joy McIntyre said primly.

"Who the fuck asked you?" young Drogue inquired.

Old Drogue kissed Joy on the thigh to soothe her.

"Ours is the best," the young director declared. "We took a great risk to honor the author's intentions. We had to reinvent a virtual chestnut because it was in the book."

"You're lucky you had a strong script," his father told him.

They watched Norman Mayne's funeral and the end of the film.

"There was another Cukor version, right?" young Drogue asked. "Before Wellman's. It had a walk to the water, didn't it?"

"There was *What Price Hollywood?* by Cukor. It's a similar plot but it doesn't have anyone in the water."

"You sure?"

"Absolutely certain," the old man said.

The chimes of the main door sounded. Patty rose to her feet and lifted the drawn shutters to peer out.

"Tell them to fuck off," said Drogue minor.

"It's Jack Best," she said. "But he doesn't look his jack best, ho ho."

"I'll bet he doesn't," young Drogue said.

"Please don't be rude to Jack," his father told him. "He's got a job the same as you. And he's been doing stills for us."

"He's been underfoot all morning with his stills," the young director said, going to the door. "Helena saw him trailing after Walker by the beach—like we're going to sell the movie with Walker's picture."

He opened the door to Jack Best, who did in fact appear ill and unhappy.

"Jack, baby," he said cheerfully, "what's this we hear about the choreographer at the Sands?"

"Ah," Jack muttered biliously. "Dumb gag."

"I didn't even know the Sands had a line," Patty Drogue said.

"It doesn't," her husband assured her. "Would you like a drink, Jack?"

Jack Best mastered a slight spasm of his jaw. Patty hastened to fix a whiskey and soda for him.

"Dumb gag," he said. He took the drink from Mrs. Drogue and swallowed half of it. "One too many."

"So what do you want here, Jack? Where's your camera?"

Best finished his drink and looked lugubriously about the room. His eyes were bright with the squamous resentment of an old snapping turtle.

"We got trouble," he said. He was holding a magazine in his hand. He opened it to reveal a photograph that had been inserted between its pages. He put the magazine aside and clutched the photograph to his breast. Everyone in the room looked at it.

"Run along, my dear," old Drogue said kindly to Joy. "I'll join you very shortly." As Joy left pouting, the old man blew her a kiss.

"I can't believe," Patty Drogue said, "that you talk to her like that."

"What's the pic, Jack?" young Drogue asked.

Best looked from father to son in a state of agitation. He showed his teeth like a frightened pony.

"Miss Verger," Jack said. "And that Walker. They been shacked up all day."

The Drogues, father and son, exchanged glances.

"Yeah?" young Drogue asked. "So what?"

Best tried to hand his picture to the old man. His son intercepted it.

"Walker been mistreating you, Jack?" young Drogue asked, turning the picture face up. "He's such a troublesome guy."

He looked down at the picture for some time. His wife came to look at it over his shoulder.

"Golliwilkins," she said. "Gag me with a spoon. And I was *so* reassuring to poor Lionel."

The photographs were sunlit shots of Lu Anne and Walker naked in bed. Walker was holding a small shiny rectangle while Lu Anne sniffed at its surface through a drinking straw.

Young Drogue handed the picture to his father.

"So what's this, Jack? A handout?"

"They got a whole bunch like this," the aged publicist croaked urgently. "It's a shakedown." He turned rather desperately to old Drogue. "Right, Wally? Like when Eddie Ritz had those pictures of Mitch? That's what it's like."

Drogue senior looked from the picture to his old friend. He shook his head sadly, put the print down and walked out of the bungalow.

Finding himself abandoned to the rising generation of Drogues, Jack Best began to shake. The ice in his glass tinkled audibly.

Young Drogue watched him with a bemused smile.

"This is odd," he told his wife. "I think these were taken very recently. I think they were taken here. On our very own location."

"It's a shakedown," Jack Best croaked.

"I see," young Walter Drogue said. "What shall we do, Jack? I mean, I've heard of these things happening in the business. But I've never actually encountered it until now."

Jack cleared his throat. He looked from side to side in a conspiratorial fashion.

Drogue put a cupped hand to the side of his mouth.

"You can talk here, Jack," he whispered. "Right, Patty?"

"Righto," Patty Drogue whispered back.

"It was Madriaga," Jack told him. Madriaga was the *jefe* of the unit's Mexican teamsters, a vicious clownish former policeman. "He come up to me. He was a cop, you see. They went to him. The ones that took the shots. He come to me. They want five big ones. Or they put it out. The reporter that's here. They would give it to him. And around. Europe. England and France. Worldwide. It's like before. You could ask your father. When Eddie Ritz had these pictures of Mitch."

"Bless my soul, Jack," Drogue said, "I can't understand a word you're saying." He turned to his wife. "Can you, dear?"

Patty shook her head. "I liked it, though. I liked it when he said five Big Ones."

"What are Big Ones, Jack?" Drogue asked.

"A grand," Jack said urgently. "A thou." His voice rose in panic. "A thousand dollars."

Drogue took Jack's empty glass from his unsteady hand.

"Jack," Walter Drogue junior said, "that's blackmail. Who would do such a thing? Not someone on our set? Not one of our own?"

Best began to titter and chatter in an almost simian fashion.

"Plenty of them. They ain't got any—they don't care anymore. They treat you like dirt. Just look around. They ain't no good, Walter. They'll make bad publicity. Shit where they eat."

"I'm no good at this," Drogue said dejectedly. "I can't even follow you. What do we have to do, Jack? Will it involve telling Charlie? Will I have to give you money?"

"I could tell you," Jack stammered, "if you ask your old man. I can handle them. Shakedown artists. I got ways. Like when they had Mitch's picture."

"Maybe we should call the police," Patty Drogue suggested.

"The inside of a Mexican jail," Drogue said with hearty indignation. "That's the place for these dirty blackmailers. How about that, Jack?"

"No," Jack said.

"No?" Young Drogue picked up the wireless house telephone on one of his bookshelves and began to dial. "You think not, Jack? Think we should pass on that one? A no-no?" When he had finished dialing, he picked up a pen and began doodling on a note pad.

"No cops," Jack said. "I mean, Mexican cops? I mean, you'd gotta be crazy. You gotta leave it to me." He stared at the futuristic telephone receiver in young Drogue's hand. "I can handle it."

"How would you do it, Jack?" He looked angrily at the wireless phone receiver. He had not obtained a connection. "Fucking thing," he muttered. The sight of his unhappy public relations adviser seemed to soothe him. "Would you do it like they did it before *Marty*? Would you do it like they did it before *sound*?"

"Hey, Wally," Jack said, "Walter—I never worked before sound, Walter. My first picture was with Dick Powell. That was sound."

Drogue was dialing again.

"Axelrod?" he said into the phone. "Put him on."

Jack turned to Patty Drogue. "Dick Powell," he said.

Drogue sat waiting for Axelrod's response, holding the miniature receiver in a clenched fist beneath his chin. Jack Best began to stare at the device with such intensity that the young director's attention was diverted.

"Did you want to see this, Jack?" he asked kindly.

In his confusion and haste to be agreeable, Jack nodded eagerly. He reached out for the sleek receiver with such gleeful anticipation that it was possible to see why he had once been called Smilin' Jack Best. At the last moment Drogue withdrew it from the old man's soiled grasping reach.

"It's a telephone, Jack," he snarled. Jack cringed. "Axelrod!" he said into the receiver. "I got this grotesque situation to cope with. You want to give me a hand?" He looked at Best. "A man's supposed to be an artist," he said ill-temperedly. "Instead you end up as a carny boss."

Jack Best could not reply. His face was trapped in the rigor of his own smile. No matter how hard he attempted to disengage his features from their merry aspect, he was unable to do so. He turned from the young director to the latter's wife. Patty twinkled back at him. She was holding a Polaroid Instamatic. Rising, she stalked the publicist.

"Now, Jack," she cooed, "we'll see what you really truly look like."

Jack wrenched his jaw into motion.

"Chrissakes," he protested. "I seen it was a phone, Walter. I mean, chrissakes. I think my glasses . . . my specs . . . I seen it was a phone, Walter."

Now the Drogues inclined together, watching for images of Jack Best to form on the blank print. They seemed rapt.

"When a thing fits in your hand," Jack explained, "you gotta be sharp. Like the pics. You aren't sharp, they'll kick your teeth in. I know, Walter, because I been there. They say—he's a nice fella and they eat you alive. Walter? Am I right or wrong?"

"Ooh," Patty Drogue said, "there he is, the old scamp." She tore free the Polaroid print of Jack's photograph and handed it to him. Jack looked down into his own smiling face.

"Walter," he said. "Honest to God, I dealt with the roughest and toughest, and the good of the organization was all that mattered to me. You could ask your father. It was dog eat dog. Murder. A jungle." He set the ghastly picture of himself on the shelf beside the strange little telephone. Beside it was the pad on which young Drogue had been doodling. On the pad he read the words: "Five Beeg Wons." He began to weep.

Patty Drogue leveled the Instamatic at him, giving no quarter.

"You shouldn't," Jack said. He raised his hands to cover his face but she made the shot. Jack fought for breath.

"It was . . ." he tried to say. "It was . . ."

Patty lowered her camera and ran at him. She thrust her face into his. Her voice, when she spoke, was a comic rasp.

"It was money talks—before *Marty*!" she growled. "It was bullshit walks—before *sound*!"

She stepped back and pulled out the print of her latest snapshot.

"Oh, see!" she cried as the print came into composition. She showed it to her husband triumphantly as though she were vindicating her position in some point under dispute. "See how he looks?"

Instead of looking at the picture, Drogue looked directly at the cringing man.

"He looks," the young director said, "like Abbott and Costello are waiting for him."

A brisk alarming triple knock sounded against the bungalow door. The sound was muted and urgent and had nothing of good news about it.

Walker had been reading *New York Arts* on the patio while Lu Anne slept. He put the magazine aside and opened the door to Axelrod.

"You're a stupid fuck," the unit manager told him.

Walker was taken aback. Openings like Axelrod's usually presaged a narrative of nights forgotten, and he was quite certain that he could account for the entire period since his arrival.

"Look at this," Axelrod said, and handed him an envelope of photographs. When he had looked at them, he went back to the patio table where he had been reading and sat back down. Axelrod followed him.

"Taken today, right, Gordon?"

"No question."

"You never heard of shades?"

Walker looked out to sea. A darkening cloud bank hovered on the horizon, supporting a gorgeous half rainbow.

"Basic precautions, Gordon," Axelrod said in an aggrieved tone. "A little discretion. You think you have nothing but friends around here?"

"I thought you got to do everything and they didn't care anymore."

"Did you, Gordon? I got news for you. Even today there are things you don't do. You don't snort in your front window with the shades up. If you do you can find yourself in a seven-million-dollar production without a dime's worth of insurance. If our insurers, Gordon— you listening to me? If our insurers had these pictures they would cancel our insurance forthwith and this thing could close down today."

"That's a worst-case scenario. Is it not?"

"Gordon, Gordon," Axelrod said with a mirthless smile, "this could have been a bad case. Remember Wright's picture for Famous? Coke on the set? There was a corporate crisis in New York at Con Intel. The stockholders went apeshit. And it's not only a matter of insurance. There's a theory around that ripped people make lousy movies."

"Lu Anne's asleep," Walker said. He rested his cheekbones on his fists and looked down at the uppermost print. "They're in color," he said. "That's far out."

"What did you think, asshole? That they'd have a black border? Look at yourself. You look like a vampire."

Walker found the image troubling.

"The drinking straw came out nice. Like a little barber pole." He looked up at Axelrod. "Who took them?"

"Jack Best."

Walker nodded. "I thought it might have been Jack. Trying to relive his heroic past."

"He used to get pictures back for us all the time. If you wanted pictures back you went to him. Half the time he probably set the people up."

"I was teasing him a little."

"You were stepping on his balls a little. He claimed his principals wanted five thousand dollars. Depression prices. So I went over and yelled at him and he folded up."

"Didn't Walter believe him?"

"Only an idiot would have believed him. You could see his mind work through the holes in his head."

"It's sad," Walker said. "I mean, he taught me how to read a racing form. I'm really sorry."

"He was some schemer," Axelrod said dreamily. "He got back those famous pictures of Mitchell Drummond and the kid. What's-his-name who was the child actor that O.D.'d last year. That was his greatest number. He knew all the mob guys and all the cops."

"Really sad," Walker said. "Poor Jack. Tell him he can take my picture any time he wants but I wish he'd leave my friends alone."

"He's finished, Gordon. He's going where Winchell and Kilgallen went."

"A tragedy," Walker said. "Do we have all the pictures back?"

"He says he put one print under Dongan Lowndes's door. Seemed kind of funny."

"It's a riot. *Confidential* closed, so he takes them to *New York Arts*. Van Epp can run them next to Nelson Eddy goosing chorines."

"It makes no sense," Axelrod said. "So I thought, well, he's senile, he's out of it . . ."

"Do we have to worry about what Lowndes thinks of us?" Walker asked. "He's supposed to be a gentleman. He'll give us the picture back."

"Gordon," Axelrod said, "let me tell you something that's also funny. I just tossed the gentleman's room again. I went through his gear as completely as I could without leaving traces. The print's not there."

"Maybe Jack was lying."

"I don't think so." Axelrod took a chair in the shade. "I think Lowndes has it. If he was going to give it back he would have done it by now."

"That's not very nice of him," Walker said. "But then he isn't very nice, is he?"

"Not in my opinion. In my opinion he's a smart prick."

"He's worse than that," Walker said. "He's an unhappy writer."

Axelrod mixed himself a drink from the setup on the umbrella-shaded table beside him.

"It's not good," he said. "These shots kick around—sooner or later they end up in print."

Walker watched the sea-borne rainbow fade into blue-gray cloud.

"It wouldn't hurt this picture," Axelrod went on. "It wouldn't help you much. But I wouldn't think it could hurt you much either."

"People would get the impression I take drugs." He turned toward the bungalow's bedroom window. The blinds were closed. "But Lu Anne may be in a divorce court presently."

"Careerwise also," Axelrod said. "If it got around that in addition to her other problems she had this—you understand me."

"We should really get the print back," Walker said.

"Definitely. We should talk to Lowndes. We should get him to do the right thing. I mean," Axelrod asked, "why should he want to keep it?"

"They're such depressing pictures," Walker said, raising one with his thumb and forefinger.

"Some things you do," Axelrod observed, "you don't want to see yourself doing them."

Walker stared at the picture and shook his head in disgust.

"She caught me with it," he explained. "It's very hard to say no to Lu Anne."

"I know that, Gordon. I understand."

"You know what they say about her, Axelrod? They say her pictures don't make money and she has no luck with men."

"I've heard that said about her, Gordon." He finished his drink and pushed the glass away. "She needed that doctor. He could say no to her."

"It's very irritating, Lowndes keeping that picture. What a cheap stunt!"

"No class," Axelrod said. "No self-respect."

Walker looked out to sea.

"Of course, it might make a good lead," Walker said, "if he was writing a certain kind of story."

"You think so?"

"I'm writing for *New York Arts*," Walker said. "Here's my lead: On the third day after my arrival at *The Awakening*'s Bahía Honda location, a package arrived at my feet having been slid under my bungalow door. Naturally I assumed it contained the daily trades . . . haha, jape, flourish et cetera. Imagine my—and so forth—when upon opening it I find it to contain a photograph of two of the principal artists naked in bed, apparently in the act of scoffing I know not what, tooting up, coke and the movies, sordidness and blackmail, hurray for Hollywood, movies as metaphor, crazy California, decline of the West, *ad astra ad nauseam*! You like my lead?"

"It's a colorful lead. Is there more?"

"Yes," Walker said, "there's more. There's effect. Charlie Freitag—the movies' answer to Bernard Berenson, the only man in California off the Redlands University campus who wears a bow tie —is deeply hurt. He subscribes to *New York Arts*. His wife subscribes, his gardener, the people next door across the canyon. His high-class flick is getting the mondo-bizarro treatment in his very favorite magazine. Sun Pix is pissed off at him. Amalgamated Can is pissed off

at Sun Pix. It's a litigious age. Van Epp is scared stiff. He calls in
Lowndes . . . Did you make this up, Dongo? A literal Dutch uncle.
The novelist's—the former novelist's—mouth is wreathed in a putrid
smile. He reaches under his cape. Observe the snap, mynheer Van
Epp."

Axelrod thought about it.

"As a completely blind item," he said, "it might not be so bad. It
might even be a little . . . good." He shrugged.

"Man, Lowndes is going to make this location look like Bosch's
Garden. If we were down here making kiddiebop with grown-ups
talking dirty and popping bloodbags, they could run that print on the
cover of *Christianity Today* and we could tell them to eat it. But what
if the story just reads as production problems? And then your lofty
scene dies the death? They'll blame it on coke."

"They'll blame it on Lu," Axelrod said.

"That's right."

"So," Axelrod said testily, "why the fuck you give her cocaine,
then?"

"Did you approve of my coming down here, Axelrod?"

"I thought it was a bad idea." He sulked, eyeing the bank of storm
cloud as though he wanted to tear it in half. "I might have been able
to stop you. I might have hung up on Shelley."

"Why didn't you?"

"Fuck you, Gordon."

"You wanted me down here. Tell me why."

"I thought we might have a few laughs."

"You figured I'd bring down some blow. You were out."

"I could've scored somewhere, Gordon. I thought maybe it would
be . . . I don't know what I thought."

"You thought it would be like old times."

"Yeah," Axelrod said disgustedly, "that's about it."

"So did I," Walker said. "Maybe they'll bring them back. They
bring everything back."

"We gotta nudge Mr. Lowndes a little. So he gives us back our print. I mean," Axelrod said, "it would be great not to have to tell Charlie about this."

"What we have to do," Walker said, "is make him understand he's playing in the wrong league. Make him understand his position."

"Right," Axelrod said.

"We have to make him look down and see where he's liable to fall. We'll tell him how we see the big ones and the little ones fall every day. Like sparrows."

"Yeah," Axelrod said. He smiled. "Let's tell him that, Gordon."

H alf an hour later Walker went into the bedroom. His first impulse was to draw open the blinds but he thought better of it. When he turned on the corner ceiling lights he discovered Lu Anne to be awake. Her hair was wet and she had changed into black lace.

"You do take a lot of showers, Lu Anne."

"I take a lot of showers for a coon-ass. Is that what you meant?"

"Let's not be crazy," Walker said.

"Let's not you be paranoid," she told him. "Goodness," she said. "I was drunk when I went to sleep and I'm still drunk."

She rolled off the bed.

"Christ," she said, from all fours, "there's crawling."

Walker put on a sweatshirt and went into the bathroom to shower.

"How long will you stay?" she asked him through the open door.

"I thought I'd go back on Monday. Leave you to work."

"Stay longer."

"Lu Anne," he said, "I can't afford this hotel. I'm here on Sun Pix and Amcan."

"So short a time," she said, "after so long."

"It's been hard for me to get away. The chance came. So I grabbed it."

"No, no," Lu Anne told him. "It was more elaborate than that. You connived. What were you thinking of?"

"Honest to God, I don't know. Maybe of cheating time. Throwing a two-by-four in the treads."

She sipped from a glass of *mezcal*, shivered and handed it half finished to Walker. He put it aside.

"Come back," she said.

He took off the trunks and sweatshirt he was wearing and climbed into bed with her. In the vulgar half light she seemed to draw away as he approached. She did so without moving, with a silent, subtly visible retracting of herself. It was as though she drew in all softness, took up her own slack and curled the flesh around her long bones. Her eyes went dull, her lips were shadows. He could not tell whether it was something she was doing or some warp in his abused perception.

Gallic severity. A crucifix. Charlotte Corday.

"Come in, Gordon," she said.

He found the game for him. The game for him was to ease through the ivory casing, to loose the bound flesh, draw out the woman and beyond the woman some creature of another sort.

The creature was inside, it fucked like pure madness. It *was* madness and it frightened him. Down the gullet of fear itself, he charged with a silent hurrah.

"How nice," Lu Anne said.

When she turned her face to his, she looked flushed and dimpled and happy. The Lady of Mortifications was fled home to Port Royal, madness appeased. Lu Anne was at home.

She seems so young, he thought. Her face was smooth, the skin beneath her eyes was sound. It struck him then how good the doctor and the children must have been for her.

"*Allons,*" Walker declared. "*Laissez le bon temps . . .*"

She put her hand over his mouth.

"I forbid you to use that idiotic phrase," she told him. "It's for morons. Only cretins use it. And people from Shreveport."

"I was feeling moronic. Happy in my sex life. A stud once more."

"You were always a stud, Gordon."

"Ofttimes," he said, "of late not always."

Suddenly she said, "How are your boys, Gordon?"

He fell silent inside. Her question fell upon his inward man like frost. He swallowed the pain.

"They're fine."

"In school?"

"Stuart's in school. Deak's on his own."

"Deak is the funny one, right? The pretty one."

"Stuart," Walker said. "He's the funny one now."

"They're the only ones you love," she said. "You always fretted over them."

"Hostages to fortune," he said. He was thinking that if they began to talk about their children they would drown in a sea of regret. Walker had always pictured regret as something like vomit. The association was not gratuitous.

"I think I'll do a little more coke," he said brightly. "It might sober me up for dinner." When he got up and looked in the mirror he thought of Lowndes and the pictures. He assembled his works, feeling more sober than he could possibly be.

"I shouldn't have any more," Lu Anne said uncertainly.

"Good thinking," Walker said. He was trying frantically to get his hit and put the stuff away.

"Well," she said finally, "if you're having some I want some too."

"You're on half rations," he told her. "Recuperating."

"There are some would have me drink," she said mysteriously, "there are those who would have me dry."

He chopped two narrow lines for her and handed over the equipment, the mirror and the drinking straw whose festive colors had shown up so well on the color photographs.

For the drawn blinds and the dim light, it might have been any hour. How foolish of him, he thought, to have forgotten about the blinds. On locations people were always watching, peering in trailers, looking for lighted windows.

"Don't think about your kids," she told him earnestly. She leaned her head on one arm to lecture him. She was wearing a pair of silver-

rimmed aviator glasses he had not seen before and he suspected she
had appropriated them to use as a prop when she felt admonitory.

"Seriously," she said, "your kids don't care about you. Don't care
about them."

Walker did not answer her. He reached down, took a pinch of
coke under his fingernail and touched it to his gum.

"I saw you do that," Lu Anne said. "Now listen to me—you don't
care a damn about your daddy, do you?"

"My father is dead," Walker said. "And my mother is dead. And
my brother is dead."

He repeated this statement, this time as a little song, to the tune of
an Irish jig.

"There was a time . . ." Walker began. He managed to stop, shut
up before it was too late. He had been about to discourse on the subject
of his father. Without trying to conceal it from her he put the mirror
on his pillow and took some more. She took the straw from his hand
and snorted until he thought she would pass out. He put it back down
quickly before she could exhale on it.

"But honestly, Gordon! They won't be worrying about you. You
ought not to worry about them. I've got children myself, Gordon."

"I know that, love."

"Yessir. Four." She held her hand, the long fingers splayed and
trembling, before his face. "Four counting the dead and I insist on
counting the dead, that's the custom in Louisiana, Gordon, where the
living and the dead are involved in mixed entertainments. And are
not tucked away in the ground but dwell among us. Their hair grows
and their fingernails and they go on getting smarter in those ovens
under their angels. Which represent the angels that attended them in
life. Or their crosses. Or their *Médailles miraculeuses*."

"Stop," he said.

"Life too much for you, brother? Huh? What says the gentleman?"

"The gentleman allows that things are tough all over."

"Gordon," she demanded, "are you listening to me?" She took her
glasses off and gave him a look of pedagogic disapproval. "Show the
courtesy to listen to the person in the same bed as yourself. I have

four!" Her hand quavered before his eyes. "They don't care about me. I'm a biological function of their lives. That's it. Three lives, one death. That's all, man. Would I let them destroy me? No, I would not, Lionel. Gordon, rather. You wrote the book, Gordon. She doesn't let them dominate her life! She will die for them, sure, but she won't live for them. Isn't that the way it goes? *They need not have thought that they could possess her*. Isn't that what you wrote, Lionel?"

"Lionel didn't write it and neither did I. Madame Chopin wrote it."

"A red-necked Irishwoman who would trade her kids for a pint of Jim Beam. That's the big secret, you know. She didn't care about her kids. What she really wanted to be was an actress. Isn't that right, Gordon?"

"I don't know what's right, my love. I'm drunk and you're bananas. That's the score."

"I want more now, please, Gordon."

"Well, honeychile," Walker said, "you ain't getting no fuckin' more. Because you have degenerated into a goddamn lunatic. What kind of party has a lunatic at it?"

"Plenty," she insisted. "Plenty of parties do. And I want more. Damn it, Gordon!" she said. Then she cocked an ear as though she had heard something.

"Listen, Gordon. A recitation. Sir King, we deem that 'tis strange sport, to keep a madman as thy fool at court."

"Rest easy, Lu Anne."

"This is the forest primeval." She paused thoughtfully and repeated the line. "Gordon, do you know how long it took me to understand that *Evangeline* was *not* a good poem?"

He put her arm under his head and wrapped his arms around her. His thought was to suffocate her fire, keep her from burning up.

"Longer than most, I bet."

"That would be about right," she said. "Late in life.

"Do you know why I take so many showers?"

"Yes," he said, "sort of."

"Say why."

"Because you have hallucinations in which your friends advise you to take showers."

"They hardly advise me, honey. French," she breathed confidentially, "can be the vehicle for some very low observations. And Frenchman French, well!"

"They aren't really there, Lu Anne. That's all there is to it."

"They aren't there in your life. They're in mine."

"Lu Anne," Walker said. "Do you understand that I love you?"

"Yes, yes." She patted his arm. "Yes, I understand."

"Does that penetrate the . . . whatever it is?"

"Whatever it is," she said, "I guess love penetrates it."

He took his arms from around her and kissed her hand.

"Gordon," she whispered, "what I said about our children . . ."

A long time ago he had learned to watch for a catch in her voice, a look in her eyes. He had learned what it portended. He had called it shifting gears. Once he had told her that she had two speeds: Bad Lu Anne and Saint Lu Anne. There on the bed beside him he saw her slide into Bad Lu Anne. Bad Lu Anne was not in fact malign, but formidable and sometimes terrifying. As soon as he saw her eyes, he jumped.

He body-checked her as she rose, and like a coach miming a tackle, eased her in his grip across the foot of the bed and held her there. It took all his strength and weight to keep her down. Her face was pressed against his chest, her mouth was open in a scream of pain, but not a sound came out of her. Panting, he held on. If she chose to bite him he would have to give way. Sometimes she bit him, sometimes not. This time she only kept on screaming, and in the single moment that his grip relented she drove him off the bed and clear across the room and into the beige cloth-covered wall. He hung on to her all the way. His body absorbed her unvoiced scream until he felt he could hardly contain, without injury, the force of her grief and rage.

At last she stopped thrashing and he loosened his grip. He backed away, and they lay together on the floor. She cradled her hands prayerfully beneath her cheek; she was facing him. Her lips moved, she prayed, mouthed words, sobbed. He put his hand on her shoulder, an inquiring hand, to ask if she wanted him there or not. When he touched her, she drew closer to him.

"Hey, now," he whispered absurdly. He put his arm around her, his every move seemed feeble and irrelevant to him. "Hey, now," he kept repeating, like a man talking to a horse. "Hey, now."

A round sundown, Axelrod walked into the Drogues' bungalow with his envelope full of photographs. Young Drogue and his wife were watching a Spanish-language soap opera on their television set. Axelrod set the envelope before them.

"Should I be overjoyed?" Drogue asked. "Is this all of them?"

"All except one print. Dongan Lowndes has it."

"Jack gave it to Lowndes? But that's ridiculous." He looked from Jon to his wife, with an expression of pained mirth. "Isn't it?"

Axelrod presented Walker's theory of the Picturesque Lead with Jack's photograph to support it.

"Somehow," Drogue said, "I find it hard to take this dopey snap-shot seriously."

"According to Walker, Lowndes is gonna really dish it to us. He says the NYA story will make this location look like Butch's Garden."

"What's that?" Drogue asked. "Some S & M joint known only to weirdos?"

"I don't think it's in L.A.," Patty said.

"He means Lowndes is gonna make us look bad. That's what he thinks."

"The hell with what he thinks. He got the whole thing started with his dissolute ways. Anyway, no story in New York Arts is going to hurt us. Or is it?"

"It wouldn't hurt to get the picture back," Axelrod said. "Lowndes is unfriendly. The Europeans might go for it. *Oggi* and those clowns."

"Christ," Drogue said irritably. "Does Charlie know about this? He'll make the night horrible with his cries."

Axelrod shook his head.

"I think it's a minor matter," Drogue said. "It would be nice if we could sort it out without bothering Mr. Freitag."

"Don't tell him while he's eating," Patty said. "He's had a bypass."

"Not only that," Axelrod said. "He's got guests."

"Well," Drogue wanted to know, "can you get the damn thing back?"

"We're gonna suggest to Mr. Lowndes that he do the right thing."

"Don't start bouncing him off walls. Then we'll really be in the shit."

"What I'd like to do," Axelrod said, "I'd like to have the local police athletic league take his head for a couple of laps around the municipal toilet bowl. Except we'd have to pay *mordida* and the pigs would probably swipe the print."

"If he's unfriendly," Drogue said, "be my guest. Put the screws to him. Just don't give him anything to sue about."

"We're gonna make him sweat," Axelrod said. "If he doesn't deliver maybe we should throw him off the set and tell Van Epp he's unethical. That way we might kill the story before he writes it. Then Van Epp has nothing to fight for."

"Let's see how it goes tonight," Drogue said. "But I don't want to get involved. If you want him off the set you have to go to Charlie."

"Charlie should be outraged," Axelrod said. "The guy's supposed to be high-class and he deals with blackmailers."

"Charlie's instinct will be to buy him out. Put him on the payroll. Option his next book. Wait and see."

"You should advise him not to do that."

"I can't advise him," Drogue said. "My father can advise him. Not me."

"What are you gonna do with Jack?"

"I should pour salt down his throat and make him walk to Tijuana. But since he's Dad's old pal I guess I'll pay him off and fly him home. For my father's sake."

"Wow," Patty said, "that's Christ-like."

"Damn right," Walter Drogue junior said. He picked up one of the photographs and examined it. "This is a truly ugly picture," he said. "I'll never be able to look at these two turkeys in the same light."

"Walker's into it."

"Walker's a bum," Drogue said. "He's going to end up like Jack."

"A lot of them do," Axelrod said.

"He's got no survival skills," the director said. He looked at the picture again. "Neither of them have."

Patty Drogue lit a joint and took the picture from her husband.

"If any kind of shit hit any kind of fan," Drogue asked Axelrod, "not that I think it will—do you suppose Walker has some kind of moral turpitude thing in his contract? Some kind of Fatty Arbuckle-type thing?"

"That would cut him out and take his points? I don't know, Walter. It's not my department. I doubt it."

"I'm not trying to take the guy's points, Axelrod. Why does everybody suspect me of being other than a nice person? I just wondered what kind of risk he ran."

"Not much," Axelrod said. "Not like she does."

Walter took a drag on the joint and gave it back to his wife.

"Sometimes I'm inclined to think this is all Charlie's fault," he said. "Charlie's a silly man. Silly shit happens around his pictures."

"Really," Patty Drogue agreed.

"The sixties," Walter Drogue said to them. "You think they were that great?"

Axelrod shrugged.

"Everybody shoplifted," Patty Drogue said. "People handed out flowers. You could get laid three times a day with an ugly body."

"That's all over now," Axelrod said.

B athed, anointed, as cool and clean as chastity, she climbed the lighted path. Walker came behind her, walking carefully. They passed a garden bar and lighted tennis courts, following a yucca-bordered path that led to Charlie Freitag's casita.

The casita's sunken patio was lit by flickering torches, set at intervals along its border of volcanic stone. A party of grim mariachis was performing; their music seemed strangely muted to Lu Anne, as if each brass note were being instantly carried off on the wind.

Axelrod appeared from the darkness. He smiled at her and hurried past, approaching Walker. The Long Friends, jubilant, fanned out among the guests. She thought it odd that they seemed happy there.

Across the patio from the musicians was a walled barbecue pit where white-capped chefs labored over a spitted joint. The air was smoky with roasting beef. A great cauldron of boiling sauce stood to one side of the pit and, nearby, a company of men in *toques blanches* sharpened carving knives. The waiters had set up a buffet and a long well-attended bar.

Axelrod and Walker were conspiring.

"Fuck him then," she heard Walker say. "Is he here?"

"Not yet," Axelrod answered. He turned to Lu Anne. "How are you, Lu?"

"A little tired," she said. He was studying her. His hard features were firelit. "Will that do?"

"It'll do fine," Axelrod said. "Remind her, Gordo. She looks beautiful but she's a little tired."

She tried working with them.

"When they ask me how I am," she assured them, "or how I feel, I'll say a little tired."

"Smile," Walker told her, "when you say it."

"I'll try it with the smile," she said dutifully, "and if it works I'll keep it."

She thought some quarrel might be breaking out among the Long Friends, some dispute over precedence or family history. Her anxiety quickened.

"Is everything all right?" she asked. In the patio below, Freitag's guests were mingling, carrying their drinks among the cloth-covered buffet tables. There were not so many of them as she had thought at first. Her Friends hung on the edge of the light.

"It's fine," Walker assured her. "It's nice here."

"It's just friends," Axelrod said. "Just . . ." He paused; both he and Walker were watching Dongan Lowndes descend into the lighted garden, making for the bar.

"Just buddies," Walker said.

"Let's get down there," Axelrod told them.

Smiling, unclear of vision, Lu Anne strolled among the guests with Walker at her side. He was conducting her to Charlie.

She went to him in expectation of elaborate greeting but he simply took her by the hand. His fondness seemed so genuine that it made her sad. She thought she could feel Walker beside her grow tense with a suitor's unease, as though Charlie were his rival.

"You lovely girl," Charlie said. "You champion." He turned to Walker. "Want to ask me if I like it?"

A tall horse-faced woman with prominent front teeth stood at Charlie's elbow. Next to her was a stocky Latin man with a dour Roman face and straight black Indian hair that fell in a sweep across his forehead. He was in black tie and dinner jacket, the only man present in formal clothes.

"You like it," Walker said. "Have you spoken to Walter?"

In the grip of his emotion, Charlie Freitag turned and sought Walter Drogue among his guests.

"Walter," he fairly shouted. "Call the director!" A few people turned toward him in alarm. "Get over here, Drogue!" The party recognized his good humor and relaxed.

Walter Drogue made his way to Freitag's side and a circle began
to form around them. Lu Anne saw Lise Rennberg, Jack Glenn and
Eric. George Buchanan sipped Perrier. Carnahan and Joy McIntyre
were dissolved in rowdy laughter. When he had gathered his principals about him, Charlie raised his glass. "Here's to all of you," he
proclaimed. "Artists of the possible!"

"And absent friends!" Joy McIntyre cried. Freitag, who had no
idea who she was, looked at her strangely for a moment, his smile on
hold.

"Like father, like son," Charlie told Walter Drogue junior when
they had quaffed their cup of victory.

The young director gave forth with an insolent simper, the malice
of which was lost on Big Charlie Freitag.

"It ain't over till it's over, Charlie."

Freitag's eye fell on Dongan Lowndes.

"Mr. Lowndes," he said, "you've been lucky. You've seen this business at its best. You've seen a fine picture made by serious people and
it doesn't get any better than that."

"I wouldn't have missed it for the world," Lowndes said thickly.

"Maybe we can get you to come out and work with us someday."

Ignoring Charlie, Lowndes looked at Lu Anne for a moment and
turned on Walker.

"Would I like it?" he asked. "What do you think?"

"Well," Walker told him, "it beats not working." Everyone laughed,
as though he had said something funny.

Charlie performed introductions for the Mexican and Dongan
Lowndes. The others were known to one another. The tall woman
was Ann Armitage, a former comic actress and the widow of a blacklisted writer. The Mexican was Raúl Maldonado, a painter.

The thuggish musicians played their way into darkness. A pair of
violinists stepped out of the void into which the mariachis had vanished and commenced to stroll. Freitag went off to speak with Lise
Rennberg and the attendant circle dissolved.

"Let's go talk," Axelrod said to Lowndes. The novelist was disposed to remain beside Lu Anne. He gazed at her with drunken ardor. Lu Anne returned his look, pitying his flayed face, his sores and fecal eyes.

"Is it important?" Lowndes asked, without disengaging his gaze from Lu Anne's.

"Not exactly important," Axelrod said. "Scummy."

He slid his hand under Lowndes's arm and drew the man aside. Ann Armitage was asking Lu Anne how she was. Lu Anne stared at the old actress blankly.

"Line!" she called.

"A little tired," Walker told her.

Lu Anne smiled confidentially. An expression of weariness passed across her face.

"The truth is," she told Ann Armitage, "that I've been feeling a little tired."

Ann Armitage did the double take for which she had once been famous.

"What are you two? An act?"

"Yes, ma'am," Lu Anne said.

Miss Armitage looked them up and down, world-wearily.

Before the guests could make their way to the seating, young Helena stood on a wooden bench and raised her hands for silence.

"We don't want you sitting with your worst enemy or your ex-spouse or their lover," she told the guests. "So as some of you may have noticed, we've had lovely little place cards with your many famous names inscribed thereon. So—sorry about the milling. Wherever your card is—after you've helped yourself to the buffet—that's where you'll sit. And you may in fact want to take note of your place before you fill your plates with all this delicious food."

There was some smattering of applause punctuated by a harsh raspberry. Joy McIntyre had made her way, unerringly but unsteadily, to Charlie Freitag's side.

"I mean," she demanded in a nasal croon, "I mean, what is this, Charlie? High tea with Rex?" She seized his dinner gong and marched off to accost the violinists.

"Who is that woman?" Charlie Freitag demanded of those nearest him. He was told she was Lee Verger's stand-in.

People walked about carrying their western-style metal plates, colliding with each other and adjusting their spectacles, trying to see in the light of tiny table lamps or flickering torchlight.

"Bang bang went the trolley!" Joy McIntyre sang at the top of her voice. The strolling violinists backed away from her like a pair of ornamental fowl. Charlie returned to his guests.

"That woman," he said to Walker, "is she actually a stand-in?"

Before Walker could answer, the patio echoed to a horrendous screech.

"My God," Freitag said. "It's her again."

It was Joy again. Bill Bly, uninvited but on watch, was attempting to relieve her of the dinner gong. Joy declined to surrender it.

"Get your bloody hand off me fucking wrist, you great fucking poofta bastard!" she protested. The guests had fallen silent. Joy's struggle, the crackling of cooked meat and the violins, sweetly paired to "Maytime," were the only sounds in the patio.

"The press is here," Freitag said. "This looks like hell." He looked about him in the dimness for Dongan Lowndes and saw the man squared off with Axelrod as though the two of them were at the point of blows.

"Jesus wept," the gentleman producer cried. Walker took the opportunity to slip away.

Lu Anne sat at the head of one of the buffet tables playing with people's name cards. Maldonado and Miss Armitage had attempted to enlist at a more congenial sector of the party but, encountering outbursts and angry voices at every turning, had been driven back into the shadows. In the shadows Lu Anne ruled. She had discovered that she, Miss Armitage and Maldonado, Walker and Lowndes, Charlie, Axelrod and the Drogues were all seated together at the very table beside which Charlie had introduced them.

"Do you think," she asked the couple, "that some table game might be played with these? Something along the order of Authors or Old Maid?"

Miss Armitage smiled sweetly.

"Yes, I do," she said. She seized the stack of place cards from Lu Anne's grasp until she had her own and her escort's, and put them on the next table. "It's called Switcheroo."

She picked up two place cards from the same adjoining table and handed them to Lu Anne.

"I'm too old to sit still for silly women, Miss Niceness, just as you're too old to be one. I'm going to leave you to the luck of the draw."

Maldonado replaced their cards.

"I want to sit here," he said heavily. Miss Armitage pursed her lips and looked at the ground. The Mexican took his chair and slowly undid the knot of his dress black tie.

"You're welcome here, Mr. Maldonado," Lu Anne said.

Maldonado looked at her.

"Am I?"

"Oh yes," Lu Anne said. "You and your companion are both welcome. You have the good opinion of my friends."

Maldonado graciously inclined his head. Ann Armitage gave a comic grimace. "Well, praise God and shut my mouth. If that's not . . ."

The painter raised a flabby hand, bidding his friend to silence.

"You all are admired in secret places," Lu Anne told them. "In quarters that you mustn't imagine, they think well of you and they give good report."

"How very mysterious," Maldonado said. "What does it mean?"

Lu Anne was at a loss to explain. Never in her life had she seen the Long Friends so unafraid of sound or light, almost ready, it seemed, to join her in her greater world and make the two worlds one. Seeing them gathered round, shyly peering from between their lace-like wings, murmuring encouragement, she could only conclude that they approved of her new acquaintanceship with Charlie's two friends. Moreover, they were beautiful, the two, the elegant old actress and the sad-faced handsome man who had removed his dinner jacket. They were as beautiful and charged with grace as Lowndes was hideous and unclean.

Charlie Freitag came to their table like a man seeking refuge from the field of defeat. There was a meager ration of salad and beans on his plate. He looked sweaty and unwell. Lu Anne, who loved him as her friend, was concerned.

"What's this?" Charlie asked. "No one's eating?"

"Charlie," she asked, "Charlie, dear, aren't you well, my poor friend?"

He took her by the hand. "Me? I'm fine. I'm thinking of you."

"I'm well enough, Charles." She smiled. "A little tired."

"You must be wiped out, for Christ's sake," Charlie said. "We have you in and out of the water thirty times a day. You're living on hotel food and missing your family." He looked about the torchlit patio uneasily. "Everyone's overworked. But I thought, what the hell, we're over the hump. I thought since Gordon was coming down and we had this man from *New York Arts* . . . and I thought we could all use a lift."

"Indeed we could," Lu Anne said. "And it's my birthday."

Charlie was surprised. "Well, for heaven's sake," he said. "But I thought your birthday was last month."

Lu Anne gave him a conspiratorial wink. Ann Armitage stared at her, unblinking.

"Where *is* Gordon?" Charlie asked quickly.

"Well, he was just here," Lu Anne said. She could not remember his leaving; she was suddenly anxious. "I don't know." To her horror she saw Dongan Lowndes approaching the table, followed with a vigor bordering on pursuit by Axelrod.

"Isn't anyone going to eat?" Charlie asked them in mounting distress.

As though in benison, Walter Drogue junior and Patty arrived, their plates piled high. Charlie and Patty Drogue exchanged kisses.

"Where's your old man?" Charlie asked young Drogue. "Won't he be joining us?"

Patty, who had hastened to stuff her mouth with food, attempted unsuccessfully to speak.

"He's having a little trouble with his date," young Drogue said.

"Yeah?" Charlie asked. "Who's the lucky lady?"

"You must have seen her, Charlie," Drogue said. "The little Australian job with the dirty mouth?"

Freitag covered his eyes with his hand for a moment.

"Hilarious," he said softly. He looked about guiltily as though old Drogue might catch him gossiping. "What a riot!"

"Best body on the unit," young Drogue said. "Present company excepted."

"That's Wally," Ann Armitage said. "I take it he's in good health?"

"He damn well better be," Freitag said. "I had a look at that little dollop."

Lu Anne, knowing that in time she must, turned toward Dongan Lowndes. As she did so she felt what could only be his hand against her knee.

"Walking the bones, Mr. Lowndes?" she asked him.

His damp hand slithered off like a cemetery rat. She watched his face as the rat-hand fled home to him. His blunt features were momentarily elongated and rodentine as he reabsorbed it, the rat within. For all the effort in the world she could not tear her eyes from his nor could she feel a grain of pity. Let the rat stay wherein it dwelled, she thought. Let it gnaw his guts forever, feed behind his eyes. So long as she was safe from it.

Lowndes's eyes were moist as he stared down her rebuke. She saw in them what he himself must take for human passion, desire, infatuation, an impulse to master the beloved. The trouble was that he was not a man. Not human.

"Mr. Lowndes," she heard Axelrod say in a low voice, "you want to look at me when I talk to you?"

At last she tore her eyes free from Lowndes's, a rending.

"Mr. Maldonado," she asked the man across the table from her, "are you a good painter?"

Miss Armitage started to speak but fell silent.

"One's never asked," Maldonado said.

"Lu Anne," Charlie said sternly, "Raúl is one of Mexico's very finest painters. He shows throughout the world."

"I should say so," Miss Armitage said.

"I myself," Charlie declared, "own some choice Maldonados. They're on display in my home and to me—they mean Mexico. The sunshine, the sea. The whole enchilada."

Maldonado and Miss Armitage looked at him coldly.

"You know what I mean," he stammered. "Everything we so admire about . . ." He fell silent, looked at his plate and mopped his brow.

"Dad owns about a ton and a half of them," young Drogue said.

"In bohemian company," Lu Anne said, "or some equivalent, in some demimonde like ours—one faces the deliberately tactless question."

Maldonado smiled faintly. "*Mierda*," he said.

"You better believe it," Ann Armitage said.

"Everybody here knows whether they're good or not," Lu Anne told him. "Given the least encouragement, everybody here is ready to say."

"I am not a good painter," Maldonado told the company. There was a momentary silence, then a chorus of demurrers.

"The great ones," Charlie said with an uneasy chuckle, "they're never happy with their work. They need us to encourage them."

"I wish you were a good painter," Lu Anne said to Maldonado. "Maybe you are, after all."

"If for you I could be," Maldonado said gallantly, "you may be sure that I would. Maybe for myself as well. But I think it would make my life difficult."

Lowndes's presence had quieted the Long Friends; they were out of temper again, out where she could not control them and where they might cause her some embarrassment. She began to feel panicky.

"Oh God," she said, "where's Gordon? I need him."

"Jon," Freitag said to Axelrod, "would you do me a favor and find your friend Walker? Be a pal."

Even in the unsteady light it was apparent that Axelrod was red-faced with anger.

"Sure, Charlie," he said. He put a hand on Lowndes's shoulder again. "What do you say, Dongan? Want to help me find our pal Gordo?"

Lowndes brushed his hand away violently. "I don't go for this tinseltown familiarity," he told Axelrod.

"That's not nice, Dongan," Axelrod said.

"Mr. Maldonado," Lu Anne said, "would you find him for me?"

"Can't you walk?" Miss Armitage asked. "Find your own god-damn friends."

Lu Anne was carefully pouring the decanted red wine into her glass. She drank it down.

"I can't see so well," she explained. "And there's such a crowd."

"Of course," Maldonado said. "Mr. Walker. I'll find him. I'll go now."

He touched his napkin to his mouth, although he had not been eating, and went off.

"Christ almighty, Charlie," Miss Armitage said to her host. "Where do you get these people?"

"The same place I got you," Charlie Freitag said brightly. There were no laughs for him at the table.

Walker was in the pool-house lavatory, sniffing cocaine from the porcelain surface of the sink, when the door opened behind him. In the mirror over the sink he saw a man framed in the doorway, discovering him *in flagrante*. The man appeared wild-eyed and disheveled; he was wearing a white dress shirt unbuttoned at the neck and dark trousers. It was an unwelcome sight.

"*Cocaína*," the man said.

Walker turned slowly toward the man in the mirror and recognized Maldonado.

"It's all right," he said slowly, having no idea himself what he might mean.

"Among my friends," the painter explained, "it's frowned on as bourgeois. As gringo. My companion—Miss Armitage—is very bitter on the subject."

"I'll bet," Walker said. He went past Maldonado to lock the door. "I thought," he explained, "I had locked this."

"No," Maldonado said, "it was open. This is difficult," he told Walker. "To have some or not?"

"Do have some," Walker suggested. "I mean, it's your decision of course."

"I shall," Maldonado said. "Why not?"

They took some. The painter paced, frowning.

"A case could certainly be made," Walker said, "that it's bad for the Indians. In terms of exploitation."

Maldonado waved the argument away.

"It's neither good nor bad for the Indians. It makes no difference for them. It's ourselves and our societies that we're destroying."

"That's as it should be," Walker said.

They had more. Instead of pacing, Maldonado fixed Walker with a grave stare.

"Who is the woman, Walker?"

"Do you mean Lee Verger? You were introduced."

"Lee Verger," Maldonado repeated. "An actress?"

"A very good actress. Quite well known."

"Is she acting now? Tonight? Performing?"

Walker hesitated.

"Not tonight," he said. "Not really."

"She's your woman?"

"Yes," Walker said.

"She sent me to get you. I'm not some house cat to be sent on such an errand but I obeyed her. She asked me if I was a good painter and I replied that I was not. I wanted to humiliate myself."

"Well," Walker said, "you've probably fallen in love with her."

"I can explain," Maldonado said. "I can explain to her. With your permission."

"Oh, absolutely," Walker said. "Let's go back and talk."

The party seemed to be going well as Walker and Maldonado made their way back to Charlie Freitag's table. The violinists patrolled unmolested; happy conversation bubbled up from every quarter. Only at the party's core, in the circle around Freitag, a dark enchantment prevailed.

Maldonado resumed his seat across from Lu Anne. He and all the others at the table watched in silence as Walker guided himself into a chair beside her and she moved to steady him. When he was down beside her she took his hand and kissed it and put her arm around his neck.

"I want to explain myself," Maldonado said. "I want to explain what I said against my painting."

"There's no need for that," Miss Armitage said. "Everyone knows how wonderful you are. And everyone can see you've been drinking."

The voice of Joy McIntyre rang again through the patio.

"The choreographer at the Sands is dead!" she bellowed. "The choreog—" She began the phrase again but was cut off in mid-word, somewhat disconcertingly.

"Why are people always saying that?" Lowndes asked.

" 'Cause we're in tinseltown," Axelrod told him. "And they're sending you a message, Dongan."

"I want to speak about my painting," Maldonado said. "This lady has challenged me and I dedicate my remarks to her."

"The lady will excuse you," Ann Armitage said firmly. "She knows there are things not to say in public. She understands that sometimes we say things that can hurt us in important ways."

"All the same," Maldonado said softly.

Walker finished the drink at his place.

"We are true artists here," he explained, "we work without a net."

Old Drogue came out of the darkness; there appeared to be dark welts on his neck. He made his way to the table to sit between his son and Patty.

When Charlie rose to welcome him, he raised his right hand in a kind of benediction and sat down.

"Yay, Pops," Drogue junior said. Patty enfolded his arm in hers.

"I come from Colima," Maldonado told them. "My people were dust. I went to school and studied art because art is prized in this country. My teacher had been a student of the American William Gropper, so he painted like Gropper and so did I. In Tepic I have a roomful of my early work—all very realistic and political."

"Passionate," Miss Armitage told the people at the table. "Fierce and full of rage. It's wonderful work."

"It resembles the cartoons of Mr. Magoo," Maldonado said. "A Mr. Magoo passionate, fierce and full of rage."

"He tortures himself," Ann Armitage lamented.

"I torture myself by enduring banalities in silence. I wish on my mother's grave I had never learned the English language."

"You probably went too far," Walker suggested. "You should have learned a little restaurant English. Enough to order flapjacks. Certainly not enough to understand Miss Armitage on the subject of Mexican painting."

"What's he doing here anyway?" Miss Armitage asked Charlie of Walker. "Why isn't he somewhere chained to a hospital bed?"

Charlie muttered soothingly and looked at the table.

Maldonado turned to Lu Anne.

"Before you there should only be truth. Because of your eyes."

"How serious everything's become," Lu Anne said. "First the choreographer at the Sands and now this."

"You started it," Walker pointed out to her. "Ask a tactless question and you get the long answer."

"The choreographer at the Sands?" Lowndes asked.

"I've never spoken the truth in English," Maldonado told them. "Is it possible?"

"Oh yes," Lu Anne said. "But very Protestant."

"I've taken to diving," the artist told her. "I take pictures wherever there's coral. Then from the pictures I paint. Can you imagine what it's like to vulgarize the bottom of the ocean? The source of life? When you know the difference?"

"Courage," Walker told the artist, "you're talking to the right crowd. There are people at this table who can vulgarize pure light."

"I want to tell you more," Maldonado said. "More of the truth."

"Isn't he beautiful?" Lu Anne asked the people at the table.

"Great face," old Drogue said. "Good bones."

"Mr. Maldonado," Lu Anne said, "if you were the god of good bones it wouldn't matter what you told me. The truth is no concern of mine."

"Can't you see she's crazy?" Miss Armitage asked her friend.

"Because I lie so well in your language," Maldonado said, "and because I listen so well to lies, I'm successful. Perhaps also because I'm beautiful and have good bones. Now I have an arrangement with a very prestigious department store. They sell my paintings there and my prints. They also use my designs. So I can look forward to the day, Miss Verger, when my visions will be stamped on every shower curtain in America. In every swimming pool, Jacuzzi and bathtub. On the toilet wallpaper and in the toilet bowl. Wherever sanitation is honored—Maldonados. Standing tall."

"Somebody's got to do it," young Drogue told him.

"Hey, man," Patty said to her husband, "you know we own a lot of this guy's stuff and he's telling us it's all crapola."

"We can fix that tomorrow morning," young Drogue said. "One phone call."

"Do you want me to forgive you, Mr. Maldonado?" Lu Anne asked. "I would forgive you if I could." The Long Friends gathered round her. "But I myself am no more than good bones. A rag, a hank of hair and good bones."

"Just a minute," Maldonado said. "We have a bargain. This is the time of truth among truth tellers. You people," he told the people at the table, "you who know how good you are! Tell us!"

"Come off it, man," Axelrod said.

"Yeah, man," Dongan Lowndes said. "Come off it." He seemed restored to full vigor and he was doing an imitation of Axelrod.

Axelrod looked at him pensively.

"I don't want anyone to leave," Maldonado said with a hint of menace. "I want everyone to explain themselves."

Lowndes raised his glass, which contained tequila *au naturel*, in Charlie's direction.

"Thank God it's Freitag," he declared.

"This is fun," Walker said. "This is better than poker. Who opens?"

"What do we need?" Ann Armitage asked. "Do alcoholism and impotence make a pair?"

"Miss Armitage," Walker announced, "was the only person in America actually hanged during the McCarthy period. She was strung up at the height of her career from the witching elm at the Hamilton horse trials."

"You louse," Ann Armitage said in her cultivated voice. "You eunuch."

"Miss Armitage is a student of sexual prowess in males," Walker continued, "and a major Mexican art critic. She combines in her single self the principal attributes of Eleonora Duse, Eleanor Roosevelt and Eleanor of Castile. Also Rosa Luxemburg, Sacco and Vanzetti. If a passing divine hadn't noticed her dangling there during the dressage competition and recognized the visible manifestations of grace, her poor alcoholic impotent husband might be alive today. Pretty soon she's going to write her memoirs and we'll see a parade of virtue as long as Macy's at Thanksgiving but with twice as much gas and imagination."

"Everyone's under a lot of strain," Charlie Freitag said grimly.

"They're all drunk, Charlie," Axelrod explained. "That's what it is."

"Tell him about yourself, Gordon," Walter Drogue junior said.

"Walter's a wonderful dresser," Walker told the Mexican, "and he's a feminist and he's not taking a writing credit on this movie because he hasn't written it."

"Watch it, buster," Patty Drogue said.

"These are only insults," Maldonado complained. "It's childish to insult people for being only what they are. I want to hear about ability."

"Laughter," Lu Anne said. She looked radiant in the firelight and everyone watched her. "Ability and sighs."

"For Christ's sake, Maldonado," Walker said, "everybody here is at least pretty good." He took Lu Anne by the hand. "This one thinks the owl was a baker's daughter but she's as pure as country water." He turned to Freitag. "And Charlie—Charlie," he said, "are you O.K.?"

"Everyone's under a lot of strain," Charlie Freitag said.

"Charlie's under a lot of strain," Walker explained.

"Tell him about yourself, Gordon," young Drogue said again.

"He knows, Walter. He and I are *compañeros* in crime. Two flash acts. Where did we go wrong? Who knows? Who gives a shit? We've done O.K." With a sweep of his arm he encompassed the patio, the neat lighted pathways and the dark bay. "Here we all are, man. On top of the hill."

"Top of the world, Ma," Axelrod said.

"Then there's Axelrod," Walker said, "who should have been pushed out of a ninth-story window of the Half-Moon Hotel at an early age."

"Your momma," Axelrod said.

People were coming by in various stages of intoxication to eavesdrop and to bid Charlie Freitag farewell. The fires were being banked and the meat wrapped in foil to keep it warm.

Maldonado sagged in his chair. His charge was wearing down, fatigue and drink weighed down on him. He looked at Lowndes, who was wide awake at the end of the table, an unsound smile on his face.

"What about *him*?" Maldonado asked Walker.

"He's a bone god," Lu Anne said.

"We're not going to talk about him," Walker said. "He's dangerous work for the likes of you and me."

Axelrod slapped Lowndes on the back.

"He's a collector. He collects art."

Everyone at the table looked at the former novelist.

"It's been heaven," Patty Drogue said. "Can we go now?"

"I'm going to turn in," Charlie said. "I think we all should. When all is said and done," he told them, "we still have a lot of work to do."

"Oh," Lu Anne said, "but not tomorrow, Charles. We're free tomorrow."

"Damn right," Lowndes said. Everyone turned to him. "This lady doesn't need some damned Freitag to tell her when to retire."

"Hey, Dongan," Axelrod said, "that's not polite."

Freitag appeared not to have heard himself insulted.

"Dongan . . ." he began, "I hope you'll bear with us."

"Don't call him Dongan," Axelrod said, "he doesn't go for tinseltown familiarity. Hey, Charlie," he said, taking Lowndes by the arm, "how long has it been since we had to buy pictures off some wise fuck?"

"What kind of pictures?" Freitag asked.

"Yes," Ann Armitage asked, "what kind of pictures, Mr. Lowndes?"

"I don't know what you goddamn people are talking about," Lowndes said. "What are you so worried about? Isn't there a clear conscience in the crowd here?"

"I have to tell you," Lu Anne said, "that we played with the bones. Yes, we did. Gordon." She looked beseechingly at Walker and then at each of the others in turn. "Mr. Lowndes. Walter. Charlie. Sir. And you, sir, and you, madam, whose forgiveness I implore. We went to the cemetery, and where the ovens—the crypts—were broken, we played with the bones."

"You go ahead, Patty," young Drogue said. "We'll be right there."

"Don't follow the counsels of drink, Lowndes," Walker said. "Liquor's not your friend. Tomorrow, we'll have a conference call—you and Axelrod and Van Epp—it'll work out great. Everybody will make out great."

"What pictures?" Charlie Freitag asked. "What pictures have you got, Mr. Lowndes?"

"Charlie," old Drogue said, "let them work it out. Don't put your health at risk."

Lu Anne got up and went to Freitag and took his arm. Lowndes watched her hungrily.

"They said it would make us sick and we didn't listen," she told Freitag. "All summer we would creep over in the middle of the day.

Inside it was cool and awful-smelling. We played with the bones until old black Pelletier come yelling at us. You all know how kids are. My sister would run across the street, eat a Sno-ball—never even wash her hands."

"Go to bed, Lu Anne." Charlie turned to Walker. "Gordon, please."

Walker stepped beside her.

"Pictures?" Maldonado asked.

"He's a reporter," Ann Armitage explained to her friend. "He has a hot picture and he wants to be paid off."

The information seemed to depress Maldonado utterly.

"How do you like the sound of that, Lowndes?" Walker asked. He turned to Maldonado. "He can write the birds out of the trees, this guy. The good fairies brought him insight and invention and sound. But the bad fairy took his balls away."

"Don't provoke him," Lu Anne said. "You only think he's a man. He isn't really."

"So here he is," Walker said. "He's got all this great stuff going for him. He's a first-class writer and a fourth-rate human being. He doesn't have the confidence or the manliness to manage his own talent. He doesn't have the balls."

"But you would, would you?" young Drogue asked Walker. "If you were as good as you claim he is, you'd be one terrific human being. Is that what you're telling us?"

"If I was that good," Walker said, "I would never waste a moment. I'd be at it night and day. I'd never take a drink or drug myself or be with a woman I didn't love."

"Listen to him," old Drogue said. "You try to tell people writers are assholes and nobody listens."

The Drogues turned away into the darkness.

"Good night, all," Ann Armitage said. She drew herself up and waited for Maldonado. "You guys slay me," she said, "with your going on about balls." Sadly, the portly Mexican rose and went with her.

"I did get sick," Lu Anne said. "I breathed them inside me from a cemetery wall. Playing with the bones. Them, there."

She pointed to the Long Friends who were clustered about Lowndes trying to touch him with their long, delicately clawed fingers, affecting to enfold him in the fine tracery of their dark wings.

"Little sister," Lowndes said. "You're a long way from home."

"I've come a long way from my cemetery wall," Lu Anne said. "Sometimes I think I've ceased to be God's child. I think you found me out, Mr. Dongan Lowndes."

Axelrod and Lowndes stood up at the same time, Axelrod placing himself between Lowndes and Freitag. Freitag stepped back with Lu Anne on his arm.

"You're a sweet woman," Lowndes said. "You don't belong with this pack of dogs."

Freitag gasped.

"All right, fucker," Axelrod said. He tried to take hold of Lowndes but the writer got by him.

"You have found me out," Lu Anne screamed. "The shit between my toes has stood up to address me."

Lowndes had bulled his way past Axelrod and was headed for Freitag and Lu Anne. He had lost his glasses and he staggered as though blinded by Lu Anne's light.

Her teeth clenched, Lu Anne made a swipe at Lowndes's face.

"He's all filth inside," she said. "Look at his eyes."

Lowndes raised his hands to protect himself. Walker stepped in and gently pulled her back.

Lowndes had backed up against an adjoining table. He had lowered his head into something like a boxer's stance and his fists, only half clenched, were raised before his face. His pale brown myopic eyes, tearful and angry like a child's, darted from side to side, trying to focus on the enemy center.

It was enraging to see the man in such a posture, Walker thought. His insides churned with anger, and with pity and loathing.

"Get away from me, you crazy bitch," Lowndes shouted at Lu Anne.

Walker was uncertain whether Lowndes had tried to strike her or not. He hesitated for a moment, decided the loose fists were provocation enough and decided to go, coke-confident. He felt drunk and sick and ashamed of himself; Lowndes would pay for it. He heard Axelrod shout something about the picture and Charlie Freitag cry that enough was enough. Walker had lived through some dozen bar fights. He was not an innocent and Lowndes was offensive and, he imagined, easy. He was making fierce faces, his right hand floating somewhere back of beyond in the ever-receding future, when Lowndes decked him with a bone-ended ham fist all the way from Escambia County. There was a brief interval during which he was unable to determine whether he was still or in motion.

"You pack of Jew bastards," Lowndes was screaming. "You blood-suckers. I'll kill every one of you."

Walker felt for the side of his head. After a moment he concluded that he had not been mortally wounded, but he was bleeding and there was not much vision in his left eye. He struggled to stand and after an effort succeeded. No one helped him. He reached into his pocket for a handkerchief; his hand came out glistening with coke crystals. He licked them off.

When he stood up he saw that Bill Bly had Lowndes by an arm and was forcing him to his knees. Bly's free hand was outstretched to keep Axelrod from closing on the fallen man. Charlie Freitag, his face frozen in an icy bitter smile, had placed himself between the struggle and Lu Anne.

She had kicked off her sandals; Walker saw her eyes go wrong. In the next instant she turned and bolted for the pathway that led toward the beach bungalows. For just a moment, Bly hesitated in his subdu-ing of Lowndes and made a motion toward her. On impulse Walker raced down the path after her, slowing to keep his balance on the turns, his heart throbbing. He ran desperately and mindlessly, pur-suing. He could hear the padding of her bare feet on the stucco sur-facing of the shadowy walkway but she kept one turn ahead of him all the way down.

The sand slowed him as he ran along the beach. He heard her door slam and when he arrived before her bungalow a light was on inside. He rapped on the door and called her name. After a few moments he went around to the rear patio and found its door unlocked. There was no one in the house when he went inside. Her bedroom was sandy and disordered.

He had started wearily for his own quarters when he saw headlights on the turnoff that led from the hotel's highway gate to its front door. In one desperate rally he raced through the deserted lobby and burst out the front door just as one of the company limousines started away. Running after it, he pounded on the rear door. Lu Anne was in the back seat.

"Wait," Walker said. He was too out of breath to speak. "Lu. Wait."

She stared straight ahead, one hand clasped to her mouth.

"*No va sin mío*," Walker panted to the driver. "Lu, *no va. Sin mío.*"

She nodded. The driver pulled over to the side of the driveway. Running back to his room, Walker heard Bill Bly calling her.

He took his cocaine stash, his roll of bills and a green windbreaker that was on the bathroom door. Securing this much, he ran full tilt back out to the limousine and climbed in beside Lu Anne.

"Go," she said to the driver, "please."

As they drove to the gate, she leaned against him, trembling with his trembling. He fought for breath.

"I have to get away, Gordon," she said quietly. "I need a day or two. I need a quiet hour."

He nodded, unable to speak.

"I wanted you to come," she told him. "I think I did. I wasn't running from you, was I?"

He tried and failed to answer. He shook his head, his chest heaving.

At the highway they stopped while the driver opened a locked gate, drove over a cattle grid and locked the gate behind them. Peering through the rear window, Walker saw no pursuing lights.

"Where are you going, Lu Anne?" he asked her as the car sped south along the highway. "I mean, where are we going?"

Lu Anne smiled wearily.

"They'll think you made off with me," she said.

"Yes," Walker said, "they will."

"What pictures were they talking about, Gordon? Some pictures that . . . some picture he had?"

"Yeah."

"Was it of me? It was, wasn't it? It was of us."

"Maybe he had a picture. Maybe not. It doesn't matter now. He's fucked."

Walker watched the dry brush race past in the car's headlights. After a while he patted his pocket to be sure his drug was there. There was a box of Dr. Siriwai's pills in the same pocket. He sighed.

"Are you going to tell me where we're going?"

"Morning," she said soberly. "We're going to where it's morning."

"Will there be something to drink?"

She had taken Lowndes's bottle of scotch and she handed it to him. He drank it gratefully.

"Bats or Birdies?" Lu Anne asked.

"It's your party, kid. You tell me."

"We'll know when we get there," she told him.

Ten miles to the south, the road on which they drove turned inland, crossed the mountains on the spine of Baja, and ran for thirty miles within sight of the Sea of Cortez. At the final curve of its eastward loop, a dirt track led from the highway toward the shore, ending at a well-appointed fishing resort called Benson's Marina. At Benson's there was a large comfortable ranch house in the Sonoran style, a few fast powerboats rigged for big-game fishing and a small airstrip. Benson ran a pair of light aircraft for long-distance transportation and fish spotting.

Early on during production, Lu Anne had been told about Benson's by Frank Carnahan; she and Lionel had hired Benson's son to fly them to San Lucas for a long weekend. The flight had produced much corporate anxiety after the fact because the film's insurance coverage did not apply to impromptu charter flights in unauthorized carriers. Charlie Freitag had been cross and Axelrod had been upbraided.

In the early hours of the morning, their car turned into Benson's and pulled up beside his dock. Walker had slept; a light cokey sleep, full of theatrical nightmares that had his sons in them.

Lu Anne walked straight to the lighted pier and stood next to the fuel pumps, looking out across the gulf. Walker climbed from the car and asked the driver to park it out of the way. In the shadow of the boathouse, he had some more cocaine. The drug made him feel jittery and cold in the stiff ocean wind.

After a few minutes, Benson's son Enrique came out looking sleepy and suspicious. He was a Eurasian, the son of a Texas promoter who had realized his dreams and a Mexican-born Chinese woman. When he recognized Lu Anne he smiled.

"You two want to go to Cabo again?" he asked. He shook hands with both of them and Walker watched him realize that it was not the same man who had been with her on the last flight.

"No," Lu Anne said. "We want to go to Villa Carmel."

He was looking down at the ground in embarrassment, an un-worldly young man.

"I don't know, ma'am. There's a *chubasco* over the mountains. I have to get the weather."

"Of course," Lu Anne said.

The youth stood with them for a minute or so and then went back inside the main house.

"We should go back," Walker said.

She shook her head.

"You're screwing them up," Walker told her, taking a slug from the bottle of scotch. "You should be back at work tomorrow. I should be gone."

Lu Anne kept looking out to sea.

"I don't think I want to go back to work tomorrow. And I don't want you to go."

"It's senseless," Walker said.

"Then why did you come?"

He thought of the bird trilling in the Hollywood hills.

"Where's he gone?" Lu Anne asked. She meant young Benson.

"I guess he's gone to find out the weather."

"Pig'll come after us," she said. "He'll figure out where we've gone to."

"Who will?"

"Billy," she said. "Bly."

"I don't know why you want to go to Villa Carmel. What's there?"

She smiled at him quickly, surprised him.

"Wait until you see."

"Weren't we near there once?" Walker asked. "You were shooting somewhere in the Sierra. A long time ago."

"We were miles away. We were shooting a Mexican setting of *Death Harvest* in Constancia."

"Was it Constancia?" Walker asked. "Or was it Benjamin Hill?"

"It was way the other side of Monte Carmel. Villa Carmel is on this side. The Pacific side."

"Why do you want to go there?"

"The reason . . ." she began, and paused. "The reason is a pretty reason. You'll have to trust me." She took hold of his hand. "Do you?"

"Well," Walker said, "we're out here together in this storm of stuff. What have I got to lose?"

"We'll see," Lu Anne said.

Young Benson came back with his map case and climbed to the small room above the boathouse that was his operations shack. He was sporting the leather jacket and white silk scarf it pleased him to wear aloft. When he turned on the lights, an English-language weather report crackled over the transmitter. Walker and Lu Anne on the pier below could not make it out.

She looked through her tote bag and came up with a white bank envelope filled with bills and handed it to Walker.

"What's this?"

"To pay him."

He started to protest. She turned away. "My party," she said.

Climbing the wooden stairs to Benson's office, he put the envelope beside his wallet, still stuffed with his winnings from Santa Anita. Both of them had so much money, he thought. It was so convenient.

"How's the weather?" he asked young Benson when he was in the office.

"*Garay!*" young Benson said, looking wide-eyed at him. "Man, what a shiner you got!"

Walker put a hand to his swollen face.

"Is it real?" the young pilot asked. Walker looked at him in blank incomprehension.

"I thought it might not be real," the youth explained. "I thought maybe it was fake."

"Ah," Walker said. "It's real. An accident. A misstep."

"Yeah," Benson said. "Well, let's see. Reckon I can get you all over there. We might have a problem coming back. When you need to be back?"

"I don't know. Can you wait for us?"

"That's expensive," the young man said uncertainly. "If the *chubasco* settles in we might get stuck."

"When can we leave?"

"When it's light," Benson said.

Walker took five hundred-dollar bills out of the envelope.

"Take us over for the day. If we're not back by sunset tomorrow we'll throw in a few hundred more."

"Three hundred for the day, if I wait. Five hundred if I have to wait overnight."

"Good," Walker said. He gave the youth five hundred. "Hold it on deposit."

She was waiting for him at the foot of the steps.

"Will he take us?"

"He'll take us at first light. He says the weather might keep us over there. Is there a hotel in Villa Carmel?"

She did not answer him. He looked at the sky; it was clear and lightening faintly. The moon was down. The autumn constellations showed. Venus was in Taurus, the morning star.

He asked her if she knew what it meant because it was the sort of thing she knew. Again she failed to answer him.

After a while she pointed to their driver, who was asleep behind the wheel of his parked limousine.

"Pay him," she said. "Pay him and send him back."

"You're sure?"

"Gordon, I'm going to Monte Carmel. Do you want to be with me or not?"

He went over and woke up the driver and paid him and watched the car's taillights bounce over the road between Benson's and the highway.

"Why there?" he asked her.

He thought, to his annoyance, that she would ignore his question again.

"Because there's a shrine there," she said. "And I require its blessedness."

"That'll be lost on me," Walker said.

She looked at him with a knowing, kindly condescension.

There was light above the Gulf of California, gray-white at first, then turning to crimson. It spread with all the breathtaking alacrity of tropical mornings. Walker found its freshening power wearisome. He was a little afraid of it.

Morn be sudden, he thought. Eve be soon.

Benson came out of his office and clattered down the steps to the dock, sweeping his scarf dashingly behind him in the wind.

"Let's go, folks."

"Is it a Christian shrine?" Walker asked. "I mean," he suggested, "they don't sacrifice virgins there?"

"Never virgins," Lu Anne said. "They sacrifice cocksmen there. And ritual whores."

"If you could give me a hand with the aircraft, mister," young Benson said over his shoulder as they fell in behind him, "I would appreciate it a whole lot."

Benson hauled open the hangar's sliding door and moved the wheel blocks aside. Then he and Walker guided the aircraft out of the hangar and into position. By the time they were ready to board, the morning was in full possession. The disc of the sun was still below the gulf, but the morning kites were up against layers of blue and the lizard cries of unseen desert birds sounded in the brush until the engine's roar shut them out of hearing.

"She's a real sparkler," Benson said when they were airborne. Walker, who had been sniffing cocaine from his hand, looked at the youth blankly again. Was he referring to Lu Anne, buckled into the seat behind him?

Benson never took his eyes from the cockpit windshield.

"I mean the day is," he explained. "I mean you wouldn't know there was bad weather so close."

"Yes," Walker said. "I mean no. I mean we'll never get enough of it."

A few minutes out, they could see the peaks of the coast on the eastern shore of the gulf and the sun rising over them. The whole sea spread out beneath them, glowing in its red rock confines, a desert ocean, a sea for signs and miracles.

He turned to look at Lu Anne and saw her crying happily. The sight encouraged him to a referential joke.

"Was there ever misery loftier than ours?" he shouted over the engine.

She shook her head, denying it.

"Everybody O.K.?" Benson asked.

"Everybody will have to do," Walker told him.

Within the hour they were landed on a basic grass airstrip in the heart of a narrow valley rimmed with verdant mountains. The air was damp and windless. A knot of round-faced, round-shouldered Indian children watched them walk to the corrugated-iron hangar that served the field. A herd of goats were nibbling away at the borders of a strip. Through a distant stand of ramon trees, Walker could make out the whitewashed buildings of town—the dome and bell tower of a church, rooftops with bright laundry, a cement structure with Art Deco curves surmounted with antennas. Villa Carmel.

While Benson did his paperwork, a middle-aged Indian with a

seraphic smile approached Walker to inquire whether a taxi was de-
sired. Lu Anne was out in the sun, shielding her eyes, squinting up
at the ridgeline of the green mountains to the east.

Walker directed the man who had approached him to telephone
for a car and within ten minutes it arrived, a well-maintained Volks-
wagen minibus with three rows of seats crowded into it. He bought
a bottle of mineral water at the hangar stand and they climbed aboard.

They drove into the center of Villa Carmel with two other
passengers—Benson and an American in a straw sombrero who had
been lounging about the hangar and who never glanced at them. In
the course of the brief ride, Walker underwent a peculiar experience.
He was examining what he took to be his own face in the rearview
mirror, when he realized that the roseate, self-indulgent features he
had been ruefully studying were not his own but those of the man in
the seat in front of him. His own, when he brought them into his line
of sight, looked like a damaged shoulder of beef. The odd sense of
having mistaken his own face remained with him for some time thereafter.

When they pulled into the little ceiba-shaded square of Villa Carmel, Benson and the American got out and the driver looked ques-
tioningly toward Lu Anne and Walker.

"Tell him the shrine," Lu Anne said.

Walker tried the words he knew for shrine—*la capilla, el templo.*
The elderly driver shrugged and smiled. His smile was that of the
man at the airport, a part of the local Indian language.

"Monte Carmel," Lu Anne said firmly. *"Queremos ir ahí."*

Without another word, the driver shifted gears and then circled
the square, heading back the way they had come.

They drove again past the airstrip and followed the indifferently
surfaced road into the mountains. As they gained distance they were
able to turn and see that the town of Villa Carmel itself stood on the
top of a wooded mesa. The higher their minibus climbed along the
escarpment, the deeper the green valleys were that fell away beside
the road. They passed a waterfall that descended sheerly from a piñon
grove to a sunless pool below. Vultures on outstretched motionless

wings glided up from the depths of the barrancas, riding updrafts as the sun warmed the mountain air.

When they were almost at the top of the ridge, the minibus pulled over and halted at the beginning of a dirt track. They could see across the next valley, which was not wild like the one from which they ascended but rich with cultivation. A railroad track ran across its center. There were towns, strung out along a paved highway. Miles beyond, another range of mountains rose, to match the range on which they stood.

"We've been here," Walker said to Lu Anne. "Haven't we?" He got out of the bus and walked to a cliffside. "We stayed in that valley, at a hot springs there. You were working in these hills. Or else," he said, nodding across the valley, "in those."

Her attention was fixed on a winding rocky pathway that led up a hillside on their right, toward the very top of the hill. Walker saw her question the driver, and the driver, smiling as ever, shake his head. He walked back to the bus.

"Is he saying," Lu Anne asked, "that he can't drive us up there?"

Walker spoke with the driver and determined that, indeed, the man was cheerfully declining to take them farther.

"He says he can't make it up there," Walker told Lu Anne. "He says the bus wouldn't go up."

Looking the track over, Walker saw that it appeared to be little more than a goat trail, hardly a road at all.

"Pay him," Lu Anne said.

He had nothing smaller than a twenty. Shamefacedly he put it in the driver's hand. The driver responded with no more than his customary smile.

"I want him to come back this evening," Lu Anne said.

When Walker suggested this to the driver, the driver said that it would be dangerous for them to spend the day in the mountains alone. There were bad people from the cities, he said, who came on the highway and did evil things.

"We won't be near the highway," Lu Anne said.

So Walker asked the man to return before sundown and the man smiled and drove away. Walker suspected they would never see him again.

Lu Anne walked across the road to the foot of the path.

"Hey, bo," she said. "Don't you know we're going up?"

Walker knew. He fell into step with her.

"The next hill," he said to her when they had gone a way, "that never was a thing that troubled me."

"No," Lu Anne said.

"I was always hot for the next hill. Next horizon. Whatever there was. That's why I came along now."

He paused, looked around and took a pinch. It was very wasteful. When he had satisfied himself, he took a drink of bottled water. Lu Anne took some cocaine from him.

"Yes," she said. "You're Walker."

"They don't call me Walker for nothing," Walker said. "It's a specialty."

"Of what does it consist?" Lu Anne said.

"Well," he said, "there's the road. And there's one."

"And how does one approach the road?"

"One steps off confidently. One in front of the other. Hay foot, straw foot. Briskly."

"Oh," Lu Anne said, "that's you, Gordon. That's your style all right." She linked arms with him. "Tell us more."

"Well," he said, "there are things to know."

"I knew there would be. Tell."

"There's to and fro. There's back and forth. There's up. Likewise down. There's taking care of your feet."

"And the small rain," Lu Anne said.

"And mud. And gravel and sand. And shit. And wet rot and dry rot. And going over fences."

"Can you look back?"

"Never back. You can look down. You have to see where you're going."

"But is there a place for art?" Lu Anne asked with a troubled frown. "It's all so functional."

"There's whistling. That's the principal art. The right tunes in the right places. Whatever gets you through the afternoon."

"How sad," Lu Anne said. They walked on, winding upward along the hillside. "How sublime."

"The road is never sublime," Walker told her. "The road is pedestrian."

When they had walked for half an hour, they could see both valleys—the plains to the east and the forested barranca through which they had come.

They stopped to drink the rest of their water and take more of the drug. The road over which they had driven ran close to the summit; the top of Monte Carmel was only a quarter mile or so above them.

"Your road is mine, Walker," she told him.

"Right," he said. He glanced at her; she was clutching the collar of the army shirt she had thrown on after the party. Her eyes were bright with pain.

"It was always me for you."

"I knew that," he said. He was thinking that, of course, they would never have lasted three months together by the day. Arrivals, departures, fond absences and dying falls were all there had ever been to it. Bird songs and word games, highs and high romance. "We weren't free."

"Oh, baby," she said, "there ain't no free."

"Only," Walker said, "the comforts of philosophy."

"Which in your case," Lu Anne said, "is me."

Walker laughed and so did she.

"Likewise the consolations of religion," Lu Anne said, "which is why we are out here . . ."

"Under the great vault of heaven," Walker suggested.

"Under the great vault," she repeated, "of heaven." She stopped and began to cry. She knelt in the dust, her eyes upturned in absurd rapture, doing the virgin's prayer. Walker was appalled. He bent to her.

"Can't you help me?" she asked.

"I would die for you," he said. It was true, he thought, but not really helpful. He was the kind of lover that Edna Pontellier was a mother. At the same moment he realized that his life was in danger and that he might well, as he had earlier suspected, have come to Mexico to die. His heart beat fearfully. His sides ached.

"I don't require dying for," Lu Anne said. He considered that she deceived herself. Weeping, she looked childlike and stricken, but even in his recollection she had never been more beautiful. She had grown so thin in the course of the film that her face had contracted to its essential lines, which were strong and noble, lit by her eyes with intelligence and generosity and madness. The philosophy whose comforts she represented was Juggernaut.

He knelt breathless beside her and realized that he was happy. That was why he had come, to be with her in harm's way and be happy.

She looked into his face and touched his hair. "Poor fish," she said. "I was always there for you."

"Well," Walker said, "here I am."

"Too late."

She raised her eyes again.

"And nothing up there, eh? No succor? No bananas?"

He helped her to her feet.

"Who knows?" Walker said. "Maybe."

"Maybe, eh?"

She stayed where she was; Walker was above her on the trail, which grew steeper as it ascended.

"Do you know why I was an actress?" she asked him.

"Why?"

A sudden luminous smile crossed her face. He could not imagine what force could drive such a smile through tears and regret.

"You'll see," she said, and took him by the hand. She climbed with strong sure steps. Just short of the crest, she released his hand and fell to her knees.

"This is the way we go up," she said. He watched her struggle up the last rise, one knee before the other. When he tried to help her, she thrust his hand away.

"This is how the Bretons pray," she told him. "The Bretons pray like anything."

So it was on her knees that she mounted the top of the hill. Walker went on before her, to find a featureless building of the local stone with a thatched roof. Over the door, a wooden sign rattled on the unimpeded wind of the mountaintop, lettered to read *Seguridad Nacional*. There was a noxious smell in the thin air.

He stood panting before the building, and he realized at once when he had seen it last and why the landscape to the east had seemed so familiar. Ten or perhaps twelve years before, he had come down from Guadalajara by limousine to visit her on the set of a Traven remake. The unit had been based on the Constancia Hot Springs in the cultivated valley to the east. He had worked many Mexican locations and sometimes confused them in memory, but he remembered it quite well now, seeing the homely building with its sign. The unit's laborers had thrown it up in a day or two.

Lu Anne crawled over the coarse yellow grass of the hilltop on her knees. A long slow roll of thunder echoed along the mountain range. An enormous bank of storm clouds was drifting toward them from the coast.

"This is a holy place," Lu Anne said. "Sacred to me."

"This is the police post from that Traven picture," Walker told her. "It isn't anything or anywhere. It's fake."

"It's holy ground," she told him. "The earth is bleeding here."

Walker went around behind the building; the ground there was muddy and stinking. He found an empty wooden trough with a litter of corncobs around it. There was a barred window through which he could see stacked ears of maize and heaped grain sacks.

He went back to where Lu Anne was kneeling.

"For God's sake, Lu Anne! It's a fucking corncrib on a pig farm."

Lu Anne leaned forward in her kneeling posture and pressed her forehead into the dirt.

Walker laughed.

"Oh wow," he cried. "I mean, remember the ceremony they had?

The governor of the state came out? They were going to make it a film museum." He stalked about in manic high spirits. "It was going to be a showplace of cinema, right? For the whole hemisphere, as I recall. Second only to Paris, a rival collection. Oh Christ, that's rich."

Lu Anne raised her head, filled her hands with dry earth and pressed them against her breasts.

"A film museum," Walker shouted. "On top of a hill in the middle of a desert in the middle of a jungle. Funny? Oh my word."

He lay down in the spiky desert grass.

"So everybody went away," Walker crowed, "and they turned it into a pig farm."

He lay crying with laughter, fighting for breath at the edge of exhaustion, shielding his eyes against his forearm. When the first lightning flash lit up the corners of his vision he had a sense of lost time, as though he might have been unconscious for some seconds, or asleep. He raised his head and saw Lu Anne standing naked over him. He scurried backwards, trying to gain his feet. A great thunder-clap echoed in all the hollows of their hill.

"What have you done to me, Walker?"

There was such rage in her eyes, he could not meet them. He looked down and saw that her feet were covered in blood. Streaks of it laced her calves, knees to ankles. When he looked up she showed him that her palms were gouged and there was a streak of blood across her left side.

"I was your sister Eve," she said. "It was my birthday. Look at my hands."

She held them palms out, fingers splayed. The blood ran down her wrists and onto the yellow grass. When he backed away, rising to one knee, he saw a little clutter of bloodstained flint shards beside the pile of her clothes.

He turned to her about to speak and saw the lightning flash behind her. The earth shook under him like a scaffold. He saw her raised up, as though she hung suspended between the trembling earth and the storm. Her hair was wild, her body sheathed in light. Her eyes blazed amethyst.

"Forgive me," Walker said.

She stretched forth her bloody hand on an arm that was serpentine and unnatural. She smeared his face with blood.

"I was your sister Eve," Lu Anne said. "I was your actress. I lived and breathed you. I enacted and I took forms. Whatever was thought right, however I was counseled. In my secret life I was your secret lover."

Propped on one knee, Walker reached out his own hand to touch her but she was too far away. The lightning flashed again, lighting the black sky beneath which Lu Anne stood suspended.

"I never failed you. Other people begged me, Walker, and they got no mercy out of me. My men got no mercy. My children got none. Only you. Do you see my secret eyes?"

"Yes," Walker said.

"Whose are they like?"

"I don't know," he said.

"Only truth here. It's a holy place."

"It's not a place," Walker said. "You're bleeding and you're going to be cold." He stood up and took off his windbreaker to cover her but she remained beyond his reach. "It's nowhere."

"Gordon, Gordon," she said, "your road is mine. I own the ground you stand on. This is the place I want you."

"There's nothing here," he said. He looked around him at the stone, the bare hilltop. "It never was a place."

"Panic, Gordon? Ask me if I know about panic. I'm the one that breathed in the boneyard. I've had the Friends since I was sweet sixteen. I can't choose the music I hear, whether it's good music or bad. I'm your actress, Gordon, this is mine. I know every rock and thorn and stump of this old mountain. I may be with you somewhere else and all the time we're really here. Did you think of that?"

"No," Walker said.

"Don't be afraid, Gordon. Look at me. Whose eyes?"

He only stared at her, holding his windbreaker.

"Gordon," she said, "you cannot be so blind."

"Mine," he said.

"They are your eyes," she told him. "I'm your actress, that's right. I'm wires and mirrors. See me dangle and flash all shiny and hung up there? At the end of your road? Mister what-did-you-say-your-name-is Walker? See that, huh?"

"Yes, I see."

"Yes? Hey, that's love, man."

"So it is," Walker said.

She cupped a hand beside her ear. "You say it is?"

"I said it was, yes."

"Well, you're goddamn right it is, honey."

Walker was compelled to admit that it was and it would never do either of them the slightest bit of good.

"Why me? I wonder."

"Why?" She looked at him thoughtfully. "Oh la." She shrugged. "One day many years ago I think you said something wonderful and you looked wonderful saying it. I mean, I should think it would have been something like that, don't you?"

"But you don't happen to remember what?"

"Oh, you know me, Gordon. I don't listen to the words awfully well. I'm always checking delivery and watching the gestures. Anyway," she said, marking a line with her finger between his eyes and hers, "it's the eyes. Down home they say you shoot a deer, you see your lover in his eyes. A bear the same, they say. It's a little like that, eh? Hunting and recognition. A light in the eyes and you're caught. So I was. So I remain."

"If a hart do lack a hind," Walker said, "let him seek out Rosalind."

She smiled distantly. The lightning flashed again, farther away. "What good times we have on our mountain," she said. "Poetry and music." She closed her eyes and passed her bloody hands before her face, going into character. "If the cat will after kind, so be sure will Rosalind."

Walker took a deep breath.

"But it never worked out."

"Things don't work out, Gordon. They just be."

Walker stared at his friend. "You're all lights," he said. He was seeing her all lights, sparkles, pinwheels.

"Oh yes," she said cheerfully. "Didn't you see? Didn't you?" She shook her head in wonder. "How funny you are."

"I never did," he said.

"This is the mountain where you see the things you never saw. There are eighty-two thousand colors here, Gordon. I've been your mirror. Now I'll be more. And you'll be my mirror."

"More and a mirror," Walker said. "How about that?"

"Gordon, Gordon," she said delightedly, "your two favorite things. More and mirrors."

"It's a kind of cocaine image, isn't it?"

"No, my love, my life. It's the end of the road. It's through the looking glass. Because there's only one love, my love. It's all the same one."

"I'm not going to make it," he told her. "I can't keep it together."

With her lissome arms and her long painterly fingers she wove him a design, resting elbow on forearm, the fingers spread in an arcane gesture.

"All is forgiven, Gordon. Mustn't be afraid. I'm your momma. I'm your bride. There's only one love."

"I've heard the theory advanced," Walker said.

"Have you? It's all true, baby. Only one love and we'll fall in it."

"O.K.," Walker said.

"O.K.!" she cried. "Aw-right!" She stepped toward him; he still saw her against the sky and the storm. "So you might as well come with me, don't you think?"

"On that theory," Walker admitted, "I might as well."

Her limitless arms embraced him. He went to her. She pursed her lips, briskly business, and took the wad of cocaine and the Quaalude box from his pocket.

"Put your toys away," she said. She flung them over her shoulder into the dry brush. "We don't take our toys when we fall in love. We'll be our toys when we fall in love. We'll be our own little horses."

He looked over her shoulder to where she had tossed the drug.

She frowned at him and pulled at his collar.

"And we take our clothes off. We don't require clothes."

Walker took off his windbreaker. As she was unbuttoning his shirt it began to rain. He shivered. He watched her unbuckle his trousers, smearing blood across them.

"I know there's a reason," he said, "that we don't require clothes, but I can't remember what it is."

"Gordon," she sighed, "don't be such an old schoolteacher."

He watched her blood seep into his clothes as she undressed him. He could not believe how much of it there was.

"Rain," he said to her.

"We'll pray," she answered. "And then we'll sleep."

He looked up into the storm and saw the black sky whirling.

"No!" he shouted. "No you don't."

His pants fell down about his ankles as he started to run. He kicked them off, bent to pick them up and ran off dragging them behind him. Lu Anne stayed where she was, watching him sadly. He ran to where she had left her own clothes and scooped them up. The clothes and the sharp stones around them were covered with blood.

The door of the building looked massive, but half of it came off in his hand when he pulled at the latch. Behind it, about four feet inside the building, the owners of the grain had built a serious door, secured with a rusty padlock. Walker huddled in the sheltered space between the broken false door and the true one.

Outside, Lu Anne stood in the hard tropical rain and shook her hair. The rain washed the blood from her wounds and cleaned the grass around her.

"Lu Anne," he called. "Come inside."

She stopped whirling her hair in the rain and looked at him laughing, like a child.

"You come out."

He picked up his windbreaker and went after her. He was wearing his shoes and socks and a pair of bloodstained Jockey shorts.

"Come on, Lu," he said. "Chrissakes."

He advanced on her holding the bloody jacket like a matador advancing on a bull. When he came near, she picked up a stone and held it menacingly over her shoulder.

"You better stay away from me, Walker."

"You are so fucking crazy," Walker told Lu Anne. "I mean, you *are*, man. You're batshit."

She threw the stone not overhand but sidearm and very forcefully. It passed close to his bruised right cheekbone, a very near miss.

"Fuck you," he said. He turned his back on her but at once thought better of it. He began to back toward the shelter with the windbreaker still out before his face, the better to intercept stones. When he was back in his shelter he discovered the whiskey in Lu Anne's tote bag.

"Hot ziggity," he whispered to himself. He took two long swallows and displayed the bottle to Lu Anne.

"Lookit this, Lu Anne," he shouted. "You gonna come in here and have a drink or stay out there and bleed holy Catholic blood?"

He watched her pick her way daintily over the sharp stones toward his shelter.

"I'll have just a little bit," she said. "A short one."

Walker was wary of attack.

"You won't hit me with a rock, will you?"

"Don't be silly," she said.

"You almost took the side of my head off just now."

"It was just a reflex, Gordon. You presented an alarming spectacle."

"Panic in the face of death," Walker admitted. "Obliteration phobia."

"You were washed in the blood," Lu Anne told him. "You'll never get *there* again." She reached for the bottle he was cradling. "I thought I was offered a drink earlier."

Walker watched her help herself to several belts.

"What was going to happen?" he asked her.

"I guess we were going to die. What's wrong with that?"

"Living is better than dying. Morally. Don't you think?"

"I think we had permission. We may never have it again."

Walker took the bottle from her and drank.

"We'll begin from here," Walker said. "We'll mark time from this mountain."

"Who will, Gordon? You and me?"

"Absolutely," Walker burbled happily. "Baptism! Renewal! Rebirth!"

Lu Anne pointed through the rain toward the road they had climbed. "It'll be all down from here, Gordon."

"Christ," Walker said, "you threw my coke away. I had at least six grams left."

"Takes the edge off baptism, renewal and rebirth, doesn't it? When you're out of coke?"

"We should have some now," Walker said petulantly. "Now we have something to celebrate."

"Screw you," Lu Anne said. "Live! Breathe in, breathe out. Tick tock! Hickory Dickory. You get off on this shit, brother, it's yours. And you may have my piece."

Walker took up some of their bloodstained clothing and placed it over Lu Anne's wounds to staunch the bleeding. The rain increased, sounding like a small stampede in the thatch overhead.

"What about your kids?" Walker said.

Lu Anne was looking up at the rain. She bit her lip and rubbed her eyes.

"Goddamn you, Gordon! What about your kids?"

"I asked you first," Walker said. "And I told you about mine."

"Mine, they've never seen me crazy. They never would. They'd remember me as something very ornate and mysterious. They'd always love me. I'd be fallen in love, the way we nearly were just now."

Walker yawned. "Asleep in the deep."

He arranged his windbreaker and his duck trousers to cover them as thoroughly as possible.

"Yeah," Lu Anne said, and sighed. "Yeah, yeah."

They settled back against the mud and straw.

"Things are crawling on us," Walker said sleepily.

"Coke bugs," Lu Anne told him.

For some time they slept, stirring by turns, talking in their dreams.

When Walker awakened, he was covered in sweat and bone weary. He kicked the false door aside. The sky was clear. He sat up and saw the yellow grass and the wildflowers of the hilltop glistening with lacy coronets of moisture. On his knees, he crept past Lu Anne and went outside. The *chubasco* had passed over them. The wall of low gray-black clouds was withdrawing over the valley to the east, shadowing its broad fields. An adjoining hill stood half in the light and half in the storm's gloom. Its rocky peak was arched with a bright rainbow.

Walker examined his nakedness. His arms, torso and legs were streaked with Lu Anne's blood; his shorts dyed roseate with it.

"Sweet Christ," he said. There was no water anywhere.

When he heard her whimper he went inside and helped her stand. She was half covered with bloody rags and her hair matted with blood, but her stigmatic wounds were superficial for all their oozing forth. She had been making her hands bleed as much as possible, the way a child might.

She came outside, shielding her eyes with her forearm.

"How's your Spanish?" Walker asked her.

"I can't speak Spanish. I thought you could. Anyway, what's it matter?"

"Sooner or later we're going to have to explain ourselves and it's going to be really difficult."

"Difficult in any language," Lu Anne said. "Almost impossible."

"How do you think I'd make out thumbing?"

"Well," she said, "you don't seem to be injured, but you're covered with blood. Only people with a lot of tolerance for conflict would pick you up. Of course, I'd pick you up."

"We'd better have a drink," Walker said.

"Oh my land," Lu Anne said when Walker had given her some whiskey, "look at the rainbow!"

"Why did you have to throw my cocaine away," Walker demanded. "Now I can't function."

"It's right back there somewhere," she said, indicating the brush around the stone house. "You can probably find it."

"It's water-soluble," Walker told her. "Christ."

"I have never been at such close quarters with a rainbow," Lu Anne said. "What a marvel!"

"You know what I bet?" Walker said. "I bet it's a sign from God." He went to the shelter where they had lain and sorted through their clothes. There was not a garment unsoiled with Lu Anne's blood. "God's telling us we're really fucked up."

Lu Anne watched the rainbow fade and wept.

"What now?" Walker demanded. "More signs and wonders?" He held up his bloody trousers for examination. "I might as well put them on," he said. "They must be better than nothing."

"Gordon," Lu Anne said.

Walker paused in the act of putting on his trousers and straightened up. "Yes, my love?"

She came over and put her arms around him and leaned her face against his shoulder.

"I know it must all mean something, Gordon, because it hurts so much."

Walker smoothed her matted hair.

"That's not true," he told her. "It's illogical."

"Gordon, I think there's a mercy. I think there must be."

"Well," Walker said, "maybe you're right." He let her go and began pulling on his trousers. "Who knows?"

"Don't humor me," Lu Anne insisted. "Do you believe or not?"

"I suppose if you don't like my answer I'll get hit with a rock."

She balanced on tiptoe, jigging impatiently. "Please say, Gordon."

Walker buckled his belt.

"Mercy? In a pig's asshole."

"Oh dear," Lu Anne said. She walked away from him toward a rock against which he had left the whiskey and helped herself to a drink. When she had finished drinking, she froze with the bottle upraised, staring into the distance.

"Did you mention a pig's asshole?" she asked him. "Because I think I see one at this very moment. In fact, I see several."

Walker went and stood beside her. On a lower slope, great evil-tusked half-wild pigs were clustered under a live oak, rooting for oak balls. A barrel-size hog looked up at them briefly, then returned to its foraging.

"Isn't that strange, Gordon? I mean, you had just mentioned a pig's asshole and at that very moment I happened to look in that direction and there were all those old razorbacks. Isn't that remarkable?"

Walker had been following her with her faded bloodstained army shirt. "It's a miracle," he said. He hung the shirt around her shoulders and took hold of one of her arms. "The Gadarene Swine."

Dull-eyed, she began walking down the hill. Walker started after her. She tripped and got to her feet again. He followed faster, waving the shirt.

"Lu Anne," he shouted, "those animals are dangerous."

She stopped and let him come abreast of her. When he moved to cover her with her shirt, she turned on him, fists clenched.

"Who do you think it was," she screamed, "that breathed in the graveyard? Who was bound in the tomb?"

Walker stayed where he was, watching her, ready to jump.

"You don't think that filthy tomb person with the shit for eyes, you don't think he saw who I was? Answer me," she screamed. "Answer me! Answer me, Walker, goddamn it!"

Walker only stared at her.

She threw her head back and howled, waving her fists in the air.

"For God's sake, Lu Anne."

"Talk to me about Gadarene Swine? Who do you think it was, bound in fetters and chains? Where do you think I came by these?" She pointed around her, at things invisible to him. "Don't you torment me! Torment me not, Walker!"

"C'mon," he said. "I was joking."

Her lip rolled back in a snarl. He looked away. She turned her back on him and went to a place beside the house where the mud was deep and there was a pile of seed husks, head high.

"Jesus," she cried, "Son of the Most High God. I adjure thee by God, that thou torment me not."

"Amen," Walker said.

She clasped her hands and looked at the last wisps of rainbow. "I adjure thee, Son of the Most High God. I adjure thee. Torment me not." She buried her face and hands in the pile of chaff. After a moment, she got up and went up to Walker. She seemed restored in some measure and he was not afraid of her.

"You're a child of God, Walker," she said. "Same as me."

"Of course," Walker said.

"That's right," Lu Anne said. "Isn't it right?"

"Yes," Walker said. "Right."

"But you can't take the unclean spirit out of a woman, can you, brother?"

She touched his lips with her fingertips, then brought her hand down, put it on his shoulder and looked at the sky. "Ah, Christ," she said, "it's dreadful. It's dreadful we have spirits and can't keep them clean."

"Well," Walker said. "You're right there."

"No one can take it out. Man, I have watched and I have prayed. And I've had help, Walker."

"Yes," Walker said. "I know."

"If you don't believe me," Lu Anne said. "Just ask me my name."

"What's your name, Lu Anne?"

"My name is Legion," she said. "For we are many."

For a minute or so she let him hold her.

"Is it all right now?" he asked.

"It's not all right," she said. "But the worst is over."

He was delighted with the reasonableness of her answer. He went to get himself a drink. When he returned Lu Anne was lying in the stack of seed husks.

"Well," he said, "that looks comfortable."

"Oh yes," she said, "very comfortable."

He lay down beside her in the warm sun and buried his arms in the seeds.

"Downright primal."

"Primal is right," Lu Anne said. She laughed at him and shook her head. "You don't know what this pile is, do you? Because you're a city boy."

She sat in the pile, sweeping aside the seed husks with a rowing motion until the manure it covered was exposed and she sat naked in a mix of mud and droppings, swarming with tiny pale creatures that fled the light.

"There it is," she told Walker. "The pigshit at the end of the rainbow. Didn't you always know it was there?"

"You'll get an infection," Walker said. He was astonished at what Lu Anne had revealed to him. "You're cut."

"Out here waiting to be claimed, Gordon. Ain't it mystical? How about a drink, man?"

When he bent to offer her the bottle she pulled him down into the pile beside her.

"I had a feeling you'd do that," he said. "I thought . . ."

"Stop explaining," Lu Anne told him. "Just shut up and groove on your pigshit. You earned it."

"I guess it must work something like an orgone box," Walker suggested.

"Walker," Lu Anne said, "when will it cease, the incessant din of your goddamn speculation? Will only death suffice to shut your cottonpicking mouth?"

"Sorry," Walker said.

"Merciful heavens! Show the man a pile of shit and he'll tell you how it works." She made a wad of mud and pig manure and threw it in his face. "There, baby. There's your orgone. Have an orgoneism."

She watched Walker attempt to brush the manure from his eyes.

"Wasn't that therapeutic?" she asked. "Now you get the blessing." She reached out and rubbed the stuff on his forehead in the form of a cross. "In the name of pigshit and pigshit and pigshit. Amen. Let us reflect in this holy season on the transience of being and all the stuff we done wrong. Let's have Brother Walker here give us only a tiny sampling of the countless words at his command to tell us how we're doing."

"Not well," Walker said.

"Yeah, we are," Lu Anne told him. "We're going with the flow. This is where the flow goes."

"I wondered."

"Yeah," Lu Anne said, "well, now you know."

"I suppose anything would be better than this," Walker said, but he was not so sure. He had come chasing enchantments. After all, he supposed, he would as soon be blessed in pigshit by Lu Anne as in holy water by some sane woman's hand.

"I'll tell you what we can do now that we're here," Lu Anne suggested. "We can have a pigshit fight. How's that sound?"

"That'd be fine," Walker said.

For a while they exchanged handfuls of pigshit, heaving it toward each other in an increasingly halfhearted manner.

"This is the scene they left out of *Porky's*. The pigshit fight scene. We should have one in *The Awakening*."

"When you're washed in the blood," Lu Anne said, "the shit is sure to follow." She looked down at her bare breasts, fondling them. "And milk. But I have none and never will." She held each breast between her filthy fingers and squeezed her nipples. "I should have tits all around," she said. "I should have seven like a dog." She lay back resting her head and shoulders in the chaff; her lower body stayed in the muck. "I wish they could take me out for fertilizer with the pigshit. I'd be worth more as fertilizer than I ever was as an actor." She sat up, looking at Walker with cool curiosity. "What's with you, Gordon? What you all seized up about?"

Walker tried to compose himself.

"I'm a little tired," he said.

Walker saw her gaze sweep past him toward the top of the road. When he turned he saw two Mexicans in the green uniform of the tourist police. One of them was holding a shotgun pointing in their direction—not quite aiming it, but coming close. Both of the policemen wore expressions of profound melancholy.

"Hi, you all," Lu Anne said to them.

A cluster of little brown children were at the foot of the *posada* stairs waiting to watch them as they passed. Walker led the descent, holding Lu Anne by the hand. Both of them stared straight ahead, affecting a sort of blindness. A woman shouted from the kitchen and the children scattered to conceal themselves.

The woman who had shouted came out to be paid. She had the physique of the valley people; dark and round with high cheekbones and bold intelligent eyes. Her husband was hiding in the kitchen.

Walker gave the woman fifty dollars. She raised her chin and lowered it.

"Ochenta," she said. Walker gave her the extra thirty dollars without complaint. It was good, he thought, to be in a place where people knew what they needed.

When she had been paid, she backed away without turning, her eyes downcast. The afternoon sun streamed in through the open front door and it seemed to Walker that she was avoiding the shadow Lu Anne cast.

Outside, the two tourist police were waiting and the man who had driven them to Monte Carmel, standing at something like attention beside his car. Walker and Lu Anne got in the taxi and the policemen into their cruiser.

"How much did you give her?" Lu Anne asked.

"Eighty," Walker told her.

It had not been a bad buy. They had been able to shower at the *posada* and children were sent out to buy clothes for them. The tourist police and a state policeman in town had been paid a total of four hundred dollars.

"Fortunately," Walker said, "money's waterproof."

They were both barefoot. Walker was wearing a pair of Mexican jeans he could not button and an aloha shirt with red palm trees on it that said MAZATLAN. Lu Anne had a white rayon blouse and a wide print skirt that was too small for her.

At the airfield, young Benson was pacing beside his plane, drinking a can of Sprite. He managed a warped smile and a silly little wave as they drove up. When they got out, the taxi driver turned at once for town. The police parked beside the runway and stayed there.

As they took off into the sun, a score of children and teenagers broke from cover and ran out for a closer glimpse of them. The goats that had been grazing beside the strip fled. Not until they were truly airborne did the police car drive away.

Within minutes they saw the dazzling sea ahead. They were both in the rear seat. The Benson boy pulled his headphones from his ears and turned to speak to them. His expression was one of grave perplexity.

"Don't ask questions, son," Walker said to him. "Fly."

One of the Benson drivers took them back to Bahía Honda. When they passed China Beach, just outside the mouth of the bay, Lu Anne said that she wanted to get out and walk.

"I'm exhausted," Walker said. "I can't believe you're not."

"I'm fine," Lu Anne said. "I walk here all the time at low tide. It's a much shorter distance at sea level."

The driver pulled over and they went to the edge of the bluffs.

"See how low the tide is?" Lu Anne said to Walker. "And we can be back at my bungalow before dark."

Walker looked into his friend's eyes. It was obvious enough that she was bone weary. Only exhaustion was keeping her devils in check. The easygoing tourist who stood before him contemplating a stroll was an illusion.

Yet, he thought, it would be horrible to arrive at the hotel's front door in broad daylight. He decided it would be unthinkable. They could walk slowly, bathing in the surf, watching the sunset colors, and then he would put her to bed.

"O.K.," he said to her. "Why not?"

He helped her down the short thorny path from the highway and they walked across the beach to the edge of the surf.

China Beach was altogether different from the beaches on the bay. The unbroken Pacific landed there and that afternoon there was a strong west wind, a tame follower of the storm. It gathered great rollers before it to break against the black sand.

"What a sight you are, Gordon," she said. "In your sexy trousers and your rip-roaring sport shirt from the sin city of surf. Devil take the hindmost, Gordon Walker. My one true pal."

"That's me," Walker said.

"Don't you love the black sand?"

"I do," he said. They walked on the sand at the tide line, beyond the waves' withdrawing.

"Black is enough," Lu Anne said. "Basalt. Obsidian."

"I think," Walker said, "we have got beyond fun."

"I don't know about that, Gordon. It doesn't sound good."

"We're going to have a sunset," Walker said. "Can we handle it?"

"As long as our money holds out," Lu Anne said.

"If it costs more than two hundred we can't have one."

"We've got to," Lu Anne said. "Otherwise the fucking thing will just sit there."

"I'd like that," Walker said. "It would be wonderful, wouldn't it, if the sun just . . . ?"

She put a hand against his chest to interrupt him. They stopped at the water's edge.

"We can't be apart now," she said.

He nodded.

"Of course, we could never be together."

"That's true," Walker said.

He started on but she stayed where she was.

"Oh, I am rather tired now," she said. "Let's rest."

They lay side by side on the dry black sand. It was cooling beneath them as the disc of the sun declined.

"Hey, Lu Anne," Walker said, "can I ask you a question? It's about your concepts."

"You mean my delusional system, do you not?"

"Yes, of course. You're insightful."

"My insightfulness," she said, "has been remarked upon."

"So—what's a bone god?"

She put her hand across his mouth, but after a moment she laughed. The laugh was strange; it seemed not quite her own.

"Well," she said, "a bone god is a little old African knuckle deity."

"I should have known that when the son of a bitch hit me."

"Poor man," she said. "Poor thing that thinks it's a man and plainly isn't."

"He's one of us, really," Walker said.

"No, sweetheart," Lu Anne said. "He's one of what I am."

The sun sank. The sea and sky ran colors unimaginable.

"How about that," Walker said. "It went down for free."

She was running the black sand through her fingers.

"It's still on me," she said. "My milk. The blood and shit."

"I haven't been thinking," Walker said. "You need antiseptics." He yawned. "You need a tetanus shot at the very least."

He stood up wearily and offered her his hand. She took it and stood and opened the clasp of her schoolgirl's skirt to let it fall away. She had a man's cotton boxer shorts beneath it.

"I feel dirty, Gordon. I want a dip in the ocean."

"Come on, Lu," Walker said nervously. "I don't want you to."

"Look there, Gordon," she said, "you can see the hotel's lights."

She had pointed beyond the darkening headlands of Bahía Honda to a wide cove where the hotel stood on its private peninsula. The tiki lights had blazed on and the little covered lights along the walkways. When he turned back to her she had removed her blouse and was kicking the formless boxer shorts aside.

"I'm sorry," he said, "I don't want you going in. If you go in I have to and I would just hate it. I mean, I'm done for, babe."

"It's my birthday," she said.

"No it's not."

In three lovely backward steps, she danced beyond his reach. He advanced toward her, his arms spread as though it were basketball and he was guarding her.

"Stop it now, Lu!"

She feinted to the left, reversed and performed her three-step retreat. They were such beautiful moves, Walker thought. Straight-
legged steps from the hip. She was in shape and he, to say the least,
was not. He had gone in on the feint and lost her. Faked out.

"See the world, Walker? How it goes?"

"Stop!"

Smiling, she shook her head. She pivoted, pointing left and right
as though she were working out her blocking. Walker backed toward
the ocean, deciding to play deep. He realized at once that it had been
a mistake. He would be depending on his speed and she was faster.

"Cut it out," he said.

"Give me my robe," she said. "Put on my crown. Hey, it's Shakespeare, Walker."

She crouched, hands on her thighs, dodging.

"Immortal longings," she said. "Here comes your dog Tray, Gordon, lookit there."

If she went, he thought, the water would slow her down. I'll get
her in the water, he thought.

"Want to marry me, Walker? I see a church."

"I beg you," he said.

She clapped her hands. He blinked and stepped back. She feinted
left, then right.

"Give me your answer, do!" she sang. "I'm half crazy, all for the
love of you!"

He shouted and charged. She spun away. He held the incorporeal
air. He turned without stopping and saw her hip deep, backing into
the surf. The left side of his chest exploded in pain. He stopped open-
mouthed, fighting for breath. He could no longer see her face. She
was a dark form against the fading sky.

"This is the last," she laughed, "of the *Gestae Francorum*." He held
his chest and stumbled toward her.

"Come with me, Gordon. This is best."

"Yes," he said. He sought to trick her. By the time he reached the
water she was under the tuck of a wave.

The tide was low and the drop precipitate. He tried to shake the pain off. Step by step he lurched toward her into the water. Each step hurt him and each wave's surge threatened to throw him off balance.

"It's bliss," he heard her say. She was standing on a bar, her hair wet down. The light gave her an aura of faint rainbows.

"Come," she called. "Or else save me."

Walker lost his footing. He was swimming free. He saw her ahead of him and to the left, perhaps twenty feet away. A tall wave rose behind her and she was swept away. A second later the same wave hit him at its breaking point; he tried to slide beneath it and hit sand. He was in two feet of water over the bar where she had stood. The wave smacked him down, drove him off the bar into deeper inshore water and held him down in it. When he surfaced he was afraid he had breathed seawater. For a moment he could not draw breath. When he was able to swim, the pain subsided.

He thought he heard her voice on the wind. Then the rip drew him out, a tiger of a rip that brought him to the edge of panic, and if she called again he never heard her.

He could only just make out the beach in the darkness, and it seemed farther away each time he looked. In the end he settled into a stroke that kept him parallel to shore, and after what seemed a very long time, he rode the waves in.

Staggering up on the beach, he stepped squarely on her skirt. It surprised him; he thought he had swum miles along the shoreline. When he lay down he found that she had weighted the skirt down with a stone and his heart rose. It made him certain that she would be back and he had only to wait for her. It was another stunt of hers, another death-defying leap. She was the better swimmer.

He called her name until his voice was gone. Then he lay down and tried to pray her back and went to sleep. Hours later the tide came in and woke him. He struck out along the dark beach toward the hotel, guiding his steps by the phosphorescent surf. The waves beat him back when he tried to wade around the point of the bay, so he sheltered against the low bluffs to wait for light. When it came he started again and got around the rocky point dry-footed. He walked, staggered, ran in short bursts, stopping when the pain forced him to.

He was terrified that she was gone. That she might be nowhere at all and her furious loving soul dissolved. He could not bear the thought of it.

When he saw a runner up the beach, he had a moment's hope. It was so quickly dispelled that he tried to bring it back for examination. The runner was a man out for a morning jog.

The moment's hope had been a grain of mercy. A shred of hope, a ray. There were a thousand little clichés for losers to cling to while they lost. Why should they seem so apt, he wondered, such worn words? Why should they suit the heart so well?

Watching the runner's approach, he wondered what mercy might be. What the first mercy might have been. She had asked him if there was one and he had denied it with an oath.

He should have told her that there was, he thought. Because there was. As surely as there was water hidden in the desert, there was mercy. Her crazy love was mercy. It might have saved her.

Jack Glenn pulled up and wiped the sweat from his eyes.

"Shit," he said breathlessly. He placed his hands palm out over his kidneys and began to walk up and down quickly. "Like . . . where you been? They're having kittens, you know. Where's Lu Anne?"

"Not back?" Walker asked.

"She's vanished," Glenn said. "Wasn't she with you?"

"Yes," Walker told him.

"So where is she?"

"In the water," Walker told him.

"Hey, I don't see her, Gordon."

Walker saw another figure running up the beach toward them. It was the stuntman, Bill Bly.

"Hey, Gordon," Jack Glenn said, "I don't see her." He turned to look Walker up and down. "Your eye looks bad. Where'd you get the weird duds?"

Walker did not answer him.

"Oh my God," Jack said. "Something's wrong, isn't it? Because I'm looking, Gordon, and, you know, I don't see her. Something is wrong, isn't it?"

Walker nodded.

"Oh my God," Glenn said. "Oh Jesus Christ, Gordon."

Walker looked at the young man's face. It kept changing before his eyes. Glenn was looking at the water, horror-stricken. For a fraction of a second, Walker thought he might be seeing her there. But when he turned there was nothing.

"I lost her," Walker said.

Around two o'clock on a Sunday afternoon Shelley Pearce, Jack Glenn and a French actor named Celli were at the bar in Joe Allen's. Because it was a rainy, chilling day and because they had spent the morning at a memorial service, they were drinking brandy and each of them was somewhat drunk.

They had begun to talk about the drunk-driving laws and about accidents friends of theirs had had when Gordon Walker came in. They watched in startled silence as he came up to join them.

"Well, hello, Gordon," Jack said.

He introduced Walker to Celli. Celli gave Walker a hearty American handshake while the others watched him to see whether he knew who it was that he was meeting.

"How was it?" Gordon asked Shelley.

"Oh, it was good, Gordon. Real good as those things go."

Walker nodded.

"I was gonna say you should have been there, but of course you shouldn't."

"I wasn't asked."

He signaled the bartender and ordered a Perrier.

"I mean," Shelley said, "what do you mean, 'How was it?' It was god-awful. Her kids cried. He looked relieved, which he damn well was. There was press but they didn't stay." She took a long sip from her snifter. "The press likes a coffin and we didn't have one."

"It was a long time afterward to have it," Celli said. "Because in France we do everything right away. The memorial, two months, it seems different."

"Well," Shelley said, "maybe they were waiting for her to . . ."

"Right," Jack Glenn said quickly. "That was another blow. That she wasn't found."

"It wasn't a blow," Walker said. "It was better. I thought it was."

"Did you, Gord?" Shelley asked. "That's good. I see you're drinking Perrier."

"I had hepatitis," he explained. "If I hadn't had the gamma globulin shot I would have died." He ran his finger around his glass. "So my drinking days are over."

"Isn't it tough?" she asked him.

"What have you been up to?" Walker asked her.

"Isn't it tough not drinking? How do you manage it?"

"Oh," Walker said. "Well, I watch television." He laughed in embarrassment. "Evenings it's hard, you get blue. And I drink a lot of tomato juice with Tabasco." He cleared his throat. "I drink unsalted tomato juice because my blood pressure's a little high."

"That's neat," Shelley said. "That's prudent. Do you jog?"

"Not yet. They say I might start in a month or so. When my blood pressure's better. I'm starting to write again."

"So you never really had a heart attack?" Jack asked.

"Apparently not."

Shelley ordered another round and another Perrier for Walker.

"What brings you to the coast?" she asked him. "What'd you do, lurk outside? The mystery mourner?"

"I hear you opened your own shop," Walker said to her.

"That's right, man. Power to the people."

"She says they'll only represent women," Jack said. "The truth is, she's taking two-thirds of Keochakian's clients. The poor guy's on the phone twenty-four hours a day begging people to stay."

"Did you go with her?" Walker asked Jack Glenn.

"You bet I did."

"I don't understand why you're in town," Shelley said. "You doing deals or what?"

"We're moving out," he said. "We're relocating East."

"We are?" she asked. "Who are we?"

Walker sipped his Perrier.

"Connie came back from London when I got sick. So we're together. We're relocating. East."

"Oh, Gordon," Shelley said. She put a hand to her chest as though it were *her* heart that was at risk. "Is that ever neat! Connie came home. For heaven's sake! How about that, fellas?" she asked her friends. "Isn't that neat?"

"Really glad to hear it," Jack said.

Gordon thanked him. The Frenchman raised an eyebrow and looked into his glass.

"I haven't been reading the trades," Walker said. "How's the picture?"

"It's on the bottom of the Pacific," Shelley said. "With the late Lee V."

"They're recutting it," Jack said. He shrugged. "They shot some scenes with Joy. Lots of luck."

"It's wonderful that Connie came home," Shelley said. "Hey," she said delightedly, "how about that for a title? *Connie Came Home?* But I suppose people would think it was an animal picture."

Jack Glenn laughed and bit his lip.

"I think it's wonderful, Gordon," Shelley said. "Plumb wonderful. Really."

Walker looked away.

"When she died, Gordon, did you think of any great quotes from Shakespeare? He can quote Shakespeare from here to Sunday," Shelley explained to her friends. "He's a walking concordance. So was she. Come on, Gordo," she insisted. "You stood on the shore when she went down for number three. What did you say?"

"I was very drunk the night it happened. The truth is, I remember very little of what went on. What I remember is pretty bad. Anyway, why don't you stop?" he said.

"You're no fun anymore now that you stopped drinking. Drunks aren't fun when you're not drunk. I bet nobody ever told you that before."

"Often," Walker said. "Repeatedly."

"I can think of a quote," Shelley said. "Too much of water hast thee, maid." She reached across the table and pushed his Perrier into his lap. "How's that grab?"

Walker tried to dry his clothes with his napkin.

"The reason I came here after the service," he told Shelley, "was to see you."

Shelley swallowed hard.

"Oh," she said brightly. "Oh, me."

"I was hoping that in future . . . I was hoping that in future you might represent me."

She blinked and looked around Joe Allen's as though she were expecting someone. She was smiling brightly.

"Sure, Gordon. Absolutely."

"I have some things in mind," he told her.

"Oh yeah?" her voice came as a croak. "Excuse me," she said, and cleared her throat. "Like what?"

"We can talk another time. I have to go." He stood up and shook hands with Jack and Celli. "I thought that at my present age I might stop going with the flow."

"We'll do good stuff," Shelley said, not looking at him. "You better believe it. Hey. I'm sorry about your drink, Gord."

"It's just water," he said. "So long."

"Right," Shelley said as he went toward the door. "And I paid for it too."

"Goodbye, Shelley," Walker said.

When he was outside they sat in silence for a while.

"Excuse me," Celli said. "But I don't know how to make of it."

"You were pretty tough on the guy," Jack Glenn said. "Pretty tough on Lu Anne too."

Shelley turned on him.

"Goddamn it," she said. "I mourned her. You think I didn't mourn her? I thought she was wonderful. I always thought it was like somebody fed her a poisoned apple."

She took out her handkerchief and cried into it. Jack ordered another round.

"One more," he said. "One more can't hurt."

When the drinks came Jack handed Shelley hers. "Drink me," he said. Shelley drank.

"She used to talk about her big night as Rosalind," Jack said. "I think it was a student thing."

"I was there," Shelley said. "I had applied to Yale Rep, so I drove down from Northampton. I saw her do Rosalind."

"And was it, like, tremendous?"

"Yeah," Shelley said. "Yeah, it was nice."

"Sweet are the uses of adversity." Jack asked, "That's *As You Like It,* right?"

"That's it," she said. She put her handkerchief away. "Men have died from time to time and worms have eaten them, but not for love."

"Great line," Jack Glenn said.

A NOTE ON THE TYPE

This book was set in a digitized version of Granjon, a type named in compliment to Robert Granjon, but neither a copy of a classic face nor an entirely original creation. George W. Jones based his designs for this type on that used by Claude Garamond (1510–61) in his beautiful French books, and Granjon more closely resembles Garamond's own type than does any of the various modern types that bear his name.

Robert Granjon began his career as typecutter in 1523. The boldest and most original designer of his time, he was one of the first to practice the trade of typefounder apart from that of printer. Between 1557 and 1562 Granjon printed about twenty books in types designed by himself, following, after the fashion, the cursive handwriting of the time. These types, usually known as *caractères de civilité,* he himself called *lettres françaises,* as especially appropriate to his own country.

Composed by Crane Typesetting Service, Inc., Barnstable, Massachusetts
Printed and bound by Fairfield Graphics, Fairfield, Pennsylvania
Typography and binding design by Iris Weinstein